At first, Kingston thou
coming from the edge
over the noise of the en
something hitting the fu_____ __der them. In a few
seconds, he realized what was happening. Someone was
firing at them.

Norton shot him an alarmed look as he put the chopper
through a violent emergency maneuver that thrust
Kingston into his seat back. For a moment they were
climbing rapidly, the engine screaming at maximum
power, then banking at an impossible angle. Straightening
up, Chris ran his eyes over the instrument cluster, then
looked at Kingston again.

"Sod it! We're losing fuel. Crazy bastard!"

Kingston knew what it portended but wasn't exactly sure
how serious it might be. Given the circumstances, he was
surprised that he was not shaking like jelly. "Do we have
enough to make a landing somewhere?"

"We'll know in a few seconds," said Chris. "If we have to
go to autorotation, we've got to find a place to land, real
quick." No sooner had the words left his mouth than the
engine coughed and the fuselage shuddered. Less than half
a minute later, the engine spluttered and died. It was eerily
quiet as the helicopter continued its forward motion, the
rotor blades propelled by the air forced through them.

---★---

THE WATER LILY CROSS

Anthony Eglin

W🌐RLDWIDE®

TORONTO • NEW YORK • LONDON
AMSTERDAM • PARIS • SYDNEY • HAMBURG
STOCKHOLM • ATHENS • TOKYO • MILAN
MADRID • WARSAW • BUDAPEST • AUCKLAND

For my friend John

Recycling programs
for this product may
not exist in your area.

THE WATER LILY CROSS

A Worldwide Mystery/February 2013

First published by St. Martin's Press

ISBN-13: 978-0-373-26837-5

Printed in U.S.A.

Acknowledgments

I am deeply grateful to the following people and organizations for providing advice, research and data that helped make my story come to life.

University of Florida Center for Aquatic and Invasive Plants: Karen Brown and Dr. Ken Langeland.

Oxford Air Services Ltd. (helicopter scenes): Michael Hampton, pilot, Aircraft Management and Sales.

Hampshire Constabulary: Sarah Julian (Media Services) and DC Claire Chandler.

Hampshire Police Air Support Unit: Bob Ruprecht, manager.

Peter Kennedy, Peter Kennedy Yacht Services, Marine Electrical Systems.

Land Registry: Carmel Austin, Customer Information Centre.

Chelsea Physic Garden: Rosie Atkins, curator.

Sissinghurst Castle: Excerpts from *Sissinghurst: Portrait of a Garden* (New York: Harry N. Abrams, 1990).

Levens Hall, Powis Castle, and Hatfield House: adapted from the video productions *The Great Gardens of England* and *Britain the Garden Kingdom,* written by the author and produced by the Larkspur Company, 1995/1997.

The Trustees of the Royal Botanic Gardens, Kew: Excerpts from various materials published by Kew.

Times crossword puzzles: from *The Times* newspaper, London.

Thanks to Zoe Langridge for permission to use the Antelope as Kingston's local in Belgravia.

Last but by no means least, my sincere thanks to Pete Wolverton, my editor at Minotaur/St. Martin's Press, and to my friend, writer and editor, John Joss, who upbraids me whenever I use five words when three will do "nicely."

ONE

ANOTHER FICKLE JUNE DAY was ending. The stubborn rains had let up at last, and the streetlamps were lit when Lawrence Kingston pulled up facing the shoebox of a garage he rented on cobbled Waverley Mews, Chelsea.

With the handbrake on and the engine running, he swung open the door of his pampered 1964 TR4 and extricated his long-limbed body from the cramped driver's compartment with practiced agility. After disabling the alarm, he opened the door and got back in his car. The garage was so small that as soon as the TR was inside, there was barely enough space to open the driver's-side door. It was all he needed, though—spotlessly clean and secure. Long gone were the days when he would do his own car's maintenance. Minuscule as it was, the garage cost him a small fortune every month but he didn't begrudge a penny of it. The only alternative was a resident street-parking permit, which, for his of all cars, would be a gilt-edged invitation to thieves and yobbos who would think nothing of vandalizing it or ripping off parts. The car safely inside, he turned the key in the jimmy-proof deadlock, reset the alarm, and in ten minutes was walking across Cadogan Square to his two-story flat.

He went into the living room, picking up the mail from the doormat on the way. Dropping the letters and junk mail on the coffee table, he took off his jacket, draped it on the back of the sofa, and crossed the room to the butler's table that served as a bar. Opening a bottle of Macallan single-malt whisky, he poured a liberal measure into a crystal glass, topping it off with an equal amount of water. On his way back to the worn leather sofa, he pressed the PLAY button on the answerphone, put his drink down next to the small stack of mail, and sank back into the bosom of the sofa. He sat, legs outstretched, staring at the ceiling, waiting for the tape to rewind.

"Hi, Lawrence. It's Sally." Kingston tilted an ear to the machine. *"Just a reminder about Andrew's birthday dinner Friday night. Benihana, seven thirty, okay? Bye."*

Kingston took a sip of the whisky and reached for the top envelope. A short beep and then a young man's voice: *"It's Dave at Bell's Appliances—Tuesday, 'bout three o'clock. Wanted to let you know we got the part for your vacuum. Okay?"*

Kingston opened the envelope and pulled out the letter. It was from the Royal Botanic Gardens, Kew. He read the first couple of lines then stopped abruptly. Engrossed in the letter, he caught only the tail end of the next message. At first, the woman's voice was not familiar.

"...The police have been round to see her and she's worried stiff. You know him as well as any of us, Lawrence—it's not like Dad at all. I'm going down on Friday. Could you call her, please—as soon as you can? I know she would want to talk with you. Thanks, Lawrence. Bye for now."

Kingston dropped the letter on the table, got up, reached for the answerphone, pressed REWIND, and remained standing while listening to the full message.

"Hello, Lawrence. It's Sarah, Rebecca's daughter. Sorry to bother you, but something awful has happened." Her voice was oddly subdued. It certainly didn't sound like the bubbly young woman he knew. *"Mum called me about ten minutes ago. Dad's gone missing. Apparently*

*he left three days ago to attend a conference in Bristol
and she hasn't heard from him since—he never got there.
The police have been round to see her and she's worried
stiff. You know him as well as any of us, Lawrence—it's
not like Dad at all. I'm going down on Friday. Could you
call her, please—as soon as you can? I know she would
want to talk with you. Thanks, Lawrence. Bye for now."*

Kingston glanced at his watch—it was nine-thirty; not
too late to call, given the circumstances. He picked up the
address book next to the phone, found Stewart and Rebecca
Halliday's entry, picked up the phone, and punched in the
numbers.

Becky Halliday answered after the second ring. She was
clearly glad to get his call but her voice quickly lost all its
energy. He listened without interrupting as she recounted,
unable to hold back a sob now and then, a drawn-out version of Sarah's message. The upshot: still no word from
Stewart, and the police, who had been in contact with her
since day one, had no further leads. Stewart had simply
disappeared.

"I think I'd better come down," said Kingston.

"I'd like that, Lawrence. I really do need someone to
talk to." He heard another muffled sniffle, and this time it
brought a lump to his throat. It pained him to imagine her,
usually so self-composed and in charge, being thrust into
such desolation. "I'm going round the bend here by myself." She hesitated. "Sarah's driving down from Shrewsbury on Saturday, and my sister Margaret was supposed
to come down," she said, her voice now a little more like
the Becky he knew, "but wouldn't you know it, she's got
the flu and doesn't know if she can make it now."

He could tell she was trying to put on a brave front.
"I'll drive down tomorrow morning first thing," he said.

"Thanks, Lawrence, you're an angel."

"If you like, I can pack a bag, just in case you want me to stay over."

"Yes, I'd like that."

"That's settled. Should arrive about noon, I would imagine. Remind me—just after Fordingbridge, I make a left turn by the pub, as I recall."

"The Cricketers, that's right. We're about a half mile up on the left. White roses over the front gate."

"Good. Until tomorrow, then."

He put the phone down and stood by the table for a moment, weighing the enormity of what had just happened, wondering what logical explanations there could be for Stewart's disappearance.

STEWART HALLIDAY AND KINGSTON had been colleagues and friends for more than thirty years. They had first met at the University of Edinburgh, where, in the early days, both of them were teaching undergraduate courses in plant science. In later years both had served on the board of the Royal Botanic Garden, Edinburgh. In those days, Becky and Kingston's wife, Megan, had also become close friends, and the four of them had shared many wonderful times together—on one occasion, a ten-day vacation in Cornwall. Later, when Megan was killed in a freak boating accident, Becky had been Kingston's proverbial pillar of strength. Without her ability to fuse compassion and resolve, his recovery would have taken twice as long. When Kingston moved to London, the three of them had drifted apart, but more recently, whenever Stewart came up to London to visit his older sister, who was in a nursing home in Putney, they would get together for lunch.

When Stewart had retired, some three years after Kingston had packed it in, he and Becky had moved to an early-nineteenth-century farmhouse called The Willows, near Fordingbridge on the edge of the New Forest. Becky made no secret that they'd spent a mint in restoring it and would chide Stewart in a playful way for being so penny-pinching about the remodel. He was good about it, though, letting her have the final say on most of the decision making. When it was all finished, even he agreed that it was money well spent.

Like many retirees, and fitting for one who had spent the best part of his life teaching and lecturing on plant biology, gardening quickly became the center of Stewart's new life in the country. Over the years, he had transformed the original barren space at The Willows into a showplace. With its central lawn, wide perennial borders, roses, box and yew hedging, vine-covered arbors, a small orchard tucked in one corner, and good-sized pond, the one-acre garden was typical in its "Englishness." The garden was Stewart's domain, the house, Rebecca's—a seemingly happy arrangement for both.

On the drive down, Kingston tried to recall when he was last at The Willows. It had to be at least three years ago. Or was it four? He hadn't seen either of them since then. It had been Stewart and Becky's thirtieth anniversary; that he did know. He remembered giving them an antique Meissen porcelain figure of a drummer boy. The weather had been quite dreadful that weekend, but one of the unforgettable high points was Stewart's collection of hellebores in full bloom—huge clumps of them. The dusty red, cream, and pink blooms of the Ballard strains with their starry, bright yellow stamens were show-stoppers. Those and the ruby-blossomed flowering quince were the only color in the garden at that gloomy time of year. It would be interesting to see how the garden had matured since that time.

Kingston slowed to make the turn at the Cricketers and in a couple of minutes pulled up and parked alongside the arbor gate festooned with snow-white clusters of Iceberg roses. It was mid-June, and from what little Kingston could see of the garden, everything appeared to be going full bore. He got out of the car carrying his leather overnight bag, opened the gate, and started up the path. Becky was waiting at the porch. She must have been watching for his arrival. They met at the front door.

"It's so good to see you, Lawrence," she said, with a wan smile, as they embraced. Kingston brushed her cheek with a kiss and then held her at arm's length, looking into her lackluster gray eyes. They said it all—a sad reminder of why he was there.

"You, too, Becky," he replied.

Average in height, she was slight and fine boned, her hair shoulder length, dark, and shiny, longer than he remembered. She wore little makeup and her only jewelry was a plain gold wedding band and a single strand of pearls that rested austerely on her black turtleneck sweater. She had changed little since his last visit. He followed her along the entrance hallway, where the roughhewn beams brushed the top of Kingston's head, obliging him to stoop a couple of times. Passing a row of engraved botanical prints on the wall, he could smell coffee brewing, reminding him that Becky was, without question, the best nonprofessional cook he knew. She was one of those enviable people who made everything in the kitchen look so effortless. Stewart had once mentioned in passing that she had taken a Cordon Bleu course at the London Culinary Arts Institute. Pricey, but worth every penny, he had said with a wink, at the time.

With coffee, and scones baked by Becky, they sat across from each other in a sunlit conservatory off the living room, separated by a glass-topped coffee table. Painted antique wicker seating was plumped up with assorted pillows in a mix of understated colors, the limestone tile floor partly covered by oriental throw rugs. Anduze planters with arching palms added a leafy, tropical look and a brass-ornamented baker's rack displayed Becky's collection of glazed terra cotta confit and oil jars. The open French doors gave them a full view of the garden.

For the best part of five minutes, clearly reining in her emotions but handkerchief at the ready, she related the events of the past three days. Kingston listened attentively, saying nothing until she had finished.

"This conference you mentioned, what was it about?" asked Kingston.

"I understand it was something to do with ecology. Global warming, that sort of thing. I wrote it down somewhere if you'd like to know."

Kingston nodded. "Yes, I would—later, perhaps."

She paused to reach for her cup and saucer, and then, after a sip of coffee, she continued. "Since Stewart retired, I regret to say I never paid much attention to his academic activities. Not that there were many. To tell the truth, he's been called on less and less over the last few years. Ninety-nine percent of the time I could count on him being in the garden," she said, smiling wistfully, taking another sip of coffee. "Except when he was at the garden club, that is."

"Do you know if the police contacted the event organizers in Bristol?"

"They did. Yes." She shrugged and bit her lip to hold back the tears. "He simply didn't show up. That was all they said."

"If it's too painful to talk about it right now, I understand, Becky."

Her attempted smile quickly withered. "No, I'm fine," she said.

Kingston slowed the conversation by taking a longer-than-usual sip of coffee, lowering the cup gently to the saucer. "What about Stewart's office, phone numbers, or messages, his calendar?" he asked.

"I've been through his things and so have the police, and very thoroughly, I might add. They were here for a good three hours." She paused, resting her cup and saucer on her knee. "Not much in his datebook, which doesn't surprise me. A dental checkup, lunch with a friend, as I recall." She looked away momentarily. "Oh, yes, a service for the Jag and a reminder about repairing some plaster." She looked back at Kingston, frowning. "If the meeting was important, you would think he'd have made a note of it, wouldn't you?"

Kingston thought for a moment. "He could have had it committed to memory, I suppose."

She shook her head. "It's unlikely. Even Stewart would be the first to admit that his memory wasn't up to snuff. As a matter of fact, he was forever writing notes to himself. It became a joke between us. I'd find them in the damnedest places, scribbled on those horrid, colored sticky things."

Kingston continued asking questions, trying to be solicitous and to not make it sound as if he were interrogating her. He knew he was probably going over the same ground the police had already but there was always the off chance that, speaking to him, she might recall something now that she had overlooked earlier.

"Had he been acting any differently of late, any subtle changes in his behavior or habits?" he asked, at the risk of sounding like a shrink.

She returned her cup and saucer to the table. "No. The inspector asked the same question. Everything's been perfectly normal, as far as I can tell. Boringly normal, I might add."

"Boringly?"

She shook her head. "Lawrence, I didn't mean Stewart was boring. Though we both know that he's not exactly the life of the party. What I meant was that there's not much going on down here. One day is much like the next. So any changes, even small ones, tend to be even more noticeable."

"I understand, Becky."

"With my being gone three days a week, I was even less aware of what Stewart was up to."

Kingston raised his considerable eyebrows. "Are you working part-time again?"

"No. Last year I joined a local ladies' auxiliary—originally more for something to do than anything else. We're part of the hospital here. I find it very rewarding."

"Well, good for you."

Her expression became pensive. "I suppose if I'd been home on those days and a trifle more attentive, I might have sensed that something was wrong."

"Hard to say, really. You can't blame yourself."

"I suppose not," she said wistfully. "Would you like some more coffee?"

"No thanks, I'm fine."

There was a brief lull in the conversation, and when Kingston next looked at Becky, she was frowning.

"There was one thing. I didn't mention it to the police—I saw no reason to. Stewart had mentioned a couple of days before he went missing that he was going to give you a call. He asked me to remind him."

"Did he say why?"

She shook her head. "No. It was just a casual remark. I didn't think much of it at the time. Why would I?"

"Hmm. This conference—how many days was it supposed to last?" he asked, rubbing his chin. "I mean, did Stewart tell you how long he was going to be gone?"

"I believe it was three days but he said he was only

going for the one day. Apparently, most of the lectures, panel discussions—you know, whatever they were talking about—were of no interest to him, only the one on Friday."

"We should find out the agenda for that day."

"I'm sure the police know by now."

"So, the last time you saw him was…early on Friday morning?"

"Yes. He left at seven-thirty, saying he'd be back in time for dinner, which is usually around seven. We discussed how long it would take for him to get there. I said it was at least a two-hour drive but he thought he could do it in a lot less at that time of the day."

Kingston smiled. "If he's still driving the XK140, he probably could."

She nodded. "I worry about him driving that thing sometimes."

"After…what? It has to be at least ten years he's had that car. I wouldn't worry if I were you. In any case, the police will certainly have checked all the hospitals along Stewart's route by now."

"They told me they already had."

Kingston leaned forward, placing his hands on his knees. "At the risk of appearing nosy, Becky, would you mind if I took a look at his desk?"

"Of course not." She paused, then with a knowing smile said, "I see you haven't changed, Lawrence."

Getting up from his chair, he returned the smile. "As the saying goes, 'Man changes often but seldom gets better.'"

She led him from the living room down a short hallway to a small room that could only be a man's refuge. One entire wall was book-filled shelves. Books, magazines, folders, and sheaves of papers were stacked on every available surface. Multicolored Post-it notes were stuck on a scarred oak roll-top desk that had its share of clutter. On the wall behind the desk were three framed diplomas and a couple of watercolors, all slightly askew. Kingston, a stickler for orderliness, was tempted to straighten them but held back. He looked more closely at one of the paintings. It was dreadful, even worse than it looked from a distance. He turned to Becky. "Did Stewart dabble in watercolors?"

"Yes, those are his."

"Hmm, he has a good feel for it. Yes, quite a nice touch."

Standing by the door behind him, Becky sighed. "It's quite a mess, isn't it?" Kingston nodded, taking in the small space. Even if he started poking through Stewart's things, what could he possibly hope to find that could further explain Stewart's whereabouts or what had happened to him? He turned to Becky. "Did you go into his computer?"

"Me? Good Lord, no! I wouldn't even know how to turn the damned thing on. The police did, however. Apparently, they didn't find anything worth mentioning—at least for now. One of their technical people is coming back to take out the hard drive— whatever that means."

"That figures," he mumbled.

Becky watched, saying nothing, as Kingston—more to give the appearance that he was at least doing *something*—picked absently through the pieces of paper strewn across the desk, glancing at some, discarding others. He opened the top drawer of the desk to reveal a mishmash of pencils, pens, paper clips, pads, Polo mints, and assorted office-type stuff. He closed it quickly and continued to poke around. After a minute or so, he gave up and was about to join Becky at the door when he glimpsed the edge of a folded newspaper tucked under two magazines. It wasn't so much the newspaper but the all-too-familiar black-and-white checkerboard squares of a crossword puzzle that grabbed his attention. Not any puzzle, though—he knew, without unfolding the paper, that it was *The Times* Saturday jumbo puzzle. He had been doing the mind-bending, cryptic puzzles for as long as he could remember. What was more, so had Stewart. At one time they used to call each other every weekend to see who had solved the most clues. Rarely did either of them complete an entire puzzle.

Out of curiosity, he pulled out the paper to see how many answers were filled in. Not many—fewer than a dozen. He gazed around the small space one more time, not knowing where else to look or even what he was looking for. Remembering Becky's remarks about the entries in Stewart's datebook, he flipped through the pages for June:

Thursday, 1: *Dental appt.*
Saturday, 3: *Lunch with Jeremy—the Cricketers.*
Tuesday, 6: *Oil change/lube.*
Friday, 9: *Plaster needs fixing.*

Then, scribbled directly under that: *Fork.*

Kingston stopped, his hand resting on the page: Friday, June 9, the day Stewart went missing. What did "fork" mean? he wondered. It looked odd, somehow, on its own.

"Any idea what 'fork' means, Becky?" he asked. "You didn't mention it."

"Sorry. Yes, I saw that. The policeman asked me, too. I've really no idea. Maybe he was going to buy one—for the garden, I mean."

"That would make sense, I suppose," said Kingston. "How about Jeremy? Who is he?"

"He's our accountant. The police said they were going to talk with him."

Kingston took one last glance at Stewart's untidy office before closing the door behind him. He was wondering whether they should check to see how many forks Stewart already had in the garden shed, then dismissed the idea.

They went out into the garden. It was warm, though with the slightest murmuring of a breeze, and all around them was a heady confection of color and fragrance. "I must say, Stewart's done a marvelous job knocking this place into shape," said Becky. "I don't think you saw it when we first moved in. It was a wilderness, a total shambles."

"I didn't, no. It's exceptionally beautiful. There's no doubt about it. I wish now I'd brought my camera."

They walked in silence for a moment, Kingston admiring Stewart's well-chosen selection of plants overtaking the gravel path on both sides: catmint, lamb's ear, cottage pinks, and several hybrids of hardy geraniums intermingled with other perennials.

Crossing the new-mown top lawn, its distinct grassy whiff still in the air, they passed under the long wisteria-covered pergola and down a shallow flight of stone steps to the lower lawn. Kingston looked up at the hanging clusters of lilac-blue flowers. "Gorgeous," he said.

"It is," Becky replied. "I only wish it would last longer."

Kingston nodded in agreement as they continued across the lawn, the pond on their left, demarcated by a curve of weeping willows. They stopped at the bottom of the garden, on the edge of the ha-ha, a deep ditch spanning the width of the garden intended to keep the neighboring sheep from straying into the garden, while at the same time maintaining an uninterrupted view of the landscape. The bucolic scene across the sheep-dotted pasture to the golden fields beyond made conversation seem superfluous. Becky broke the spell.

"That's the village of Stoke Magna, way over there," she said, shielding her eyes with her hand. "It won a prize several years ago as the prettiest village in Hampshire. We walk there, across the fields, for Sunday services, sometimes." She glanced at her watch then turned to face him. "Goodness, it getting quite late," she said. "I haven't even shown you your room. We redecorated it since you were last here. You'll be pleased—it's not quite so frilly." They turned and headed back to the house. "By the way, I booked the table at the King's Head for seven o'clock," she said. "The food's excellent. I thought we could have a drink here before leaving. We still have that bottle of your favorite whisky."

"Becky," he said, taking her hand. "I don't want you to go out of your way on my behalf. You have enough to worry about already."

She looked up at him with a forced smile. "We do have to eat, you know. I'm just sorry I'm not up to cooking right now."

Their table was ready when they arrived at the King's Head. Each with a glass of Vouvray, waiting for the first course—both of them had ordered the Waldorf salad— they continued to speculate about Stewart's disappearance and his odd behavior. Kingston did most of the talking, using his considerable way with words and soothing manner to try to convince Becky that there had to be a simple explanation for everything and, most of all, for her not to give up hope so early in the game. Soon, he became aware that he was starting to repeat himself, and by the time the salads arrived, they'd reached an unspoken agreement: further discussion on the subject served no useful purpose. Throughout the remainder of the meal, Kingston kept the conversation from flagging with a recounting of the year that he had spent in Somerset restoring a large garden for a young American woman who had inherited an estate there. Becky, of course, had read all about it in the newspaper, but with Kingston's telling, it became another story entirely. The dinner ended with coffee and updates on their respective daughters' lives and careers: Sarah and her new baby in Shrewsbury, where her French husband owned a successful restaurant, and Kingston's daughter, Julie, who lived in Seattle and worked for Microsoft.

The next morning, after a tentative hug at the front door, they said their good-byes and Kingston drove off. Just before the turn at the end of the short street, he looked in his rearview mirror. Becky was still standing there waving.

He eased back into the leather bucket seat, ready for the drive home, and shook his head. He was none the wiser now than he had been when he'd arrived yesterday as to why her husband should have suddenly disappeared without a word or trace.

TWO

WITH HIS KNIFE, Kingston deftly removed the crown of the soft-boiled brown egg cradled on its china cup. He'd first purchased the Cornish free-range eggs a year ago at Harrods, on a whim. From that day he was hooked. It was the Platonic essence of egg. Taking a bite of buttered toast, then a spoonful of egg, with the barest sprinkle of salt, he read the 9-across *Times* crossword clue one more time: *Plain cake might be seen (7).** It made no sense—hardly unusual. This morning, he was finding it hard to concentrate—a prerequisite for anyone entering "the territory of addictive, potentially delusional compulsions that make the puzzles anything but a harmless pastime," as one cruciverbalist put it.

His mind kept drifting back to yesterday, to Stewart's untidy desk, his unfinished crossword puzzle, and the appointments in his datebook. The dental visit, the lube and oil job, the lunch with Jeremy, the plastering—each was the kind of entry one would expect to find in a datebook. It was the word "fork," standing on its own, that still bothered him. He pushed aside the crossword and spooned the last of the egg from the shell, following it with the last of the toast and a sip of tea.

As he thought about it, "standing on its own" was not really accurate because the word "fork" was directly underneath the reference to the plaster that needed fixing.

---

* Answer is: Noticed (Not iced)

Perhaps the two were connected? Why? The answer eluded him. On a pad, he wrote "Plaster needs fixing," then under that, "Fork," as he remembered seeing the words written in Stewart's datebook. He stared at the four words for a moment then glanced around his own kitchen, hoping for inspiration: the counter, the cabinets, the AGA electric range, and the cream-painted plaster walls. "Plaster"? Did that mean indoor or outdoor? If, indeed, there were plaster somewhere in the house that needed repairing, wouldn't most people be a little more specific and write "plaster in kitchen" or "garage wall?" The more Kingston thought about it, knowing how precise Stewart was, the more he realized that "Plaster needs fixing" was too ambiguous, uncharacteristic.

Deciding to think about it later, he put the pad aside and started to tidy the table, picking up his plate and the folded *Times*. Seeing the unfinished crossword puzzle reminded him of the one in Stewart's office. He was halfway out of the chair when it struck him. Was Stewart leaving a cryptic clue? No, that was too fanciful—but then again, why not? He put down the plate and newspaper and tapped his forehead, as if to say "Dummy." It had been staring him in the face. It must be an anagram. In the vernacular of *The Times* puzzles, subtle hints were always provided when the answer was an anagram. Words such as "recycled," "roundabout," and "translated" tip off the solver that the relevant word in the clue is an anagram of the answer. Thus for a clue that read *Recycled pans make a photograph,* the answer would be *Snap.* If Kingston was right—and he was now certain that he was—"needs fixing" meant that it was the word "plaster" that needed fixing: it was an anagram of "plaster." He got it immediately, there was only possible answer: *Stapler.* After that, it wasn't difficult to figure that "fork" meant "for Kingston," for his eyes only.

He reached for the phone and his phonebook and punched in Becky's number. Not surprisingly, she answered right away.

"It's Lawrence," he said. "I want you to do something for me, Becky."

"Of course. What is it?"

"Go into Stewart's office and see if you can find a stapler there."

"A stapler?"

"Right. You know, a hand stapler."

"What an odd request."

"I know. But I think I'm onto something." He didn't want to tell her what it was just in case he was wrong, which would make him look even more foolish.

"All right, Lawrence, I'll go look."

In less than a minute, Becky was back. "Okay, I have it in my hand," she said.

"Do you know how to open it? As if you were adding more staples?"

"I believe so. Let me give it a try."

"There should be a release catch, probably on the base."

"Yes, here it is. Okay, Lawrence, it's open. Now what?"

"Lift the cap that covers the staples."

A long moment of silence followed. He pictured her struggling to open it, staples sprinkling to the floor.

"Here we go," she said. Another pause followed.

"What is it, Becky?"

"There's what looks like a long cigarette tucked in here."

"Unless I'm very wrong, it's a message."

"I think you're right, Lawrence. It's a tightly rolled sheet from Stewart's notepad." Another pause. "It's in his handwriting."

"What does it say?"

"Wait a minute—it's a list of herbs, a clue of some sort…but it makes no sense."

"Read it to me."

"All right, here it is: 'Sage, thyme, marjoram, and rosemary yield secret. Deadheads will lead you to a sacred place.' After that, there are the numbers two and five in brackets."

She read it back a second time while Kingston wrote it down on the top edge of his newspaper.

"Crafty old Stewart. It's in the form of a crossword-puzzle clue. Two words, the first, two letters, the second, five."

"Are you serious, Lawrence? For heaven's sake, why go to all that trouble?"

"I don't know. The only reason I can come up with is that he wanted only you and me to know what the message says. Few people would be able to decipher the clue."

"Can you?"

Kingston was reading it for a second time. "Hmm—I don't know," he muttered. "Hard to say."

"Promise to call me the minute you do, Lawrence. I pray to God that this means that Stewart is alive and well."

"Becky, never doubt for one moment that he is."

Kingston read the clue one more time. It was too long to be an anagram and unlikely to contain one. The herb references were intriguing, and the word "deadheads" would be familiar to rose fanciers—meaning the heads cut off the spent rose blossoms in deadheading, a summer-long practice to encourage the growth of new flowers. And what on earth was the "sacred place"? A cemetery, a church, a mausoleum? Could be any number of places. He put the newspaper with the scribbled clue to one side and said good-bye to Becky, reassuring her that, even if he couldn't decipher it, it should be taken as a good sign. As he put the phone down, he realized that she hadn't asked him how he knew the message was concealed in the stapler.

KINGSTON LOOKED AT HIS WATCH. It was 8:43 and he'd solved the cryptogram. It had taken him a shade over ten minutes. The written answer was in front of him: *St. Mary's*. It was hidden in the heads (first letters) of each of the first seven words. St. Mary's had to be a church. There was also the long shot that it could be a school but he ruled that out. It must be a church known to Stewart, he decided. He picked up the phone and called Becky again. As before, she answered immediately. They both knew that any news of Stewart would most likely come in the form of a phone call, and clearly she wasn't taking any chances of missing it.

Kingston told her the answer to Stewart's clue, explaining how he'd solved it.

Not that he expected a round of applause, but her response surprised him.

"I suppose I should say that it was clever of Stewart—this and the stapler thing. But considering the fact that he's missing and could very well be in some kind of danger, it strikes me as hardly the time for word games, Lawrence."

"I agree with you, Becky, but whatever all this mumbo jumbo is leading to, Stewart must have had good reason for keeping it a guarded secret. Is there a St. Mary's church anywhere near you?"

"Yes, there is. It's in Stoke Magna, the village I pointed out when we were in the garden."

"That's certainly it, then. We have to go there."

"What are we supposed to be looking for?"

"Right now, I have no idea. We can only hope that we'll

find out when we get there. Stewart wouldn't direct us there for no reason."

"Do you want me to go? I hate to have you drive all the way down here again."

"No. I'll come down first thing tomorrow. I'll phone just before I leave."

"I still can't believe Stewart would go to all this trouble," she said. "I hope this is not some twisted joke of his."

"I doubt it very much," said Kingston, ending the conversation.

St. Mary's, Stoke Magna, was lodged in a tranquil setting among towering beech and ash trees, alongside a gentle-running tributary of the river Avon. Though Becky had attended a number of services at the church, she admitted to being unfamiliar with its history. After helping her out of the TR4's cramped confines, Kingston paused to study the flint stone exterior, looking up at the square tower where the St. George's Cross, the English flag, rippled in the breeze.

"Norman, I would guess," he said. "It probably had a spire at one time, too. Over the centuries many of the smaller churches have lost them to the ravages of time and the weather." He took Becky's arm, continuing his discourse, as they walked the short distance from the gravel parking lot to the church. "The only purpose they served was symbolic, really: not so much as a symbol of piety but to proclaim a perception of supreme power, to reach up toward the sky as a gesture of being closer to God and the heavens. They also served as landmarks, of course."

Becky looked impressed but said nothing as they walked under the wooden lychgate and up the stone path toward the humble front door. Ancient headstones and lichen-encrusted memorials were scattered haphazardly on either side of the path. They passed through the open door into the cool, hushed interior.

Save for a handful of monuments, paintings of ecclesiastical subjects, and a large floral arrangement, the vaulted interior lacked ornamentation. A soft natural light played on the worn flagstones. Kingston was examining a well-preserved painting of a saint when a door to the right of the altar opened and a dark-haired young man in an open-necked sport shirt entered. He was carrying a large book and smiled effusively as he approached.

"Good morning, I'm Patrick McGuire, the new vicar of St. Mary's. Have you visited our church before?"

"Many times," said Becky, frowning. "Father Riley's no longer here, then?"

"No, he retired. He's living in Devonshire now. He was not at all well, you know."

"I am sorry to hear that."

"How can I help you?"

"Let me do the introductions," said Kingston. "This is Rebecca Halliday. She and her husband live in Fordingbridge. They've attended services here. I'm a longtime friend of theirs, Lawrence—"

McGuire's mobile rang. "Sorry," he said, juggling the book, pulling the phone from his pocket and flipping it open. A quick yes-and-no conversation followed, then McGuire closed the phone and returned it to his pocket. "I apologize," he said. "The organist—she's always late." He gave another well-practiced smile. "Please feel free to look around. If you have any questions, I'll be in the office over there," he said, nodding toward a door visible through one of the arches.

"We do have a question, as it happens," said Kingston. "I'm not quite sure how to phrase this," he said, scratching his chin, "but we believe Rebecca's husband might have left her a message somewhere here at the church. He went missing several days ago and we're following up on a hasty note that he left in his datebook."

Like raising a blind, McGuire's expression turned immediately to one of solicitude. The man would have made a good actor, Kingston thought.

"How awful," McGuire rejoined. "I apologize. I had no idea."

Kingston frowned, unsure of his meaning. "You had no idea? You know something about Stewart Halliday's disappearance?"

"No, no. I meant I had no idea that it might be you. You are...Doctor Kingston, I take it?"

Kingston nodded. "Yes, I am." He frowned. "How did you know?"

"The envelope—it's addressed to you."

"Stewart left an envelope here?" Becky interjected.

"Someone did, yes. It was in the post box last week. Wednesday or Thursday, I believe. I have it in the office. I've been trying to track you down."

"Was the envelope posted?" Kingston asked. "Was it stamped?"

"No. I didn't think that curious, though. Parishioners often drop off items in the post box. Some not too complimentary." He chuckled.

Becky took a long look at Kingston. By the kindled look in her eyes, he knew pretty much what she was thinking. "It's almost certain that Stewart dropped it off on his way to the convention," she said. "He would have driven right by here on his way to Bristol." She looked at McGuire. "And what safer place? A church."

McGuire, looking pleased, nodded. "Let me go fetch it," he said, making off toward his office.

He was back with the envelope in a matter of seconds.

"Here you are," he said, handing it to Kingston. "It arrived in another envelope, addressed to me."

Kingston looked at the face of the sealed envelope. PERSONAL was written in large letters in the top left-hand corner. In the center: FOR THE ATTENTION OF, AND ONLY TO BE OPENED BY, DOCTOR L. KINGSTON.

Kingston took Becky's arm and guided her to a nearby pew, where they both sat down. McGuire, sensing their need for privacy, said that he would be in his office if he was needed and wished them well, expressing his condolences and that he would offer prayers for Stewart at the next service. They watched him disappear. Then Kingston opened the envelope.

THREE

KINGSTON WITHDREW the folded single sheet of paper and opened it. He angled it slightly toward Becky so that she could read it, too.

"What is it?" she murmured.

He took his time in answering. "If it's what I think it is—"

He handed it to her.

On it were written the symbols and words NaCl+ H_2O+*Nymphaea* cross=H_2O.

Becky studied the symbols and words, wrinkling her nose. "What an earth does it mean, Lawrence?"

"It's a rudimentary formula of sorts. NaCl is sodium chloride or salt. H_2O, of course, is water. Together, salt water. *'Nymphaea'* is the Latin name for 'water lily.' The word 'cross' means that the native plant has been cross-hybridized or interbred, if you will, with another lily or plant."

"I still don't get it."

"As I read it, it can only mean one thing. If you take salt water and grow this particular crossbreed of water lily in it, you end up with water. Pure water. As illogical as it sounds, from a botanical standpoint Stewart's saying that the plant is desalinating the water."

"Surely that would be quite a scientific breakthrough?"

"It would, Becky. 'Quite' may be an understatement," Kingston replied, glancing one more time at Stewart's scrawl before folding the sheet of paper and replacing it in the envelope.

He stood and stepped aside to let Becky out of the pew. "Let's thank the vicar and then get out of here," he said.

Back in the parking lot, Kingston fired up the TR4, slipped into first, and exited onto the leafy street, heading back to The Willows.

Kingston took his eyes off the road and glanced at Becky. She had hardly spoken since they left St. Mary's five minutes earlier. "Are you all right?" he asked.

"This formula thing—it's why Stewart's disappeared, isn't it?"

"It certainly looks that way."

"I think we should call the police when we get home."

Kingston nodded in agreement as he downshifted, slowing for an approaching traffic light.

Neither spoke for a moment. Then, back on a straight stretch of road, he looked at her again. The puzzled look on her face had turned to one of apprehension. She pursed her lips. "It doesn't look good, does it? I mean, with Stewart making this big discovery and immediately disappearing?"

He took a long time in answering. "I don't know, Becky," he said, finally, shaking his head and looking away. "I just don't know."

A few miles slipped by, then Kingston glanced at her again. As their eyes met, she was about to say something, then stopped, as if what she was thinking was too unbearable to utter.

"What is it, Becky?" he asked quietly.

"Stewart's been kidnapped, hasn't he?"

Her question came at a propitious moment, just as they were in the middle of a roundabout, surrounded by cars jockeying for their respective exits. The maneuver required full concentration, allowing him time to think before answering.

"I don't think we can rule it out, Becky," he said. "But let's not jump to conclusions. Let's face it: as of now, we know very little, and I think that sooner or later, the police will be able to answer that question."

Becky slumped back in her seat. His answer didn't appear to have comforted her any.

They arrived back at The Willows shortly after one o'clock.

BEFORE LEAVING FOR ST. MARY'S that morning, Becky had prepared a plowman's lunch: crusty fresh bread and a selection of three cheeses with chutney and pickled onions. They ate it in the conservatory, each with a glass of shandy, going over the events of the morning. An hour later, after coffee, Kingston helped Becky clear the table and they went into the living room.

Seated in a wingback across from Becky, Kingston couldn't help noticing how much she had changed since he'd arrived. Her usual poise was gone. She looked vulnerable and afraid. It was as though the awful reality had just dawned on her: the fact that Stewart really *was* missing and the likelihood of his having been abducted, no longer a question in her mind. Earlier, before Kingston had deciphered Stewart's message about his botanical discovery, she had been able to cling to the idea that it was all some kind of mistake and that any moment Stewart would breeze through the door demanding to know what all the fuss was about.

"I'd better call the police, I suppose," she said, as if she wanted to separate herself from the reality of it all.

"You should, yes. But let's talk about it for a moment."

She brushed a strand of hair from her forehead but

Kingston caught the disguised attempt to wipe a tear from her eye. "What is there to talk about?" she asked.

Plenty, he was about to answer. What he actually said was, "You're right—at this point, not a lot, I suppose." He nodded his head silently, thinking. No point whatsoever in his rattling off a laundry list of all the things that might happen as a result of Stewart's discovery. That would serve no purpose. Becky was already distraught enough. Nevertheless, the implications of Stewart's message were starting to sink in and he needed time to think about it. He had to choose his words carefully.

An awkward pause followed while Becky waited for him to continue.

Kingston drew in a breath. "If—and let's face it, it's a big 'if'—Stewart has stumbled upon a million-to-one shot of breeding an aquatic plant that can actually extract salt from seawater, a lot of people would want to know about it."

She frowned, obviously trying to fathom what he was inferring. "And you're suggesting that somebody already does?"

"No, I'm not. That would be pure speculation. To start with, we don't know how long Stewart's known this. I take it he's never mentioned anything to you?"

"No, not a word. But that's not unlike him. Like I said, he hardly ever talked about his work. When he told me that he was going to the conference, I didn't pay too much attention to it at the time. Why would I?" She looked away for a moment, deep in thought. "A bit late in the day now—I suppose I should have asked him more about it, taken more of an interest." Another pause, then she said, "Would you like me to look for that piece of paper? I wrote it down, you know."

"Don't worry about it right now. I'm sure I can find out easily by calling the Bristol Chamber of Commerce."

"If it's true—" She paused and looked up to the ceiling. "If, for argument's sake, Stewart really *has* discovered a way to desalinate seawater, well—just how significant is it, Lawrence?"

Kingston rubbed his chin with thumb and forefinger. "It depends on several factors. Mind you, I'm no expert. I'm only going on what little I've read. There's more than one process of desalination, but distillation, while not necessarily the most common, is perhaps the easiest to understand. In theory it's remarkably simple. All one has to do is boil seawater until all the water is gone and only the salt and other residues remain. In the meantime the steam has condensed back to water and is no longer saline. All ships use the process as their basic source for drinking water—have for years."

Becky interrupted, "If it's such a simple process, why is its use so limited?"

"It's not the process that's the problem. It's the expense. The cost of the energy required to heat the massive volume of water needed to make it worthwhile is astronomical. I don't recall the exact numbers but I do know that projections for a pilot plant that I read about called for roughly a hundred million gallons of seawater per day in order to produce 15 million gallons of purified water. You can just imagine how much energy it would take to heat that much water to boiling, let alone keep it going until it's all evaporated."

"I can, yes," said Becky, looking at Kingston. But her thoughts were clearly elsewhere. "The conference had to do with global warming," she said after a lengthy pause. "Is that what it's about? Why Stewart went?"

"Not directly, no. It's not so much about climate change

but rather population growth. Some nation's water supplies won't be sufficient to keep up with the demand. It's a serious problem right now, but in the coming years it will become a worldwide crisis. More so than the shortage of oil, one could debate."

Becky said nothing so Kingston continued.

"So, if Stewart has indeed discovered how it can be achieved botanically, it would be considered an important scientific coup, at least on the surface." He paused, in thought. "Though in practical terms it would certainly present quite a few problems, one would think—quite a few."

"I'm a little surprised he didn't confide in you, Lawrence."

"Maybe he planned to, at one point. Who knows? Didn't you say that he intended to call me?"

"Yes. I wish he had."

Kingston nodded. "All we can do right now is pray that Stewart shows up or that the police find him unharmed." He forced a smile. "Look," he said, "there are probably any number of explanations. We'll know soon, I'm sure."

"God, I hope you're right, Lawrence," she murmured. "It's the not knowing that hurts the most."

Turning away, Kingston thought for a moment. "Did Stewart have any help with the garden? A gardener or handyman?"

"He did, yes. A young man called William. I don't think he was a gardener, though. He did all the heavy-lifting stuff, so to speak. The things that Stewart had given up doing himself."

"Local fellow?"

"From Verwood, I believe. Some days he would bike over."

Kingston made a mental note to talk to William. "You mentioned a garden club?"

"Right."

"A local one, I take it?"

"Yes. The Sarum Garden Club in Salisbury. We get the newsletter every month."

"Do you have one, by chance?"

"I'll take a look. I believe it's in the pile of papers in the mud room, for recycling."

"If not, I can always give them a call."

"You think someone at the club might know something?"

"It's a long shot but you never know."

Becky nodded. "I suppose so," she said resignedly.

"Will you be all right tonight? I mean, would you like me to stay longer—a couple more days, perhaps? I was to attend a friend's birthday party tonight. But I can easily make a call and tell them that I can't make it. Andrew will understand," Kingston said, standing and smoothing his trouser legs.

Becky got up and walked over to him. "No," she said, looking up into his blue eyes. "You've done enough for now, Lawrence. Don't let your friend down. You go back home and enjoy yourself tonight. And don't worry, Sarah will be here tomorrow. I'll be just fine." She summoned a tiny smile. "At least we know a lot more now than we did yesterday." Then she stood on tiptoe, leaned forward and gave him a peck on the cheek. He could feel the contours of her slender body. "Thank you for coming down, Lawrence—for today and the other day," she said. "It's meant an awful lot to me."

Kingston looked into her doleful eyes. "Promise to call me immediately if you hear anything. Sometimes I'm not too good about answering my mobile but I'll make sure I check the messages." He took her hand and held it tightly. "Meantime, I'll read up on that water lily. I know a chap who runs a nursery and water garden in St. Albans. I think a chat with him might be in order, though I doubt seriously he'll know anything about plants that consume salt," he added with a shake of his head. "He'll probably think I'm a few bricks short of a full load."

She managed another thin smile then said, "You'll convince him, I'm sure."

"As far-fetched as it is, there's no mistaking Stewart's message," he said, letting go of her hand.

Becky touched his arm. "Wait here a minute. I'll look for that newsletter," she said.

In less than a minute, she was back, newsletter in hand.

"By the way," she said as they reached the front door, "I forgot to ask you. You didn't say what 'fork' meant. And how on earth did you know the message was hidden in the stapler?"

"That's right, I didn't tell you, did I? Well, once I figured out that Stewart was leaving a clue, that was easy. It meant 'for K'—for Kingston."

She raised her eyebrows. "Who would have guessed?" she said. "And the stapler?"

"It's an anagram."

"An anagram?"

"Yes. 'Stapler' is an anagram of 'plaster.' As part of a cryptic crossword clue, 'fix plaster' would be a dead giveaway. Stewart would know damned well I would figure it out. At one time we used to compare notes every week on the crossword puzzles, remember?"

Becky shook her head. "I don't know about you two," she said as Kingston hugged her briefly and then strode off up the path.

For the second time in as many days, Kingston waved farewell from the TR4 and headed back to London.

FOUR

ANDREW'S BIRTHDAY PARTY was a drawn-out and boozy affair. Starting with drinks in the lounge at Benihana in the King's Road, their party of ten was ushered into a private dining room. Seated on three sides of a large wooden table, with a *teppan*—a flat stainless-steel grille—occupying the fourth side, they marveled at a dazzling knife-skill performance by their good-humored Japanese chef, Toshiro, who orchestrated a *teppanyaki* banquet that stretched over nearly three hours. By the end of the first hour, Kingston had lost track of the number of sake bottles that had come and gone.

The following morning, nursing a milder headache than he deserved, all things considered, he phoned the Bristol Chamber of Commerce, inquiring about the June 9 conference. He was told that it was held at the At-Bristol Complex and was given the appropriate phone number to call. In the following minutes, talking with the Complex's press officer, he learned that the event that took place on the three days in question was the tenth annual conference of the World Desalination Institute. The lecture given on Friday, June 9, was titled "New developments in the biological treatment and desalination of effluents and other marginal waters."

Kingston put the phone down and thought about the implications. This new information left little doubt that Stewart had indeed been dabbling, in one form or another, with a biological method of desalination, using water lilies. Turning to his iMac, he logged on to the Internet and, after a Google search, bookmarked a half-dozen sites with information on desalination. After an hour of scrolling through pages that described the background, different technologies, technical drawings, charts, diagrams, energy usage, waste discharges, and costs, he was much enlightened on the subject. Along the way, he had compiled three foolscap pages of notes.

With a cup of tea, he sat back and read over his notes.

Seawater in the world's oceans has a salinity of ~3.5 percent. Every liter of seawater has 35 grams of salts dissolved in it—mostly, but not entirely, sodium chloride. Other elements can include magnesium, sulfur, and potassium.

The two principal technologies for extracting salt from seawater are reverse osmosis and distillation. With reverse osmosis, high pressure is applied to the intake seawater, forcing the water molecules through a semipermeable membrane. The salt molecules will not pass through the membrane but the water does and becomes potable product water. In distillation, the intake water is slowly heated to produce steam. The steam is then condensed to produce product water with low salt concentration.

Of the two, reverse osmosis is more energy efficient, but distillation plants offer a greater potential for economies of scale. Unlike RO plants, they are not required to shut down a portion of their operations for cleaning and replacing equipment as frequently as RO plants and generate no waste from backwash or treatment filters. The principal operational costs of desalination plants are from energy usage and disposal of waste discharges.

In all cases, pure product water recovery ranges from 15 to 50 percent. For every 100 gallons of seawater, 15 to 50 gallons of pure water is produced. Based on 1992 figures, most seawater desalination plants produce pure water at costs ranging from $1,000 to $2,500 per acre-foot (326,000 gallons). This is equivalent to the amount of water that two to three households would consume in one year. Comparable costs for the same period in the Western United States for untreated domestic-use water from conventional sources (reservoirs, wells, etc.) range anywhere from $27 to $270 per acre-foot. The cost of desalinated water remains substantially higher; however, over recent years with technological advances, the gap is narrowing.

Among the Web sites Kingston had visited was one describing London's Thames Water Utilities' investment of £300 million to build the city's first reverse-osmosis desalination facility. The new plant, expected to be up and running in 2008, will have a capacity to desalinate 150 million liters per day and provide water for nearly 900,000 people. Kingston made a note to call Thames Water's public-affairs office and see if they could update his figures.

He took his last sip of tepid tea, leaned back in his ergonomic leather chair—an impulse buy that had set him back £500—and thought about Stewart. What could possibly have happened to him? Every once in a while, stories cropped up in the newspapers about elderly people who wandered off, though in most cases they were found a day or so later, often miles from home. But Stewart wasn't *that* old, and as far as Becky was concerned, his *compos mentis* was never in question.

Another thing: What would happen if the news media got wind of the story? He made a mental note to call Becky and tell her not to talk to anyone outside the family for the time being. Of course, this all hinged on whether his interpretation of Stewart's cryptic message was right. He needed a second opinion and he knew just the right person to give it.

He looked in his address book and found Desmond Scott's telephone number, the chap who owned a large water-garden nursery just outside St. Albans called Across the Pond. In the ten years or so that Kingston had known him, he had never had the courage to tell Desmond that he found names like that just too fey. What on earth was wrong with Desmond's Water Gardens? Really?

DESMOND SCOTT WAS IN his late fifties, tall and slim. Considering that he spent most of his time in the fresh air, he had an unlikely gaunt face that appeared even more pallid under a circle of dark curly hair that, on closer inspection, was becoming grizzled. With his long musician's fingers and wire-rimmed glasses, he looked the least likely person to be running a nursery.

Kingston had arrived at Across the Pond midmorning after giving his TR4 a good airing out on the M1. After a minute or so of nosing around, Kingston spotted Desmond in a far corner bending over a large galvanized tank, fishing something out of the water. At the crunching sound of size-twelve shoes on the gravel, Desmond turned his head and looked up. "Hi, Lawrence," he said. "How've you been?"

"Fine," Kingston replied, looking down at the cherry-red-and-white koi swimming around. Some were almost two feet long. "Big buggers," he said.

Desmond grunted and, with arms up to his elbows in water, went back to thinning out a tangle of submerged plants that Kingston guessed to be water wisteria. Aquatic plants were not his strong suit.

"I somehow expected a more enthusiastic welcome," said Kingston, addressing Desmond's back. "It must be at least eighteen months since we last saw each other."

Desmond stood, turned, and ceremoniously wiped his

hands on a towel that was draped over the tank. "Sorry, old chap," he said, smiling and shaking Kingston's hand. "So what have you been up to?"

"Among other things, I spent the best part of those last eighteen months down in Somerset, helping a young American woman jump-start a garden that'd been out of commission for about sixty years."

"Heligan revisited, eh?"

"Damn right."

Desmond eyed him closely, frowning and scratching his chin. "Didn't I read something about that? Weren't some valuable paintings found there?"

"There were," said Kingston. "French Impressionists. I'll tell you all about it some other time. It's a three-drink story."

"What brings you to these parts, then? Not just to see my smiling phizog, surely?"

"It's about something that happened a couple of days ago—to a friend of mine. I need to ask you a few questions."

"Same old Kingston." He grinned. "You'll never learn. So whose life are you trying to straighten out this time?"

Kingston didn't think a response was warranted and refrained from any comment.

"Okay, why don't we go to the office? You want a cup of tea?"

"No, don't trouble yourself. I won't be staying that long."

The office was unexpectedly tidy. Far from your typical nursery office, which more often than not was no more than a storage shed with a desk wedged in it. Desmond gestured for Kingston to take a wobbly-looking kitchen chair while he sat down behind his desk. "So, what is it, pray tell, that's important enough to drag you all the way up here? Away from that Belgravia love nest of yours?" asked Desmond, picking up a pencil and tapping it on his knee.

Kingston looked up to the galvanized roof and shook his head in derision. "I'll get right to the point," he replied, shifting on the hard wooden seat. "A friend of mine—Stewart Halliday, a former colleague at Edinburgh—has gone missing. His wife, Becky, called me a couple of days ago. Naturally, she was distraught, so I went down to Hampshire to see her, to offer whatever help I could. Nice comfortable place called the Willows with a big garden on the edge of the New Forest."

Desmond rested his head against the back of the chair, content to listen.

"It seems he was planning to attend a conference in Bristol," said Kingston, pausing. "But he never made it. No notes, phone calls, nothing. He's completely dropped out of sight."

"She's informed the police, I take it?"

Kingston nodded. "Yes, of course. They questioned her and went through his office looking for clues, but so far, they've come up empty-handed."

Desmond tapped the pencil on his lower lip. "So, where do I fit into all this, Doctor Watson?"

For the next five minutes, Kingston explained how, in the old days, he and Stewart used to do *The Times* crossword puzzles and how he'd found and solved the encrypted entry in Stewart's datebook. Following that, he described the second coded message, concealed in the stapler, the one that had led Kingston and Becky to St. Mary's.

In the beginning, Desmond listened patiently, without comment. But as Kingston went on, it became more and more apparent that Desmond was losing interest in what was sounding—the way Kingston was telling it—more and more like a recitation from a forties British spy novel.

When Kingston got to the part where he opened the envelope and withdrew Stewart's formula, it was clear that Desmond had had enough. "Lawrence, I hate to be a bloody bore, but where the hell is this all going?" he said, shaking his head.

"This is where it's going," said Kingston, reacting sharply. He reached in his pocket and pulled out a photocopy of Stewart's original that Kingston had left with Becky to give to the police. "Here," he said, thrusting it across the desk. "You won't be so damned blasé when you read this!"

Desmond studied it for a moment, and then, to Kingston's chagrin, he leaned his head back and started laughing. "You must be joking," he said between the peals of laughter.

Although he'd anticipated some degree of skepticism from Desmond, Kingston wasn't quite prepared for such a spontaneous outburst. For a moment he couldn't decide whether to simply let it pass or tell Desmond where to get off.

"What's so damned funny?" he asked when Desmond had calmed down.

"If I'm interpreting this correctly, Lawrence"—he had put the pencil down and held his hands in front of him as if framing his words—"somehow this water-lily cross is capable of taking salt out of—presumably—seawater. Is that right?" The grin on his face was aggravating Kingston.

"That's how I interpreted it," he replied curtly. "And give me some bloody credit, Desmond. I know as well as you that botanically it would be considered impossible."

"You're right there, chum. Who did you say this friend of yours is?"

Kingston shook his head. "That's the whole *point,* Desmond. The chap's a professor of botany, for Christ's sake.

I taught with him at Edinburgh for ten years. He, of all people, would know it's a million-to-one chance of something like this happening."

A short silence followed while Desmond weighed the implications of what Kingston had just said.

"So, let's get this right," said Desmond. "What you're suggesting is that this friend of yours who's gone missing has by some freak chance, accident…whatever…created a water lily that can desalinate seawater and that you think the two incidents might be connected, right?"

Kingston nodded. "That's what I think, yes. It strikes me as a perfectly reasonable assumption."

"And you've come to me to get *my* opinion on the whole thing?"

"Mostly the botanical part." Kingston paused, choosing his words. "Far-fetched as it sounds, why should we summarily reject the concept? Think about it, Desmond. You know that all plants absorb nutrients from soil and other sources through their leaves and roots. And we know there are plants capable of consuming insects and small animals." He shifted on the hard seat, scraping the legs of the chair on the stone floor, and continued. "What about ant plants that absorb insect parts and other debris dumped by the ant colony that they host?"

Not surprisingly, Desmond didn't look impressed. He was a horticulturist and hadn't heard anything that he didn't know already. However, Kingston wasn't finished.

"And what about all the epiphytic plants, the air plants like the orchids and bromeliads, the ones that require no soil whatsoever to grow, that derive their nutrition from the air, rainwater, and decomposing matter that gets tangled in their roots or leaves?" He drew a breath and got up. Had there been room to pace, he would have. As it was, he stood with his hands gripping the back of the chair as if it were a courthouse rail and Desmond was a one-man jury. "If I walked out of here and told the first person that I met that I'd once seen a plant over thirty feet long that had eaten and digested a rat, what do you think they'd say, Desmond?"

Desmond shrugged. "Oh, come on, Lawrence. I know what you're trying to get at. Let's not summarily reject the idea that a plant can absorb sodium chloride—right?"

"Exactly," said Kingston, snapping his fingers. "I forgot to mention the fern *Pteris vittata*. You know about that greedy little bugger?"

Desmond shook his head. "Can't say as I do."

"It consumes arsenic—in staggering amounts. It extracts the heavy metal from soil or water and concentrates it in its leaves. I understand it's being used in some countries to filter arsenic out of water supplies. Convinced?"

Another short-lived silence followed while Kingston sat down again and let his point sink in, then Desmond spoke. For the first time, he looked a little more earnest.

"So, how can I help?"

"Considering your skepticism, I'm not sure," said Kingston. "You could start by telling me what kind of aquatic plant Stewart might have been tinkering with."

"What kind of question is that? Didn't you say it was a water lily?"

"Let me rephrase it." Desmond could be annoying at times. "Among the varieties of water lily, which in your opinion would be the most likely candidate to cross? Think in terms of size, hardiness, growth, reproductive ability—those kinds of things."

Desmond's eyes moved around the room as he pondered the question. Kingston waited, arms crossed, and then Desmond finally spoke.

"I suppose *Victoria cruziana* would be my first pick."

He nodded, as if agreeing with himself that he'd made the right choice. "Yes, *cruziana*."

"Why?"

"Well, in the first place, it's large. The foliage—pads—can be as much as four to five feet across. It's hardy and very vigorous—'aggressive' might be a better word. It'll take over a pond before you can say 'Bob's your uncle'!"

"The right qualifications," said Kingston, noticing that Desmond was frowning, perhaps rethinking his choice. "There's a problem?" he asked.

"I forgot about *Nelumbo lutea,* the American yellow lotus. I seem to recall reading an article about it some time ago. Its leaves are not quite as big but it will thrive in cooler water. I think it can also tolerate both acidic and alkaline water." He paused, scratching his head. "Come to think of it, I believe the article said that it's also been grown in swimming pools to purify the water naturally, without the use of chlorides—and I'm almost sure it mentioned something to the effect that *lutea* can also absorb heavy metals from water and has been planted in ponds as a method of discharging industrial effluents—pollution management, that sort of thing. In India, I think it was." He paused again and made a poor excuse of a smile. "So, I take back what I implied earlier, Lawrence. But I still think it's a stretch of the imagination that a lotus or water lily could ingest or process salt in some way or other—particularly in large quantities—but hey, with nature, we both know that anything's possible."

Kingston looked considerably more pleased than he had at any time since arriving. "This is more like it, Desmond. What I was hoping to hear."

Desmond shrugged. "My pleasure," he said, looking away.

Kingston could see that he was thinking hard, so didn't interrupt. Then Desmond looked back at him, puzzled.

"Lawrence, if the whole idea of botanical desalination is to be practical, surely it has to be done on a large scale, millions of gallons at a time. Those bloody water lilies are going to have to be working overtime and it would require enormous expanses of water."

"Particularly if they're six feet in diameter."

"Exactly."

"You make a good point, Desmond, but that's a separate issue. And I don't see it as being insurmountable."

Desmond scooted his chair back, talking as he did so. "So, if we accept the fanciful possibility that your friend has indeed hybridized this salt-sucking plant, it opens up a bloody Pandora's box. There's no doubt a lot of people would be interested in knowing about it, right? It raises all kind of questions."

"Foremost among them: What or who is behind Stewart's disappearance, perhaps?"

Desmond frowned, pondering the question. "Could be any number of reasons. Let's face it."

"There are. I've given it a lot of thought."

"You think he's been kidnapped?"

"It's a possibility."

"He could have gone into hiding, I suppose."

"Why, though?"

"Perhaps he felt his life was in danger. How do I know? Maybe you're taking this whole thing too seriously, Lawrence. The chap's only been gone for what—three days?"

"Actually, a week now."

"Even so. He could have had an accident; he could be lying in some hospital bed as we speak; he could have gone away for a couple of days to discuss his discovery with an interested party; he could have had sudden loss of memory and be wandering the streets; he could have decided to leave his wife—there're all kinds of explanations."

"I grant you all the above, except the hospital. The police have already checked that possibility. Question is, why would he go to all the trouble of leaving cryptic messages—unless I've put two and two together and come up with five?"

Desmond scratched his head. "I dunno." He thought over the question some more. "Presumably to conceal his discovery from everyone except you. That you would immediately figure out the message and—"

"Then what? Assuming that it really was a message for me—and frankly, I don't see, really, how it could have been for anyone else."

"I'm not sure."

"That's the problem. Other than his message, which tells us only what Stewart might have discovered, we have no other clues to explain what happened to him or where he is."

Desmond's face was a blank. "You got me," he said.

"Another thing," said Kingston, pausing. "If we're to conclude that Stewart was experimenting with *cruziana* or *lutea,* where was he doing it? It certainly wasn't at The Willows."

"There's no water there, I take it, no lake or a pond?"

"Only an average-sized pond and I didn't see anything unusual about it."

"That would suggest that he was experimenting elsewhere and that others are involved. When you think about it, he would hardly be working alone."

"That's what I figured. That would also explain why there's not a single piece of physical evidence or other clues at The Willows to suggest he was working on a project with such far-reaching potential and long-range humanitarian benefit. There has to be a lab of some kind somewhere, large expanses of salt water. And, you're right, other partners or associates—and money."

Desmond twiddled the pencil between his slender fingers, his eyes fixed on Kingston's. "The more I think about it, you're right about one thing, Lawrence. Putting aside the logistical and physical problems of volume, the ramifications are pretty staggering. Someone stands to make a ton of money." He pointed the pencil at Kingston. "What's the old adage? 'Follow the money'?"

"Right." Kingston nodded.

For a moment neither of them spoke. For his part, Kingston was pleased that Desmond was finally persuaded that Stewart had somehow pulled off an improbable discovery and that it was not just a prank of some kind. At the same time, he was contemplating the ramifications.

"Here's what I think," said Kingston. "Given the date on the calendar—Friday, the day he went missing—it's more than likely that Stewart wrote that message and hid it in haste."

"You think he had some kind of premonition?"

"Right. If he wanted me to know about his discovery, why wouldn't he have simply picked up the phone and told me about it or told me over lunch on one of his trips up to town."

"If it were me, I would certainly want to keep it a secret, but if you two are as close as you say, then it would be perfectly natural or expected that he'd confide in you. You say that even his wife was not aware of what he was up to?"

"No, she wasn't, believe it or not."

"When you say 'in haste,' then kidnapping would seem much more probable."

Kingston sighed. "It would, though let's hope to God that's not what's happened."

They talked for a few more minutes, then Kingston

left the nursery with a promise to ring Desmond when he had more news of Stewart. In return, Desmond said that he would call a couple of friends who were water-plant experts and do some more research on the water lilies in question.

IN THE THREE DAYS following Kingston's trip to St. Albans, he had spoken with Becky on the phone twice, each time to find the situation unchanged. In the first of those conversations, he had told her all about his meeting with Desmond, quizzing her again about Stewart's day-to-day activities: Did he have any visitors recently? Was he gone for stretches at a time? Could she think of anything, no matter how insignificant or unrelated, that might offer clues about her husband's experiment with water-lily plants? The answers to all his questions were negative.

Following up on his request, Becky had spoken with William, the part-time gardener, who said he couldn't think of anything odd or unusual about Stewart's demeanor of late or anything different about the garden, and that there had been no recent visitors. William said he would be happy to talk with Kingston on the phone or when he next came down. Before hanging up, she told Kingston that she was planning to spend a few days with her daughter, Sarah, in Shrewsbury. She gave him the address and phone number where she could be reached, saying that she'd also given it to the police.

The only other line of inquiry left was the Sarum Garden Club. According to the eight-page newsletter, which Kingston had read from cover to cover, the next monthly Wednesday evening meeting was still several days away. Though he had a feeling it could end up being a waste of time, he still planned to go. He was determined more than ever to find out exactly what it was that had led to Stewart's disappearance.

Becky's going to Shrewsbury came at an expedient time because Kingston had an unusual assignment for the next two days—unusual for him, that is. Early the next morning, he was meeting pilot Chris Norton of Henley Air Services at Kidlington airport, near Oxford. Kingston's task was to capture aerial footage of six of southern England's most treasured gardens.

Much as he would have liked to keep up his investigation and continue helping Becky cope with her ordeal, he had little choice in the matter. Canceling was out of the question this late in the day. The company that had hired both the chopper and Kingston's services for the day was New Eden Productions, a small concern that specialized in the production of film and videotaped programs featuring prominent British gardens and country estates. It would be the first time he had viewed these gardens from the air and he was looking forward to the ride.

FIVE

THE HIGH-PITCHED WHINE gave way to a rising thrashing noise as the rotor blades became a white blur, the tail tilted upward, and the helicopter lifted off the tarmac at Kidlington airport.

The five-seat Bell 206 JetRanger carried only one passenger. In the contoured cabin, next to pilot Chris Norton, Kingston sat with a slim laptop computer mounted in front of him. The computer was linked to a gyro-stabilized digital video camera mounted on the nose of the craft. The chopper soon reached cruising altitude, climbing through the threads of light clouds that stitched the skies over the green countryside below. Their route would take them directly south over Newbury and Andover to the first garden located above Romsey, near the northern edge of the New Forest. The light buffeting during the climb had ceased and Norton turned to his passenger. "We'll be over Mottisfont in about fifteen minutes or so. You all set with that thing, Doctor?" he asked, glancing at the laptop.

Kingston nodded. "As ready as I'll ever be," he replied, nodding.

A week earlier, he had undergone several hours of computer instruction, learning how to operate the software system that controlled all camera functions. On this, his maiden outing, the first subject on which he would test his skills was Mottisfont Abbey garden—in particular the three-acre walled rose garden therein, featuring Graham

Stuart Thomas's magnificent collection of ancestral species and nineteenth-century rose cultivars.

Ten minutes had passed when Chris put the craft into a shallow bank and began his descent toward their destination. Kingston glanced at the altimeter—a little under a thousand feet. Looking out of the cockpit window, he could see the helicopter's shadow bobbing across the fields beneath them. The skies above were now clear and blue.

"Over there," Chris said, pointing at the imposing abbey set in the midst of spacious lawns, surrounded by gigantic trees.

"Magnificent," said Kingston, who lined up the videocam as Chris did a direct pass low over the lawns—the chevron pattern created by the mower clearly visible—and then swooped up over the rooftops of the former twelfth-century Augustinian priory. After two more passes over the abbey and grounds, Kingston pointed out the walled rose garden located in the northwest corner of the grounds. Ten minutes later, Kingston was satisfied that he had enough footage and instructed Norton to head for their next location, Cranborne Manor Garden in Dorset. The flying time to Cranborne in Dorset was only a matter of minutes but it was enough time for Kingston to tell Chris about Stewart's disappearance. Ordinarily he might not have brought it up, being of little or no interest to the pilot, but in this case it was apt, as their route took them directly over Fordingbridge and The Willows. Circling over the house, there were no signs of Becky or anyone else and no cars visible. They continued on their route.

Twenty minutes later, with comprehensive footage of Cranborne Manor garden "in the can," they headed southeast toward Milford on Sea and the Solent, the stretch of water separating the south coast from the Isle of Wight. The next leg of their journey was the long run across the south of England to the legendary garden at Sissinghurst Castle in Kent. Rather than fly overland, Chris had suggested a more scenic route, following the southern coastline of Hampshire, and West and East Sussex. Kingston couldn't argue with that. Their altitude was now 1,500 feet and climbing as they neared the coastline.

"Hold on," said Kingston, touching Chris's arm. "I'd like to get a shot of that little village with the thatches and the field of blue linseed we just passed. It could make a good opening for the piece."

"Sure," said Chris, already in a bank, making a wide circle and losing altitude. In less than a minute they were back, passing low then hovering over the village for a minute or so while Kingston shot sufficient footage to satisfy him. They resumed their course toward the coast.

At first Kingston thought nothing of the tiny flashes coming from the edge of what looked like a farm. Then, over the noise of the engine, he heard the sound of something hitting the fuselage under them. In a few seconds he realized what was happening. Someone was firing at them.

Norton shot him an alarmed look as he put the chopper through a violent emergency maneuver that thrust Kingston into his seat back. For a moment they were climbing rapidly, the engine screaming at maximum power, then banking at an impossible angle. Straightening up, Chris ran his eyes over the instrument cluster, then looked at Kingston again.

"Sod it! We're losing fuel. Crazy bastard!"

Kingston knew what it portended but wasn't exactly sure how serious it might be. Given the circumstances, he was surprised that he was not shaking like jelly. "Do we have enough to make a landing somewhere?"

"We'll know in a few seconds," said Chris. "If we have to go to autorotation, we've got to find a place to land, real quick." No sooner had the words left his mouth than the engine coughed and the fuselage shuddered. Less than half a minute later, the engine spluttered and died. It was eerily quiet as the helicopter continued its forward motion, the rotor blades propelled by the air forced through them.

"We're in luck," said Chris, gripping the control stick with both hands, keeping the craft stable. "Up there. See that field of yellow rape? That'll do nicely."

Suddenly Kingston felt a lot better. A few seconds earlier he had been thinking about preparing to meet his maker. He said nothing, not wanting to break Chris's concentration while he was zeroed in, fighting to keep the craft on an even keel.

Now less than two hundred feet from the ground, they were losing altitude quickly and Kingston was starting to wonder whether they would make the field. If they came up short, they would land on top of the dense woods bordering the field. From above, the trees didn't look large, but he knew they were big enough to rip the helicopter apart if they drew that straw.

Closing in on the ground, their airspeed was much faster than Kingston realized. Chris had flared the helicopter and was preparing it for the short run on landing. In seconds, they were over the woods and could hear the landing skids raking the treetops, broken branches and leaves scattering like black confetti in their wake. Chris gave him a quick sideways glance. "Could be a bumpy ride," he said between clenched teeth.

They were past the trees and less than thirty feet from the ground and the sea of buttercup-yellow rape. "Hold tight—we're going to lose the skids and land on our belly." At that instant they heard the skids collapsing as they hit the ground hard, bouncing on the crushed vegetation.

It was perhaps just as well that Kingston didn't know

it right then, but if the main rotor blades, still rotating at considerable speed, had touched the ground, the impact would have flipped them upside down. As it was, Chris managed to keep the helicopter stable. It shuddered and shimmied, then finally slowed, coming to rest at an odd angle. Kingston tried to open his door but it was jammed.

Immediately, Chris was on the radio reporting the shooting, their crash landing, and their location to air-traffic control. The information would then be dispatched to the police control room at Netley Support H.Q., Southampton. They would take it from there. Signing off, Chris released his harness, opened the cockpit door, and started to climb out. "You okay?" he asked. Kingston nodded then followed the pilot out into the fresh air, gripping the laptop and his bag.

Outside, legs a little unsteady, he looked up at the sky, closed his eyes, took a long breath, then exhaled loudly. "Had me worried there for a minute," he said. "Thanks, Chris. Hell of a landing."

By then, the pilot was busy inspecting the camera and removing the digital tape.

FOLLOWING NORTON'S radio call, the police control room had immediately dispatched two ARVs (armed response vehicles), each with two armed officers, to check out the area where the shooting took place. In addition, uniformed patrols would soon take up static points within the general area to observe and note down vehicle movements and registrations if they felt it necessary. A police Air Support, Britten-Norman Defender turboprop surveillance aircraft would also fly over the area, transmitting digital video to the police control room. On landing, the digital tapes would be bagged and tagged as evidence and working copies made.

Simultaneously, two police area cars under the command of a uniformed inspector had been dispatched from Lymington to the crash site. After briefly questioning Norton and Kingston and making sure they were not injured, they had taken initial command of the site, setting up a taped inner crime-scene cordon to preserve the scene for forensic examination, then a second outer cordon to keep the public and press back and to allow police a safe working area outside the inner cordon. Soon thereafter, Kingston and Norton had been taken by police car to nearby Lymington.

Kingston and Chris Norton sat in an office at Lymington Police Station, one of six that make up the New Forest Basic Command Unit, which was part of the Hampshire and Isle of Wight Constabulary. Norton was describing the shooting and the ensuing crash to the senior C.I.D. Officer, Detective Inspector Chisholm, and his deputy, Sergeant Jennings. In the coming hours, as Chisholm explained, a chief detective forensics inspector from the Major Crime Team, based in nearby Southampton, would also be assigned to the case.

"Well," said Inspector Chisholm, "it looks like we've got two possibilities. Either someone didn't want you snooping around or some lunatic simply decided to single you out for target practice. If I were to hazard a guess, I'd say it was the former."

"It's quite likely that whoever did the shooting saw the camera and decided that they didn't want their picture taken," said Sergeant Jennings. "That thing sticks out like a bloody sore thumb."

"At our altitude, they couldn't miss it, that's for sure," Chris replied.

"You checked out the area where the gunfire took place?" asked Kingston.

"We did and still are," Chisholm replied. "But if there *was* something that they didn't want you to see from the air, more likely it would have been somewhere else in the vicinity. I doubt very much if they'd be that careless in drawing attention to the actual location." He paused. "I forgot to ask. Was your camera running when the shots occurred?"

"I'm almost certain it was off by that time," Kingston replied.

"Nevertheless, it might be a good idea for us to make a copy before you leave."

After a moment of silence, Sergeant Jennings spoke up. "And you're sure you saw nothing else unusual? Nothing that would warrant someone firing at you?" Norton shook his head and smiled. "I was kind of busy at the time."

The sergeant looked at Kingston.

Kingston shook his head. Other than a marijuana farming operation, what could be so unusual? He was having difficulty trying to imagine what on earth could justify such a drastic, potentially deadly action. "Nothing," he answered.

Several more minutes of conversation followed before Chisholm thanked them both and got up, ready to leave. "There are some real nutters out there," he observed, shaking his head. Anyway," he said with a sniff, "we'll let you know the minute we find anything. If air support comes up with anything on video, we'll let you know."

"At one point, could I take a look at their tape?" asked Kingston.

"Very doubtful, I would think. It'll be considered part of an ongoing criminal investigation. If they deem it non-sensitive, I suppose there might be a chance of seeing a vetted working copy." He shook his head. "Truthfully, I don't know. I've never been asked that question before."

Before leaving the police station, Kingston put a call through to Martin Davis, the managing director of New Eden Productions, to learn that hc was out for a couple of days. Kingston gave his secretary, Milly, a brief account of what had happened, saying that unless he heard to the contrary from Martin, he would reschedule the remainder of the shoot as soon as he could get a new date from Henley Air—depending on the weather and most likely within the next several days.

"If that had happened to me, I'd be terrified to go up again. At least, so soon," said Milly.

"Don't worry, I'm going to insist on a different route," Kingston replied with a chuckle. "Besides, as someone once said, the reason lightning doesn't strike twice in the same place, my dear, is that the same place isn't there the second time."

It was almost dark by the time Kingston turned the key in the front door of his flat. All he was thinking of by then was the welcome-home glass of Macallan waiting for him—that and kicking his shoes off and getting a good night's sleep. On top of everything else, his back was aching, not surprising when he thought about the crash landing.

The journey by train and taxi from Waterloo had taken more than three hours, and he was thankful now that he and Chris had used the hour-and-a-half wait for the next train to grab a quick meal at the Bell, a pub close to the station recommended by the sergeant. Steak and ale and mushroom pies big enough to feed a small family, washed down with a pint of Courage best bitter, had put them both in a much better mood. As their empty plates were taken away, Chris had asked Kingston if he was sure he wanted to finish the photo shoot. "After what we went through,

I wouldn't blame you one bit if you want to opt out," he said. Kingston assured him that he was up for it and would be all the better for it as a result of the practice run. They also discussed the question of Kingston's car, which was parked at Henley Air. If the next shoot were within a few days, he would leave it there. If not, he told Chris he would try to bribe Andrew with a nice lunch to drive Kingston to Oxford to pick it up. Before parting company, it was left that the minute Chris got back to Oxford, he would have his people check the schedule for the next few days and let Kingston know when they could go up again to resume videotaping.

Kingston turned on a light in the living room, put down his leather bag containing the tape and the laptop, and re-wound the answerphone tape. He played back the messages while he poured his drink: two fingers of malt whisky (never measured) and an equal amount of Malvern water. The first two messages were of no importance. The third was from Martin Davis at New Eden. Typical of him, the message was brief: *"It's Martin, Lawrence—Milly gave me your message. What a nasty mess. Glad you're all in one piece, though. Give me a call on my mobile when you feel up to it. Here's the number."* Kingston jotted it down. He was about to reach for the phone when he paused, looking at his watch. It was by no means too late to call Martin back but he decided he'd had enough Q&A for one day.

Tomorrow was Saturday, which meant Kingston would have to wait until Monday before he could review the footage. First thing in the morning, he would call Transmedia, New Eden's post-production studio, to book an appointment, with any luck, for Monday. Being Saturday, though, he doubted they'd be open.

Kingston had a full weekend coming up. Saturday, he had tickets for a symphony concert at Barbican Hall and

Sunday was also spoken for, with lunch in Hampstead with a bohemian artist friend, Henrietta, followed by a visit to the Tate Modern to view an exhibition of naturalistic and abstract paintings by Kandinsky. He had accepted the "date" reluctantly, knowing that he would be subject to Henrietta's brazen amorous overtures, added to which, modernist painting, in particular, was hardly his cuppa. However, Hussy Henrietta—as he called her—was not one to take "no" easily.

Kingston flicked on the television and reached for his whisky.

THE BEDROOM WAS ALREADY awash with light when Kingston awoke on Monday morning. No sooner than his toes touched the carpet, the phone started ringing in the living room. Grabbing his robe, putting it on as he loped down the hall, he managed to get to the phone just before the answerphone kicked in.

"Lawrence Kingston?" a man's voice inquired.

"This is he," Kingston mumbled, running a hand through his tangled hair.

"My name's Patrick. I work for Martin Davis at New Eden."

"Oh, yes, good morning."

"Milly's out sick and Martin wanted to know if you shot any footage on Friday. If you did, he'd like to take a look at it—mainly for quality."

Kingston thought for a moment. Hadn't he told Milly that they got at least twenty minutes of good footage of the two gardens? Now he couldn't be sure. From what he was hearing, he hadn't, or why would they be calling? "We did, yes, about twenty minutes, I would guess," he replied. "Tell Martin I'll be taking a look at it at Transmedia, in Hammersmith, hopefully later this morning, if they can squeak me in—then I'll send it over. We're going to re-schedule the rest of the shoot, in the next couple of days, while this good weather is still around."

"Excellent."

Kingston paused, expecting him to go on, but he said no more.

"Well, then—Patrick—as soon as I know when that is, I'll let him know."

"Thank you, Mr. Kingston. I'll pass the message on." Then he hung up.

Not yet fully awake, Kingston thought nothing more of the call. He fetched *The Times* from the front doorstep, returned to the kitchen, and plugged in the electric kettle. Tea was always the first order of the day, Earl Grey with a slice of lemon. Waiting for the kettle to boil, he glanced over the headlines and took a quick look at the race cards for Sandown and Chepstow. The crossword came next, once tea was poured.

An hour and a half later, after two slices of toast and marmalade and ten solutions penciled in, Kingston was ready to face the day. First on the list was the call to Trans-media, to book a time to review the footage. He would look a right berk if, for some reason, the tape were blank.

The footage? He thought back to the phone call from Patrick. There was something not quite right about it. What was it? He tried reconstructing the conversation. He got to the end where Patrick had said "Excellent," but nothing more. Then, suddenly, he knew what was missing. Why hadn't he asked to see the tape, to pick it up for Martin? Now he *knew* that something was wrong.

Kingston dialed the number Martin had given him. Martin answered right away.

"Hello, Lawrence. Good to hear from you. That must

have been one scary experience. Milly told me all about it. Are you all right?"

"I am now, sure. As a matter of fact, I'm taking another shot at it in the next few days."

Martin either missed or ignored Kingston's dubious choice of words. "You know, Lawrence, if you'd rather, we can always hire a photographer. I don't want you to feel obligated."

"It's not a problem, Martin. Like I told Milly, lightning doesn't strike twice in the same place."

Martin chuckled. "Yes, she told me your little joke."

"How is she feeling, by the way?"

"Fine—as far as I'm aware."

"Your chap Patrick who called earlier this morning said she was out sick."

"Patrick?"

"Yes. He said you wanted to know if we shot any footage on Friday."

An unusually long pause followed, then Martin said, "There's no one named Patrick working here, Lawrence."

SIX

KINGSTON GOT OFF the number 10 bus at the Latymer Court stop in Hammersmith. From there, according to the personable young woman at the studio who had given him directions earlier that morning, it was only a short walk to the studio. With the digital tape, a lightweight windbreaker, and a few other bits and pieces in a black leather bag slung from his shoulder, he set off to find 23 Ovesden Terrace.

He found the address with no trouble, but wasn't prepared for a handsome three-story Victorian house. He had been expecting something more commercial for a recording studio—a storefront maybe. He checked his note to make sure he had the right address—then he spotted the discreet stainless-steel Transmedia Studios plaque on the brick wall to the right of the shiny black door. He pressed the doorbell below the plaque and waited.

As the door opened, he felt a slight tug at his shoulder. A young woman faced him, holding the door open. She put a hand up to her mouth as if she were about to scream, shock registered on her face. Then Kingston realized what had happened. His bag was gone. Turning, he saw a man racing down the empty street, the bag tucked under his arm. Kingston watched helplessly as the man disappeared round the corner. There was no earthly hope of catching up with the thief. The tape was gone.

Kingston went inside and called the police. Then, taking the advice of the duty policewoman, he took off down the street in the direction the man had fled. Chances were, she had said, that if the thief found nothing of value in the bag, then he would soon dump it. And she was right. About twenty yards from the corner, Kingston spotted his bag lying under some black-spotted roses behind an iron railing. Retrieving it, he saw that the shoulder strap was cleanly cut. A box cutter, he guessed, as he checked the contents. As he suspected, the tape was gone but everything else was intact.

Kingston walked back to Hammersmith Road and hopped on another number 10 bus headed for home. Sitting on the bus, thinking about the unlikely turn of events of the past twenty minutes, he made a snap decision to make a short detour. If he got off at the Natural History Museum stop, he could walk to Old Brompton Street and Atkinson's, the luggage shop where he had purchased the bag a year ago. A half hour later he was back at his flat, a new strap on the bag. Right away he called Martin to give him the bad news about the tape, but he wasn't in. Leaving a message for Martin to call, he then called Becky in Shrewsbury, only to get the answering machine.

Kingston had some thinking to do. Too many disturbing things were happening, and all in the space of a few days. But first, he had to have something to eat. He'd never been one to think too well on an empty stomach. Knowing that there was nothing in the fridge that had the makings of a half-decent lunch, he decided he might just as well do his thinking over a pub lunch and a pint of London Pride bitter. Fifteen minutes later, he was sitting in the upstairs bar of the Antelope, a genteel 175-year-old pub with oak floors and photos of the pub cricket team covering the downstairs wood-paneled walls. The room exuded an aroma that was hard to pin down—an impossible to describe or replicate coalescing of food, beer, spirits, and conviviality, aged over a century and a half. It now permeated the very bones of the room and its contents. Kingston found it comforting. He had chosen the Antelope as his "local" shortly after moving to Chelsea.

As luck would have it, the bar was quieter than usual. An elderly couple, hunched silently in a corner over half pints, and a small group of young business types—who seemed more intent on talking than eating—were the only other patrons. Kingston took a sip of beer, looked over the menu, and made a quick decision what to order: scampi with peas, tartar sauce, and lemon. It came with chips, one of his few dietary weaknesses, but, like with ice cream and chocolate, nowadays he only indulged once in a while.

He leaned back, staring absently at a sepia-toned photo of legendary nineteenth-century English cricketer W. G. Grace. In his mind, he was replaying the helicopter shooting. Not a word from the Lymington police, which he took to mean that their search and reconnaissance hadn't turned up anything worth reporting. Neither had he heard back from Chris Norton or anybody from Henley Air about rescheduling the photo shoot. He and Chris had gone over every single detail of the shooting, first with Inspector Chisholm and afterward at the pub in Lymington, without coming up with a single clue that might shed at least *some* light on the case. Had they all overlooked something? If they had, he couldn't think what on earth it could be. The other thing—and they'd belabored this, too: What could possibly be so important, worth keeping from the eyes of strangers, that would warrant taking down a helicopter at the risk of killing two people? He kept coming up with all questions and no answers.

What with the helicopter downing, the phony "Patrick" call, and now this morning's episode with the tape, Kingston had had little to no time to give much more thought to Stewart's disappearance. The last thing he wanted was

to give Becky the impression that he had forgotten her.
And what about Stewart? So far, that was a dead end, too.
He thought back to his conversation with Desmond and
the idea that Stewart might have been kidnapped. Taking
another sip of beer, he mulled over that scenario. If that
were the case, then what was the reason? A couple came
to mind. The most obvious—also the flimsiest—was that
someone had found out about Stewart's discovery and had
abducted him to get the desalination formula, at the same
time preventing him from approaching other interested
parties with his ecological breakthrough. But if Stewart
was working with others—as Kingston and Desmond figured was the case—this theory became even less plausible.

The only other reason Kingston could come up with
was that Stewart had got in over his head and wanted
out. If so and Stewart wanted off the team, his partners
or associates might find themselves in a sticky situation.
One way of dealing with this turn of events—a little extreme, granted—would be for them to hold Stewart against
his will until they could sort it out or until he came round
to their way of thinking. In either case the guilty parties
would know that when Stewart didn't show up after a few
days, it would become a missing-persons case and the
police would be looking for them, too.

He finished the scampi but not the chips. Leaving a few
on the plate somehow made him feel a little less guilty,
though he knew he was kidding himself. Reaching in his
pocket for his wallet, another thought occurred to him.
How did the thief know he had the tape? And, come to
think of it, how did that Patrick bloke know that Kingston had shot the footage? He must have got the information from Henley Air. Their name was on the helicopter.
Where else would he have got it? He must have called New
Eden, too. Otherwise how would he have known Martin's

name? Kingston made a note to call Martin and then Henley to ask whether anyone had been making inquiries and to talk about picking up his car.

Leaving a larger-than-called-for tip, Kingston left the Antelope and walked back through the drizzle to Cadogan Square, glad he'd thought to tuck a folding umbrella in his jacket pocket.

His answerphone displayed two messages. The first was from Chris Norton at Henley Air, wanting to know if the coming Monday would be okay for Kingston to reschedule and reassuring Kingston that his TR4 was safely locked in one of the hangars. The second message was from a pleasant-sounding Detective Inspector Carmichael, Ringwood Police Station, leaving a number and asking for Kingston to return his call. Kingston's first thought—hope, really—was that maybe there was a break in Stewart's case. He picked up the phone, dialed the number, and was put through immediately.

"Yes, Doctor, thanks for getting back to me so quickly. I'm working on the Stewart Halliday case," Carmichael said, all businesslike.

Kingston, hoping for positive news, didn't interrupt.

"Becky Halliday tells me that you were once an associate of her husband's and it was you who found his message. She told me all about it. Clever of you, by the way."

"Thanks. I did, yes," Kingston replied, wondering why it had taken them so long to call him.

"A bit unusual, his using cryptic messages, wouldn't you say? Why was that, do you think?"

"The only explanation I could come up with was that he wanted only me to read the messages. To tell me what he stumbled on."

"Why not just pick up the phone and tell you?"

"I asked myself the same question. I can only assume that he did it in an awful hurry. At the last minute."

"A premonition of some kind?"

"That's what I concluded."

"This discovery of his—I mean the notion that some kind of water plant can desalinate seawater—is this on the up and up? Is it possible?"

"Becky told you, then?"

"She did, yes."

"Damn!" Kingston muttered under his breath. He'd forgotten to impress upon Becky not to tell anyone about the desalination discovery, after she had suggested telling the police about it. He knew from past experience, with the discovery of the blue rose those many years ago, what a Pandora's box that would open. The minute the media got wind of such an unprecedented scientific breakthrough, the news would become global overnight. It would be splashed across the front pages of newspapers, magazines, and the Internet; trumpeted on TV and radio news programs; and dissected on every current-affairs and talk show. The repercussions could be formidable, not the least of which would be the media frenzy that would descend on The Willows. Becky would become a hostage in her own home, and her life would become even more intolerable. That alone was reason enough for him to want Stewart's message kept just between the two of them. He just hoped Carmichael's knowing didn't mean that the floodgates were soon to open. Too late now, he thought to himself.

"I'm sorry, Inspector," he said. "Your question: Could this plant desalinate seawater?"

"Right."

"That's a tough one. If you were to have asked me that question a month ago, I would have said it wasn't possible. But now I'm not so sure."

"What does that mean?"

"Last week I talked to a friend of mine who knows all there is worth knowing about aquatic plants. When I told him what had happened, he all but laughed in my face. But the more we talked about it, the more we both came to realize that it wasn't totally science fiction. I won't go into all the botanical rationale but the bottom line—well, our belief—is that the possibility can't be ruled out."

"I must say, it all sounds a bit iffy to me." Carmichael sniffed. "Becky tells me you think he must have been working with other people on these experiments—whatever you call them."

"Yes. That was based on the fact that there was nothing in the house or on the property to suggest Stewart was working at home. In order to reach such a discovery, one would need large amounts of salt water and a number of water-lily plants, for starters. My friend and I think that the particular cross—new variety, that is—that Stewart had created could be quite large, as much as five feet across."

"That's what we have concluded—I don't mean the size, which is hard to imagine, but the fact that he was carrying out his experiments elsewhere and as you suggest, in all likelihood, with others."

Kingston decided to ask the all-important question. "You think he's been kidnapped?"

"Let me put it this way. The longer it goes without his turning up, the more that becomes a possibility. Either that or he's no longer alive."

An uncomfortable pause followed, after which Carmichael asked another question.

"If Halliday was able to desalinate seawater with these plants, this would be something that he—or I should say, they—would want to keep very much to themselves, I take it?"

"No doubt about it. When you consider how many countries in the world are lacking in supplies of potable water and water for irrigation, the ramifications are pretty obvious. Putting it mildly, it would be a huge scientific breakthrough. And, if—and it's a big 'if,' mind you—it could be put to practical use, it could be worth a small fortune over the long haul."

After another longer-than-usual pause, Kingston asked, "I take it you haven't had any breaks in the case, then?"

"I'm afraid not. That's really the reason for my call. Knowing of your friendship with Halliday and your expertise in the subject, I wanted to see if you had anything to offer that we might have overlooked."

"I wish I had but I keep coming up with blanks, too."

Kingston heard a muffled sneeze followed by a pause and some nose blowing. "Gesundheit!" he said.

"Sorry. Bloody cold—can't shake the damned thing. Anyway, where was I? Right. So, I gather from what you're saying that we should be looking for an expanse of water with lilies floating on it, correct?" There was the slightest trace of sarcasm in his tone.

"Bit of a tall order, I know, but—yes."

"And where do we look? It could be damned well anywhere. In any case, if this discovery is as huge as you suggest, wouldn't they attempt to conceal the pond or whatever?"

"As best they could, yes. But you have to think of it as resembling a large, low-lying greenhouse, so it's unlikely they could conceal the operation entirely."

"Sounds like a job for Air Support to me." He paused, Kingston hearing suppressed nose blowing again. "Well, Professor, thanks for your cooperation. I'll get back to you the minute we hear anything worth reporting. And if you come up with any bright ideas, let me know."

"I will, Inspector," Kingston replied. "The area *was* taped by Air Support, by the way. You can check with Inspector Chisholm at Lymington on that. They did it after our helicopter went down."

"Yes, I was coming to that. I got the report. You were damned lucky to come away unscathed. Fortunate that you had a damned good pilot, from all accounts."

"You're right about that, Inspector."

"Anyway, I'll give Chisholm a call—see what they taped." He paused, sniffling. "Five feet across, you said?"

"Right."

"Not your everyday water lily, that's for sure."

Carmichael gave Kingston his direct phone number, his mobile number, and hung up.

Kingston flopped on the sofa and reviewed the conversation. He wished now that he'd suggested discreetly that Carmichael keep the discovery from the press. He made a mental note to bring it up the next time they talked. He looked up, staring at the intricately scrolled plaster rosette in the center of the ceiling, pulling on his earlobe— a reflex action when he was thinking in overdrive. Could the two events be connected? he wondered. That the helicopter had been fired on because they flew too close for comfort to where the desalination tests were being performed? The more he thought about it, the more it made sense. The two events had occurred within an area of less than fifteen miles, from Fordingbridge to just northwest of Lymington. Why hadn't he thought of it before? If that were the case, how would it change things? Off the bat, he couldn't think how it could help the search for Stewart or to pinpoint the place where the hypothetical test facility was located. That was all speculation. He got up, wondering if he should call Inspector Carmichael back and tell him. He decided to wait. He wanted to think about it some more.

Next, Kingston returned Chris Norton's call. Told by Henley Air's manager that Chris was up flying and wouldn't return to the office until the following day, Kingston left a message confirming that Monday was fine for the videotaping and that he would pick up his car then. When Kingston asked if anyone had been making inquiries about him or the taping over the past few days, the manager said that she wasn't aware of anyone having called, and that even if there had been, she would be the person to take the calls.

Phone calls out of the way, he dashed off a quick letter to Kew Gardens confirming his appearance as a featured speaker at an upcoming symposium. This reminded him that he also had to call the Sarum Garden Club to make sure that their monthly meeting was taking place on Wednesday, a couple of days away, and let them know that he would be attending as a guest. He had already arranged to borrow Andrew's car, a cherry-red Mini Cooper S that had been garaged for most of its one-year life. Kingston was really looking forward to that spin.

SEVEN

THE SARUM GARDEN CLUB meetings took place in a back room of St. Hilda's, a picture-postcard church on a maple-lined street on the outskirts of Salisbury. Arriving about fifteen minutes before the meeting was to get under way, Kingston introduced himself to the club president, Phillip Austin, with whom he'd spoken on the phone. Austin reiterated that it had come as a nasty shock when he and other club members had read the missing-persons report in the *Wiltshire Times*. "It explained why Stewart had missed quite a few meetings of late," he said.

Because of Kingston's stature in the horticultural world and his newfound fame as a quasi-celebrity sleuth, Austin suggested that Kingston be introduced at the beginning of the meeting and again before the meeting adjourned, when he would tell the forty or so members more about Stewart's disappearance and appeal for help from among those in attendance.

Ten minutes after being introduced, Kingston sat on a folding chair warming his hands around a paper coffee cup at the back row of the chilly room. The chit-chat subsided as the club secretary, a tall, silver-haired lady with a lorgnette, of all things, hanging from her neck, approached the lectern, a simple wooden affair with a cross carved on the front panel. In a cultured and commanding voice worthy of a dog-obedience trainer, she launched into a report on recent club activities, congratulated members who had won awards at the regional flower show, announced an upcoming day trip to the Royal National Rose Society gardens near St. Albans, and last, reminded everyone that the guest speaker for the next meeting would be none other than Gertrude Pickering, a respected landscape designer, whose presentation was entitled "Hardscaping, where garden design begins."

Up next was guest speaker Nigel Sutherland, whose specialty was clematis. Along with a slide show, he spent the next hour (and then some) going through the ABC's of growing and caring for the "queen of vines," as he called them. His presentation was exhaustive and informative, and the photos, taken by him, were of professional quality. Lamentably, Nigel had a Scottish accent that you could cut with a knife. Even Kingston, who had spent most of his teaching years in Edinburgh, could grasp about one half of what Nigel was chuntering on about.

Enthusiastic applause and next it was Kingston's turn.

"Good evening, everyone," he said, standing like a preacher, both hands on the lectern. "Most of you already know why I'm here tonight. It concerns a member of your club and a former associate and good friend of mine, Stewart Halliday. As has been reported in the newspapers, Stewart has gone missing. A little over two weeks ago, he left home to attend a conference in Bristol but never showed up. He hasn't been seen nor heard from since." Kingston paused, aware that his introductory statement had contained nothing new. "I realize that if any of you had information concerning Stewart's disappearance, you would have reported it to the police by now. However, I have some new information that could have a bearing on the matter. It is the reason I'm here." He cast his penetrating blue eyes over the silent audience. "His wife, Becky, tells me that he had been working on a project involving aquatic plants. We don't know the specifics, but if any of you has any knowledge whatsoever as to what Stewart might have been up to, please let me know. Even if it's something that you might think trivial or not worth mentioning, don't keep it to yourself—it could help in finding Stewart. Anything you tell me will be passed on to the police, of course. You can tell me now or after the meeting, if you prefer." He cast his eyes over the somber-faced audience. No one spoke.

The meeting broke up shortly thereafter and Kingston found himself cornered and being peppered with questions, mostly concerning Stewart, but a few members wanted to know first-hand about his now-celebrated garden-restoration project in Somerset the year before. At the time, stories about the event had appeared in just about every newspaper and magazine in the country and on most television stations. For good reasons, it had struck a chord with the British public. What had started as an assignment to supervise rehabilitation of an abandoned garden, inherited by a young American woman, had evolved into a bona fide murder-mystery case reaching back to World War II. Kingston's investigations had culminated in an unprecedented architectural discovery: a labyrinthine complex of catacombs under the site of an old Benedictine priory and, with it, the recovery of several French Impressionist paintings that were looted by the Nazis during the occupation of Europe. Both the young woman and Kingston had become overnight celebrities.

Kingston left the church and walked up the street to the parked Mini. He wasn't aware of being followed but stopped and turned when he heard his name called. Walking toward him was a tall man, thin as a broom handle, with hair ridiculously long for his age, who in the poor light looked to Kingston to be around sixty. He was wearing a dark colored duffel coat over a Fair Isle sweater. As he passed under the streetlamp between them, Kingston recognized him as one of the club members. He remembered the sweater; Kingston's mother used to knit a similar pattern.

"Can I have a word?" he said as he caught up with Kingston.

"Of course," Kingston replied, hoping that the man wasn't going to ask more questions about the Somerset affair.

"It's about Stewart Halliday. I didn't want to bring it up back there," he said, nodding over his shoulder.

"That's fine. You know something about Stewart?"

"Not much, but it might be of help. My name's Howard Oswald, by the way." He paused, twiddling the toggle on his coat apprehensively. Then he continued, "First of all, Stewart hasn't been to a meeting for over three months— could be four."

"Yes, Phillip Austin told me but he didn't say as long as four months. That's a long time."

"It is and he hardly ever missed a meeting before. Take my word for it, Doctor. Anyway, some time back, Stewart and I got to chatting after one of the meetings and he asked me what I knew about water plants. Not much, really, I admitted. I have a small pond but I'm thinking of filling it in, actually—it's more of a nuisance than anything else. On top of which, my wife keeps on complaining about mosquitoes. She's got this thing in her head about the West Nile virus but for the life of me I can't convince her that we haven't had a single case of it yet in England."

"So where's all this headed, then?"

"Sorry. Let me get to the point. Soon after Stewart approached me, I learned that he'd hooked up with another club member, Adrian Walsh, who's quite an expert on the subject." Oswald wrinkled his nose. "Bit of a pushy sort at times. He owns a big house over by the Woodfords, not far from that nice garden there."

"Heale House."

"Yes, that's the one. I've never been to Adrian's place, though it was on one of the garden tours once. Quite a fancy pile, from all accounts. Anyway, for what it's worth, I know he has a large water feature there, with koi, bridges, and water lilies. One of the blokes from the club said it reminded him of Monet's garden in France."

"Really? Do you know what he does for a living?"

"Construction business, I believe. He might be retired now. I'm not certain."

"And you didn't tell the police any of this?"

"Well, no. It was only when you mentioned the aquatic plants that it all clicked."

Oswald shuffled his feet and thrust his hands in the pockets of his duffel coat as a gust of wind rustled the leaves in the gutter. *"Anyway"*—Kingston wished he wouldn't keep using that word—"in light of what you said at the meeting, I thought you might want to have a chat with him." He shrugged. "That's about it, I suppose, for what it's worth."

"It could be worth a lot, Howard. One never knows. I certainly will have a chat with Walsh and I thank you very much for coming forward with this information. You don't have an address for him, by chance, do you?"

"I don't, but ask anybody up around the Woodfords. They all know of him, I'm sure. He drives a red Morgan most of the summer months."

"I'll go up there in the next few days. And thanks again."

"Glad to be of help. I hope it works out," Oswald said as they shook hands and parted.

Kingston slipped behind the wheel of the Mini and

started the engine. Before he drove off, he wrote down Adrian Walsh's name in the notebook he'd brought with him. Perhaps something had come from his trip to Salisbury after all. As he reached to put the notebook back in the glove compartment, his eyes rested on Andrew's *AA Road Atlas* and an idea occurred to him. He took it out and turned to the page covering the area around Salisbury. He was right, Upper, Middle, and Lower Woodford couldn't be more than six or seven miles from Salisbury. He glanced at his watch—it was getting late but not too late to find a decent place to stay overnight, then he could run over to Adrian Walsh's house in the morning, thereby saving another trip to Hampshire. If Walsh was retired, chances were he would be home.

Fifteen minutes later, Kingston was checking in at the White Hart, a seventeenth-century hotel facing Salisbury cathedral. Despite the late hour, the hotel kitchen rustled up a light meal, which Kingston ate in the bar. An hour and a half later, having glanced through most of the magazines in the room, he nodded off on the queen-sized down pillows of the canopied four-poster bed.

THE NEXT MORNING at eight, Kingston pulled aside the curtains to peek at the weather. The sky was the color of galvanized metal, the windows beaded with moisture on the outside. Too bad, he thought, because the Woodfords were in a peaceful and unspoiled part of Wiltshire and when the sun was shining—as it had been the day he'd visited the garden at Heale House on the river Avon, some five years back—it was extraordinarily lovely.

There was no point in rushing. His plan was to have a leisurely breakfast in the Squire Room—maybe a full English, as that way he could skip lunch—and get up to the Woodfords around ten-thirty or eleven. There, he would stop at the Angler, a charming old country hotel on the banks of the Avon, and inquire about Walsh. If he got lucky enough to get a phone number, he would call Walsh first. Failing that, he would just have to take his chances and drop in unannounced, a practice he frowned on, but he might have no choice. At ten-fifteen he drove out of the parking lot, windscreen wipers on intermittently, and headed for Upper Woodford.

At that time of morning there were few customers in the bar of the Angler. Not surprising, as the weather was hardly conducive to shirtsleeves and frocks or lunching on the riverbank. Kingston ordered a Hop Back ale and took a long draught before asking Kevin, the young fellow behind the bar with a ring in his ear, if he knew where Adrian Walsh lived. The name didn't ring a bell but the mention of a red Morgan did the trick. Walsh lived roughly a mile north of Upper Woodford, he said. There was only one road in and out of the village and the entrance to Walsh's house, which was called Swallowfield, couldn't be missed, according to Kevin, who explained that it had been on his newspaper route when he was in school, when the previous owners lived there. It had two large brick pillars on either side of a wide gravel driveway, each with a bronze lamp on top. The house, invisible from the road, was about a quarter-mile in. "Big, white, and nouveau riche written all over it," he said.

A quick check of the pub's local phone directory showed no listing for Walsh, which didn't surprise Kingston, given Kevin's pithy description of the place. Kingston downed the rest of his ale, thanked Kevin, and left the Angler. Outside, the drizzle hadn't let up and the sky had darkened even more. All the tables in the beer garden were empty save one, occupied by a couple of cyclists in yellow anoraks with hoods up, making the best of a miserable morning. Waiting for the windscreen wipers to do their job, Kingston slipped into first gear and headed out of the village.

Kingston glanced at his trip odometer: it was coming up to one mile. Up ahead he could see a knot of people off to the right-hand side of the road. At first he thought nothing of it. Then, as he slowed, he saw one of the brick pillars and realized they were standing outside the entrance to Swallowfield. Behind them, a police car was parked sideways across the drive. Just beyond that, Kingston recognized the all-too-familiar TV image of blue-and-white crime-scene tape stretched across the drive. He pulled onto the verge a few yards past the gawkers and got out of the Mini; immediately he caught the smell of burning. Approaching the driveway, he saw a plume of fuscous-colored smoke spreading out over an area behind some tall trees. Red and blue flashes of light, albeit blurred in the drizzle, meant that fire-brigade and police vehicles were on the scene. Remembering that Kevin had said the house was quite a way in, he could only guess that that was where the fire was located.

A lone police constable stood by the police car. He had just finished talking to a gray-haired gentleman wearing a checked cap and a Barbour jacket. The man had a black Labrador on a leash and looked about ready to leave— obviously a neighbor walking his dog, Kingston figured. As the man passed within a few feet of him, Kingston asked what he immediately realized was a pointless question. "Where's the fire?"

"At Walsh's place. Must've been quite nasty. Apparently they had to call in equipment from Salisbury. An ambulance left about five minutes ago. I hope Adrian's all right."

"You know him well?"

"No, hardly at all, actually. I live about a quarter-mile

from here. My wife and I don't socialize much these days. Not that we've ever been asked up to Swallowfield," he added, chuckling. "Well, you know how it is. Walsh wouldn't hobnob with the likes of us. Keeps pretty much to himself, from what I hear."

The man gently tugged the Lab's leash, leaning to pat the dog's head. "Yes, Daisy, we're leaving in a minute." Then he looked back at Kingston. "You live around these parts?"

"No. As it happens, I was going to see Walsh this morning. To ask him about a friend of mine who's gone missing."

"Oh, dear."

Kingston shrugged. "Well, I suppose there's not much to be gained by staying here."

"Doesn't look like it."

"By the way, I hope you don't mind my asking, but I don't know much about Walsh. What does he do for a living?"

"I'm not certain, but I think he retired recently. Used to be in construction of some kind, I believe."

"You mean a builder, contractor?"

"I'm really not sure."

Kingston thanked the man then walked over to the policeman, who was on a walkie-talkie. As Kingston approached, he finished the conversation, put the walkie-talkie back in its pouch, and looked at Kingston in that chin-up, indifferent manner that all coppers seemed to assume when the occasion warranted it. Kingston wondered if they were taught that in training. "How can I help you, sir?" the constable asked.

"Looks like I won't be meeting with Adrian Walsh, then?" Kingston said with a shrug.

"'Fraid not, sir. A good part of his house has just gone up in smoke. No point in your waiting around."

"I'm told an ambulance left a while ago. Do you know who was in it?"

"I don't, sir. They don't tell me those sorts of things. In any case, even if I knew, I wouldn't be able to pass on that kind of information."

Kingston could see he wasn't going to learn any more about the fire or Walsh, so he thanked the constable and went back to the car. Now it had started to rain, which no doubt would please the firemen, he thought.

THE DRIVE BACK to London took much longer than Kingston had hoped, mostly due to the weather. After leaving Wiltshire, it had gone from tolerable to miserable, then to downright nasty the closer he got to town. On the Mini's six-speaker stereo system, a CD of Haydn's cello concertos performed by Jacqueline du Pré had more than its usual calming effect as he pondered the events of the morning. What a rotten stroke of luck that Walsh's house just happened to go up in smoke the very morning that Kingston was about to pay him a call. As he thought about it, he realized how selfish that was, and that he should really be feeling sorry for Walsh, a man he had never met and about whom he knew virtually nothing. The poor chap's house was partially destroyed, and for all Kingston knew, Walsh might also have been injured or burned. He hoped not.

It was going to be difficult now to find out whether Walsh's garden and its koi pond were in fact Stewart's aquatic laboratory—the place where he, or the two of them, had hybridized the salt-consuming water lily. From everything Oswald had said, that would appear to be the case.

Kingston considered his options, deciding to wait a few days, until the disruption resulting from the fire had sub-

sided, then ask Inspector Carmichael if he would grant
Kingston access to the grounds. With security doubtlessly
heightened, walking into the garden uninvited would be
out of the question.

By the time he had got off the M3 at Sunbury, Kingston
had decided he needed cheering up. That meant a bottle
of Chianti Classico and an early dinner in the congenial-
ity of his favorite Italian restaurant, Il Falconiere in South
Kensington, where he was treated like one of the family.

Two hours later, he was seated at a white-clothed corner table with a starter of mushrooms sautéed in garlic
and fresh basil. For the main course he'd chosen one of
his favorites: veal escalope with aubergine and mozzarella.
Two-thirds of a bottle of wine later, he was in a much better mood than when he'd arrived, tired and feeling a bit
peevish after what, to all intents and purposes, was looking very much like a wasted trip. After a chat with the
maitre d', Kingston left the restaurant to find that the
weather had done a typical English about-face and the
pavements were almost dry. After such a filling meal, he
was happy to get a breath of fresh air on the ten-minute
walk back to his flat.

For a change, there were no phone messages, which
suited him just fine. At the restaurant he had reminded
himself to write a much overdue letter to his daughter,
Julie, when he got back to the flat. There was certainly a
lot to write about. It would come as a nasty shock when
she learned that "Uncle Stewart," as she still called him,
was missing. Growing up, she had spent many weekends
with the Hallidays, playing with Sarah, who was almost
the same age. Julie now lived in Seattle and worked for
Microsoft as a software programmer. They e-mailed occasionally but Kingston made a point of writing a letter every now and then. For him, there was something

appealing and anticipatory about getting a letter, opening the envelope, unfolding and reading it, that could never be achieved with an e-mail.

It was seven years now since Julie had broken the news to him over lunch at the Tate Gallery restaurant that she had accepted the high-paying job and would be making a new life in the States. Even now he could picture her face as she struggled to find the right words to tell him her good news and what she knew would be unwelcome news for him. At the time he had concealed his hurt as best he could, congratulating her and saying all the things one says to a daughter one loves dearly who is leaving the country, most likely for a long time. He kept reminding himself not to be so damned selfish and to think of her happiness, her life. What had made it even more of a blow was that Julie's announcement came barely a year after the death of his wife in a freak accident while on holiday in Switzerland. The months following had been the most heartbreaking and difficult of his life. He felt doubly bereaved.

He'd made several trips to Seattle in the ensuing years and Julie had come over to see him once. He glanced across the room to the mantle where her photograph stood next to that of Megan's, his wife of thirty-five years. He let his eyes rest on them, never minding that the photos were etched so deep in his memory that he could close his eyes and see them as clear as day: the likeness of their features and complexion, the same laughing eyes and soft dimpled smile. He smiled wistfully and looked away.

Before writing the letter, he decided to catch up on the news. He hadn't read a newspaper for two days. He switched on the small LCD TV that sat on a shelf in the bookcase and went back to the sofa, looking for the remote, which he finally located under one of the pillows. He thumbed in the number for BBC London and sat back while a dark-haired lady with unlikely white teeth and penciled eyebrows droned through the weather report. He got up and went to the bureau, taking out a box of writing paper that also contained the pen he used exclusively for letter writing, a green-and-black marbled Waterman's he'd had for thirty years.

"And now for news from other parts of the country—"

Kingston went back to the sofa, put the box beside him, fluffed up the pillow, got comfortable, and turned his attention to the news.

"Police in Wiltshire are investigating the death this morning, at his home in Upper Woodford, Wiltshire, of Adrian Walsh, chairman and former managing director of AW Construction Ltd., a commercial construction company headquartered in Farnborough. Firemen responding to a blaze at his estate found Walsh's body, with a gunshot wound to the head. Police have yet to determine whether his death was a result of foul play or a suicide. Damage to the house is estimated in the region of two million pounds. Investigations are continuing. And now let's go to Audrey Wilkins at—"

"Well, I'll be damned," Kingston muttered.

EIGHT

KINGSTON COULDN'T RECALL who said it but he still remembered the quote: "Once is happenstance. Twice is coincidence. Three times is enemy action."

He hoped it wasn't coming to that, but the coincidences kept coming. No arguing that point. Whether or not they were connected to Stewart was another matter.

It was near noon and Kingston was in the kitchen preparing brunch—nearly always a fry-up on Sundays, if he was alone. As he sliced two pieces of bread to toast, waiting for the bacon to cook crispy, he was wondering how he could find out more about Walsh's death. The Woodfords would be under the jurisdiction of the Hampshire Constabulary, and he knew they wouldn't divulge information to a stranger, least of all one inquiring about a suspicious death and fire. The only other source he could think of was Inspector Carmichael in Ringwood. Kingston was going to call him anyway, about getting access to the garden at Swallowfield. While he was at it, a casual enquiry about Walsh's death shouldn't come across as unreasonable, considering that it was now common knowledge. On the downside, it would be sure to raise a few questions, the first being: Why do you want to know and why are you interested in Walsh? Then Kingston would have to go into a long song and dance about his trip to the Woodfords based on a flimsy lead provided by a long-haired chap he had met at a garden club. Next he would have to explain the tenuous Walsh-Stewart connection and how Walsh might be implicated in Stewart's disappearance. He could hear Carmichael's reaction now: "Yes, Doctor—and if pigs could fly!" Kingston would call him anyway.

Meantime, he would start looking into Adrian Walsh's background. He knew it was a fishing expedition and the chances of something turning up that might connect to Stewart's disappearance were unlikely. From all accounts, Walsh was well known in the construction industry. Add to that his standing in the horticultural world and it shouldn't be difficult to find out more about him. It was sometimes amazing what an Internet search could reveal.

He flipped the two fried eggs and slipped them onto the plate alongside the bacon, fried tomatoes, and mushrooms. The toast popped up at just the right moment and Kingston took it all to the pine kitchen table, sat down, and, without thinking, reached for *The Times*. If only briefly, he needed to give his mind a rest from the succession of unexplained events, ambiguities, and now a possible homicide since Stewart went missing. Sipping his fresh-squeezed orange juice, he smoothed out *The Times* jumbo crossword, put on his reading glasses, and started to eat.

The clue for 33-down was *Curious idyll fashioned in an absurd manner.* He figured it had to be an anagram and he was right. Thirty seconds later he penciled in the answer: *Ridiculously,* the same twelve letters as "curious idyll." That helped him solve a couple of the across clues. After ten minutes, his concentration was starting to falter. He couldn't get Walsh's death off his mind. He took a last sip of coffee, cleared the table, and went into the living room to call Becky at Sarah's in Shrewsbury. Among other things, he wanted to ask her more about Stewart's garden-club activities. As he entered Sarah's number, he was wondering how much he should tell Becky about what had been happening—the Walsh connection and his untimely death (he wouldn't mention the possibility of murder) and the stolen tape.

Expecting Sarah to answer, he was surprised to hear Becky. It was as if she were standing by the phone waiting for it to ring.

"Hello, Becky. It's Lawrence," he said.

"Nice to hear from you. How are you?"

"More important, how are you? How are things in Shropshire?"

"All considered, I'm doing fine, Lawrence. Sarah's been simply wonderful." She paused, her voice suddenly sapped of enthusiasm. "I'm afraid there's no more news of Stewart. I would have called you if there were. The police have rung a couple of times. It seems they haven't made any progress; only more questions."

There was dullness in her tone, almost resignation, as if she were becoming used to the unthinkable—that Stewart might never return.

"I wanted to ask you about the garden club that Stewart belonged to—the one in Salisbury. I went there Wednesday evening."

"You did? What did you hope to find?"

"I'm not sure, but the club president told me that normally Stewart hardly ever missed a meeting."

"He's right about that. Not only the regular meetings but all the others, too."

"What do you mean by 'all the others,' Becky?"

"Every week it seems he was meeting with someone or another from the club. Sometimes two or three times a week."

"You never told me this before."

"I did tell you about the club, didn't I?"

"Yes. But you never said he spent a *lot* of time involved in their activities."

"Well, yes, he did but I didn't think it was that important at the time. You see, many times he would be gone when I was at the hospital. I suppose I should have mentioned it before, Lawrence. Is it important?"

"It could be. I'm not sure."

"I'm sorry." She paused for a moment then sighed. "You know, Lawrence, you don't have to be doing all this for me. It must be taking up an awful lot of your time."

"Don't worry on my account, Becky. I'm determined to find Stewart, that's all."

There was a break in the conversation before Kingston spoke again. "I'm going to ask you a question, Becky. Give it some thought before you answer, all right?"

"Come on, Lawrence, you're sounding like a policeman."

"No, seriously. Answer me this: Was Stewart going to these meetings in the last three or four months before he went missing?"

She didn't answer right away. "Yes. Right up to the week he disappeared," she said, a tremor in her voice. "Often, I would call from the hospital, wanting to talk to him about something or the other and many times there was no answer."

"He could have been in the garden."

"No. He always took the cordless phone with him. It was as if he didn't want to miss a call."

"And this had been going on for some time?"

"Yes, quite a long time."

"And you never asked what these meetings were about?"

"Why would I? It was a garden club. What could be more innocuous than that?" She sighed again. "Please, Lawrence, what's this all about?"

"When I talked to Phillip Austin, the president of the Sarum Garden Club, he said that Stewart had skipped quite a few meetings of late. Another member I spoke to afterward went further. He said that Stewart hadn't attended any meetings for at least three months."

"Are you saying Stewart *lied* to me?"

"I'm afraid it rather looks that way. The question is, where was he and what was he doing when he was supposed to be at the garden club or meeting with other members?"

"I don't…I don't know what to say, Lawrence. Are you sure…"

Kingston knew that the news would come as a shock to Becky and could tell that she was struggling for words, to find justification, however vague, for what he had just told her. "Becky, my dear," he said as gently as the three words would allow, "you don't have to say anything now. I'll tell the police what you've just told me. We can talk again tomorrow, or whenever you feel up to it."

"I don't mind telling you, Lawrence, this is terribly upsetting. I'm sure there's a rational explanation for it all. Stewart just wouldn't deceive me like that."

"I don't think he would, either, Becky. There's usually an explanation for everything," he said, regretting the cliché. "Just try to put it out of your mind for now."

"All right, Lawrence, I'll try," she said quietly. He sensed she was on the verge of tears.

TOMORROW WAS MONDAY, the day he and Chris Norton were going to pick up where they had left off with the aerial photography. As arranged, Andrew was going to chauffeur Kingston up to the airport in Oxford, and on his way back to London, stop in to visit his ex-wife, whose husband owned a wine shop in Henley-on-Thames. He invariably came away with a case of mixed wines, which he shared with Kingston. After the day's shooting, Kingston would return to London in his TR4.

Kingston had made the decision not to reshoot Cranborne Manor and the rose garden at Mottisfont Abbey on this trip but instead to photograph at least two of the other gardens on New Eden's list. There were two reasons: first, Inspector Chisholm, in a brief phone conversation a few days earlier, had recommended holding off for the time being, not wanting any further low-altitude aerial activity in the area while their investigation was ongoing; second, there was the long shot that the tape might show up, though Kingston doubted that very much.

This time the gardens were spread much farther apart—a triangular route of approximately 550 miles—so it was questionable whether they would have enough time to cover more than just the two. The first chosen was the ten-acre garden at Levens Hall, halfway up Britain's west coast, in Cumbria near the Lake District. The garden was won, as the story goes, on the turn of the ace of hearts during a card game in 1688 to settle a gambling debt. Levens Hall was also judged the Christie's and Historic Houses' Association Garden of the Year in 1995.

What made Levens so special—and Kingston was betting it would look even more breathtaking from the air—was its collection of topiaries, some almost 300 years old. The more than ninety designs, most at least twenty feet tall, included giant umbrellas, chess pieces, peacocks, crowns, a judge's wig, and a jug of ale—all clipped by hand out of box and yew. The garden also boasted an original Great Beech hedge planted in 1694 still surviving and other gardens within gardens, including one with only plants known to exist in the seventeenth century.

Not that it was relevant, but Kingston had learned from the present owner, on a visit in 1996, that Levens had a resident ghost. The story, mostly concerning the owner's father, was that forty years ago a priest named Stonor had stopped at Levens to visit a sick person in an upstairs bedroom. Passing through the main hall, which was unusually dark, he noticed someone in a room to one side playing a harpsichord under the light of an electric lamp. Taking care not to disturb the player, he went upstairs to see his patient.

When Stonor came downstairs twenty minutes later, the person was still playing. As the priest was about to leave, he noticed a glimmer of light from under one of the doors and heard muted voices. Entering the room, he found the owner's mother entertaining guests by candlelight. Inquiring why they were in candlelight, she told him that there was a power failure, apparently frequent in those days. When he told her about the harpsichord player, she and her guests rushed from the room, finding no electric light and no player.

The mother then told the priest at that time that no one present could play the harpsichord except her husband, and he was away on business, due to return the next day. Both her first reaction and that of the priest was that he might have been killed in a car crash or an accident and they had seen his ghost. If he were dead, there would be no way to verify it immediately.

As arranged, the priest returned the very next day to meet the woman's husband. The moment the priest saw the husband, he confirmed it was, without question, he who had been playing the harpsichord. Indeed, the priest maintained that he would be able to recognize the piece played should the husband go through his repertoire. The husband, only too happy to comply, sat down and started playing. The third piece was a rondo, a musical canon in which the bass line constantly repeats. Immediately, the priest said, "That's it. That's the piece you were playing the other night."

"How could that be?" said the husband. "I wasn't here."

Or had he been?

Kingston always enjoyed retelling that story.

THE OTHER GARDEN scheduled was one of Kingston's favorites, the National Trust garden at Powis Castle in Wales. For sheer drama, it was hard to beat. From the valley floor, the salmon-colored grit-stone castle perches on top of a near vertical rocky slope looking eastward to England. Built in 1200 by Welsh princes, the castle's main attraction is its hanging gardens comprising four grand terraces. Constructed in 1682, the lushly planted terraces form bands across the steep castle slope, each connected by stairs to the next. The top terrace is overhung with a row of enormous clipped yew hedges. In part, the gardens are historic because they feature the remains of a great formal garden of the seventeenth century. Laid out under the influence of Italian and French styles of the day, the gardens feature an orangery, an aviary, and early Flemish life-sized lead statues. Kingston could picture the dramatic visual effect achieved by hovering over the cliff face in the helicopter and panning across the colorful terraces.

Right now he had no qualms about going up again with Chris. He hoped he felt the same way when they lifted off tomorrow morning. The weather forecast was favorable: warming and clear for the next three days or so. At least they were lucky in that department.

KINGSTON SPENT the rest of the day catching up: replying to e-mails that had piled up over the past several days; searching the Internet trying to compile a dossier on Adrian Walsh; paying his bills online—a new experience, encouraged by his daughter; and finishing the latest Peter Robinson mystery. He'd also called Inspector Carmichael, leaving a message when told he was out for the day. Dinner was leftover pasta from two nights before, washed down with a couple of glasses of an Australian Penfolds Shiraz and a slice of fruit tart made by Andrew, who fancied himself a pastry chef. When Andrew wasn't cooking or lunching at the current restaurant du jour, he could likely be found at the racetrack.

Kingston had read enough for one day; his eyelids were beginning to droop. He closed the current issue of *Gardens Illustrated* and was about to switch off the bedroom light when the phone rang. He glanced at the clock: ten-thirty. "Bit late to be calling someone," he muttered under his breath as he reached for the cordless phone.

"Hi, Lawrence. It's Desmond. Sorry to call so late."

Kingston could hear a buzz of chatter and clinking glasses in the background.

"Where the hell are you?"

"Right now I'm at the—"

Desmond's voice became muffled; he was evidently questioning someone nearby.

"The Barley Mow, Baker Street—sorry, it's bloody noisy in here. I'm staying at a friend's place in the back of Marylebone High Street for a couple of days. Wondered if you'd like to have lunch or a jar sometime tomorrow or Tuesday? My treat."

"Tomorrow's out, I'm afraid, I'm going to be up in a helicopter with a video camera. Tuesday would be fine."

"A helicopter? This I've got to hear about. But Tuesday, great—where do you want to meet?"

Kingston thought for a moment. "Look, why don't you cab it over here and I'll order something in? There's a good deli around the corner. How does that sound?"

"Not like you, Lawrence, to turn down a free lunch. But that's fine by me, if it's not too much trouble."

"Not at all. How does noonish sound? Do you still remember where my flat is?"

"Lawrence, it's been over a year since I was last invited. Don't worry, though. It's all in my little black book."

"Tuesday it is, then. If there's time afterward, we could run over to Kew. I want to look up an old colleague who works there. While we're at it, we can take a look at those giant lilies. I believe they have both *cruziana* and Longwood hybrid, a cross of *amazonica*."

"I'd enjoy that. Haven't been to Kew for ages. By the way, I've got more thoughts about your salt-sucking water lily. Has your friend shown up, by the way?" Before Kingston could answer, he said, "Sorry, I suppose I should have asked that first."

"No. Stewart's still missing, I'm afraid. I've been doing a little nosing around myself, though. I'll tell you about it."

"Who'd have guessed? See you Tuesday—bright and early, one or the other. Cheers."

KINGSTON HARDLY RECOGNIZED Desmond when he arrived at the flat. He wasn't used to seeing Desmond in anything but jeans and grubby T-shirts, and here he was looking as though he'd just stepped out of an Austin Reed catalog: stone-colored linen jacket, navy-and-camel-check button-down shirt, and tan chino slacks. Even his hair was less of a tangle than usual.

They sat in the high-ceilinged living room, Kingston sitting cross-legged in a leather wingback, Desmond leaning back on the sofa, each with a glass of Heineken. The decor was unmistakably masculine. Overstuffed and leather seating, antique furniture, books everywhere, gilt-framed oil paintings and watercolors, family photographs,

artifacts and military memorabilia dotted around. Despite
the clutter, there was surprising orderliness. A large vase of
white roses, lilies, and freesias atop a French sideboard was
the only feminine touch. Megan had always loved flowers in the house and Kingston had preserved the custom.

"So, what brings you to town?" Kingston asked.

"I'm looking for money."

"Hope that's not why you're here, old chap."

Desmond smiled. "I know better than that. No—I came
down to meet a loan officer at the bank. They're putting
together a loan package for me. I'm expanding, Lawrence."

"More space?"

"No, a second location. I did a bunch of due diligence
and figured another location closer to London would be
a no-brainer. Searching for a place big enough in a good
area was a problem but I've found a super location near
Finchley."

"Good for you, Desmond. I'm surprised there's that
much interest in water plants. By the way, I hope you're
not calling it Across the Pond Two, are you?"

Desmond grinned. "What else?"

Kingston rolled his eyes in resignation and took a
longer-than-normal sip of beer. "I'll pull lunch together
when we've finished these."

Desmond leaned forward, glass resting on one knee.
"So, how did it go yesterday?"

"As far as I can tell, very well. Unlike the first time,
uneventful, thank goodness. The gardens looked extraordinary from the air. Particularly Powis. Have you been
there?"

Desmond nodded.

"Well, I can tell you that hovering opposite the cliff face
with the terraces in full color, the massive yew hedges,

and the castle towering above it all was spectacular. I can't wait to see the footage."

Desmond was frowning. "You said 'the first time.' You went up before?"

Kingston suddenly realized that Desmond knew nothing about the ill-fated first trip and the stolen tape. He had been so preoccupied over the past few days that he'd forgotten all about Desmond. So, for the next five minutes, making it sound a touch James Bondish, he told Desmond about the helicopter crash and the tape theft, finishing with a mention of his visit to the Woodfords and Walsh's death. Desmond listened stone-faced until Kingston was finished.

"This is serious stuff, Lawrence. You should really think twice about getting more involved."

"You may be right, but given what we know now, the helicopter thing was going to happen anyway—unavoidable." He drained his glass and put it on the coffee table. "I'm getting really worried about Stewart, though. It's been almost three weeks."

"Be careful, Lawrence, that's all. If this chap Walsh's death *wasn't* a suicide and he was connected somehow to Stewart's disappearance, then these people—whoever they are—aren't the kind of people you want to mess with. Given everything you've told me, I would knock it off if I were you, before they start singling you out."

Kingston stood and picked up their empty glasses. "You're probably right, Desmond." He paused before leaving. "Though I should tell you that I still plan to take a look at Walsh's garden if I can. Want to come along?"

Desmond sighed, closing his eyes momentarily while shaking his head. "Thanks, but no thanks," he said.

"Don't worry, I'll probably have company, anyway. I've left a message for Inspector Carmichael. I'm sure he'll give me permission. He may even want to join me." He clapped his hands. "Anyway, let's have some lunch. Help yourself to another beer. I'll be back in a couple of minutes."

In short order, Kingston returned, balancing two plates with lox and cream cheese, bagels, a bowl of crisps, and a wad of napkins. "You said you had more thoughts about the water lily?" he asked, placing it all on the coffee table.

"Right." Desmond bit into his bagel and wiped his mouth, not too daintily, with the cloth napkin. "I did a little more research. I'm not so sure now that *Victoria cruziana* would be my first choice. It's more likely *Victoria amazonica*. At first I rejected *amazonica* because I was under the impression that it was an annual. It turns out it's not. I read that in its native habitat, where there is little change in water level, plants can last for several years." He paused to take another bite, munching a few seconds before finishing his thought. "Also, it's bigger— up to six or seven feet across—and much beefier. So, if size has anything to do with it, that's your water lily. The one Stewart most likely crossed." He took a gulp of beer and continued. "You do realize, of course—providing this is not some perverse stunt cobbled up by your friend to cover up his real reason for going AWOL—that cultivation would have to be done under glass. The water would have to be heated. Oxygenated, too."

"I'd hardly overlooked that," said Kingston. "Give me *some* credit, Desmond. We all know a tropical water lily wouldn't last five minutes in Hampshire's climate."

"Keep your hair on, chum. I'm just trying…well, not to overlook anything."

Mollified, Kingston continued. "As you say, size would have quite a bearing when you think about it. To desalinate large volumes of water, one would have to propagate a helluva lot of plants, so the bigger the better, so to speak."

"And that raises the sixty-four-thousand-dollar question. What kind of facility? What kind of setup and where?"

"You're asking me? You're supposed to be the water-plant expert." Kingston looked aside for a moment, pondering the question, then back at Desmond. "I don't know. A humongous glasshouse doesn't quite seem the answer. I visualize a system of large pools with glass or Plexiglas coverings that open and close mechanically. More than likely it could be camouflaged. To be practical, it would have to be reasonably near salt water, almost certainly along the south coast somewhere."

"That's an awful lot of territory."

"I know—but if the shooting was intended to scare us off, then the facility has to be somewhere in that neck of the woods."

"You said that the police flew over the area?"

Kingston nodded. "The Air Support observers relay video footage back to a control room as they over fly. They have tapes of it."

"What would *they* be looking for?"

"Good question. I don't know. All they asked was whether I noticed anything out of the ordinary on the ground at the time of the shooting."

"You didn't, I take it?"

"No."

"Will they let you look at the footage?"

"I was told it's doubtful because it's part of an ongoing criminal investigation. There may be some way around it, though. I have to call Chisholm back."

KINGSTON AND DESMOND came out of the Kew Gardens tube station, walked across the street and took the short walk alongside the gardens to Kew's magnificent ornamental wrought-iron main gate. They were headed for Clifford

Attenborough's office. He was Kew's project manager for plant cultures and a longtime friend of Kingston's.

The Royal Botanic Gardens, Kew, shouldering the south bank of the Thames near the borough of Richmond in southwest London, was founded in 1759. The original botanical gardens were created for Augusta, the Princess of Wales, around her home, Kew Palace. Seven years later, Augusta's son, "Mad King" George III, substantially enlarged the gardens. Following his death, the gardens fell into decline, and the estate was handed over to the public to become a place for the scientific study of horticulture. It now contains the largest collection of plants in the world.

Today, the scope of Kew's collections and worldwide influence is immense. The numbers alone are staggering. Kew employs more than a thousand people, and houses almost a half million species of plants. It also functions as a botanical research centre, with multiple laboratories, and a library containing nearly a million volumes.

The 500-acre gardens and landscape boast no less than seven magnificent glasshouses. The Palm House, the centerpiece of the Kew Gardens, was built in the mid-nineteenth-century to house tropical trees, shrubs, and palms. It is a classic example of Victorian architecture. The Waterlily House, built a few years later, is the hottest and most humid glasshouse at Kew. In the summer it houses tropical ornamental aquatic plants and climbers, plus plants such as rice, taro, and lemongrass. The newer, hi-tech Princess of Wales Conservatory, with its enormous multispan roof, houses ten different environmental zones, each with its own climate. It displays Kew's collection of tropical herbaceous plants. Conditions within each zone are controlled and continually monitored by a computer, which adjusts the heating, misting, ventilation, and lighting systems accordingly.

They found Attenborough's office with no trouble. Kingston introduced Desmond and they made themselves comfortable in Clifford's neat, spacious office. Attenborough looked like a scientist: thinning white hair, pink complexion, rimless glasses, and wearing a bowtie and unbuttoned cardigan. He and Kingston had once worked together and had not seen each other for a while, so there was some catching up to do in matters personal. That out of the way, Kingston told Attenborough the second reason for his visit—Stewart's disappearance and the likelihood that he might have stumbled across an ecological breakthrough while hybridizing water lilies. He avoided all mention of the purported desalination process, and had prepped Desmond, on the walk from the tube station, to be careful not to mention it. If word got out at Kew, of all places, about water lilies that could desalinate seawater, it would be front-page headlines in all the following morning's newspapers. Before the meeting ended, Attenborough called the curator of the Princess of Wales Conservatory to tell him that Kingston and Desmond would be over in a few minutes and to make sure they got the red-carpet treatment.

In the warm and humid climate simulating that of South America's Amazon basin, Kingston and Desmond looked over the railing, gazing at the extraordinary sight below. A serene, dark pool was covered edge to edge with the giant water lilies called *Victoria* "Longwood" *hybrid*. Spread out like monstrous green platters with upturned red rims, some of the lily pads were more than five feet wide, looking for all the world like something from another planet, mesmerizing in their size, color, form, and beauty. The curator had told them earlier that the pads were thick, like elephant flesh and, with their underside of sharp inchlong spines in a ribbed pattern, could support a weight of almost a hundred pounds. First discovered in Bolivia in 1901 and named in honor of Queen Victoria, the species has fragrant white flowers the size of soccer balls that turn purple after being pollinated. The pollinators, the curator said, are large scarab beetles that are drawn not only to the flower's scent and pure white color but also to its warmth. The beetles crawl inside to stay warm and consume the sugar and starch. Later, at night, the flowers close and the beetles are trapped inside. Throughout the next day, the beetles stay inside to feast, gathering pollen as they do so.

After several minutes, Kingston and Desmond turned away from the extraordinary spectacle. "Seems hard to imagine those buggers growing somewhere in Hampshire," said Desmond.

"It certainly does," said Kingston with a smile. "In Hertford, Hereford, and Hampshire, it would hardly happen."

NINE

AFTER LEAVING KEW, Kingston and Desmond stopped at the Antelope for a quick drink. Desmond had to return to his friend's flat in Marylebone to pick up his bag before driving back to St. Albans and wanted to get an early start to avoid the rush-hour traffic.

Over beers, they agreed that the subject of Stewart's disappearance and his putative discovery had been flogged to death. To placate Desmond, Kingston submitted that, despite his own investigative forays and best intentions to help Becky, the answers to all their questions would most likely come as a result of police work or a lucky break. This led to another plea from Desmond, who pressed Kingston not to get further involved, which, in turn, led to a not-too-convincing promise from Kingston that he would follow Desmond's advice—which he wouldn't, of course. They parted five minutes later, under darkening skies and rumblings of thunder. Desmond hopped into a cab, and Kingston, sans brolly, made haste for his flat before the skies opened.

Walking home, he wondered again about how Patrick knew to phone him, how he knew about the photo shoot and the tape. Henley Air had received no inquiries. The only possibility that he could think of was that the helicopter crash had been reported in the paper and his name had been mentioned.

Too late for tea and too early to think about dinner, Kingston went into the small bedroom he'd converted into an office, turned on his iMac, and logged on to the Internet.

In the search engine, he typed in *"Wiltshire Times"* and was directed to the paper's online site, *This is Wiltshire*. He clicked on archives and entered "helicopter crash." There it was:

Helicopter downed near Lymington

A Henley Air Services helicopter on a photographic assignment was forced to make an emergency landing near Lymington yesterday after its fuel tank was ruptured by gunfire from the ground. A spokesperson for Henley Air reported that both the pilot, Christopher Norton of Oxford, and the lone passenger, Professor Lawrence Kingston, were unharmed. Kingston was aboard shooting video footage of famous gardens as part of a future TV special produced by New Eden Productions, London.

A police spokesperson stated that a ground and air search of the area where the helicopter was downed has produced no results. Police request anyone having information about the incident to contact the Wiltshire and Avon Constabulary.

Kingston, a botanist of repute, gained brief celebrity status two years ago when he was instrumental in discovering a series of underground rooms on the site of a former Benedictine priory in Somerset. The landmark archeological and historical find came to light when Kingston was supervising the restoration of the estate's Heligan-like gardens.

The unearthing led not only to a cache of valuable Impressionist paintings, believed stolen by the Nazis during the occupation of France, but to solving two

recent murder cases and a suspicious death that took
place on the estate forty years ago.

Reading it a second time, Kingston realized that the
information was all there—everything that "Patrick" had
needed to know to pull off his stunt.

Curious to see what was reported about Walsh's death
and the fire, Kingston typed in "Adrian Walsh" in the
newspaper's archives search bar. Two items came up. The
first, published the day after the incident, was much like
the one he'd seen on TV: a straightforward account of the
fire and Walsh's death, along with a biographical summary, mostly concerning his business accomplishments
in the construction industry.

The second mention had appeared a week later. It read:

Prominent local businessman's death ruled a homicide

A statement released today by the Wiltshire &
Avon Constabulary announced that a coroner's post-
mortem examination into the death of Adrian Walsh,
two days ago in a fire at his home in Upper Woodford, resulted from gunshot wounds inflicted by a
person or persons unknown. At this stage in the investigation, it is concluded that, other than Walsh and
his assailant, no other persons were in the house at
the time. Police are requesting that anyone with information concerning the case to contact the Wiltshire & Avon Constabulary.

Kingston leaned back, hands clasped behind his head,
staring at the screen and thinking about what Desmond
had said: "These are not people to be messed with." He

read the first sentence again. It certainly appeared that Walsh had been murdered. If so, why?

Kingston picked up the phone and called Lymington Police Station. After a short wait, Detective Inspector Chisholm came on the line.

"Professor Kingston—nice surprise. What can I do for you?"

"It's about the helicopter incident."

"Do you have some new information?"

"Not really. I wanted to ask you about the aerial footage your people shot. If they did shoot any, that is."

"Right. What about it?"

"I was wondering if I could take a look at it."

"I seriously doubt it. Didn't you ask that before?"

Kingston ignored the question. "The investigation's ongoing, then?"

"Certainly. Shooting down helicopters is hardly a misdemeanor. What's all this with the tape, anyway? Is there something special you hope to find that Air Support didn't?"

"I'm not really sure. A friend of mine has a theory that the shooting might be connected to another case." Introducing Desmond's name had just popped into his mind. For reasons he couldn't entirely explain, Kingston didn't want Chisholm to know it was actually his theory. Interfering in police matters was not new to him and he knew not to ruffle feathers. Already the tone of Chisholm's questions had an impatient edge.

"Really? What case is that?"

"The disappearance of a professor from Fordingbridge. The events took place around the same time. He's a friend of mine."

"I see."

"Your counterpart up in Ringwood called me about it

a while ago. DI Carmichael. Wanted to know if I had any information that might help in their investigation."

"Yes, I know Robbie. I'll give him a call."

"That's why I was hoping to take a look at the video footage."

"I thought I made myself clear on that."

"Yes, you did, but if your higher-ups were assured it doesn't concern the helicopter investigation, would that make a difference?"

"Look, Doctor, I don't want to sound rude but—" A long pause followed. "All right, since you're so damned insistent, I'll make an inquiry. But I wouldn't hold your breath if I were you."

"Thanks, Inspector."

"If the answer happens to be yes, you'll have to come down here to view the tapes, of course. Technically, they'll be releasing them for our eyes only."

"That's fine. I'll wait until I hear from you, then."

"Shouldn't take long, I would imagine."

"Thanks again, Inspector," he said, hanging up.

Kingston was about to get up and retrieve the mail— he'd heard it fall through the postal slot earlier—when the phone rang again. He picked it up, hoping it wasn't someone trying to flog something or ask if he would answer a few questions for a survey. His excuse, saying that he couldn't talk because he was late for a meeting with his parole officer, usually got them off the line quickly.

"Professor Kingston?" The woman's voice was not familiar.

"This is he."

"My name's Alison Greer—you won't know me. I'm calling about your friend Stewart Halliday."

Her voice was soft and betrayed a flicker of nervousness. Kingston was caught unawares by the mention of Stewart's name, so much so that he didn't reply right away.

"It's about your friend and a man named Adrian Walsh," she said.

Kingston tensed. "Stewart and Walsh. Really?"

"You know Walsh?"

"Only by name. I never got to meet him. I do know he was killed recently. It was on television and in the paper."

"He was, yes."

"I'm curious. What made you decide to call me? How did you get my number?"

"I got it from Rebecca Halliday. She was reluctant to give it to me at first but when I told her I knew her husband, she agreed."

"I'm surprised she didn't let me know."

"I only spoke with her yesterday."

"Are you a friend of Becky's?"

"No, not at all. I've never met her."

"May I ask why you were calling her?"

"After Adrian's death, I got to thinking what a coincidence it was that he was murdered and your friend went missing about the same time, particularly after I'd seen them together several times at Swallowfield. I read about his disappearance in the paper. Calling Rebecca seemed the thing to do. She was pleased that I did—or so she said. We talked for quite a while."

She paused for a moment, as if waiting for him to say something, then continued, "Rebecca knew nothing of Adrian—which didn't come as a surprise—but told me that you were helping the police find Stewart and suggested I give you a call. I might have some information that could be of help."

"Have you spoken with the police?"

"Not yet. I thought I would talk to you first."

"So Stewart and Adrian Walsh—they were friends?"

"Friends or in business together. Possibly both, I suppose."

"Interesting."

"I was wondering if we could meet. For some reason the phone doesn't seem right to talk about something so serious. It's so impersonal."

"I couldn't agree more…Mrs. Greer."

"Alison, please. And it's Miss—I'm not married."

"Where would you like to meet? Where do you live?"

"In Hampshire. In Hartley Wintney. Do you know it?"

"I do. I had a friend there who used to own an antiques shop in the High Street, back in the eighties. There were a number of them in those days."

"Not anymore. You could count them on one hand, sad to say. I'm told it's harder to find antiques nowadays." She sighed, then paused. "You're in London, I take it?"

Kingston thought that should be obvious from the prefix she'd dialed. "Yes, but I can take a run down there."

"I would appreciate that."

"No problem."

"Is tomorrow a possibility?"

He thought for a moment. "It is, as a matter of fact."

"We could meet at my cottage—if that's all right with you."

"That's fine."

"How about mid-afternoon—about three? I'll make some tea."

"I look forward to it. How do I find you?"

"It's easy. In Hartley Wintney, take the Fleet Road off the A30. I'm on the village green. Pennyroyal Cottage."

He jotted down the directions and the conversation ended.

Kingston went into the kitchen, where the crossword puzzle sat on the pine table. He sat looking at it but not reading. He was thinking of another puzzle and whether Alison Greer might provide a clue that would help toward solving it. Tomorrow, maybe, he would get the answer.

TEN

DESPITE THE SOMBER CLOUDS that had been threatening rain all morning, it was still dry when Kingston arrived in front of Pennyroyal Cottage in the TR4. He smiled to himself, wondering if she was going to offer him mint tea. He hoped not. Pennyroyal was the common name for *Mentha pulegium,* a variety of mint, oddly enough, safe as a flavoring but poisonous in large quantities. He couldn't stand the stuff. Nor could he tolerate any of the other so-called teas—the herbal and fruit ones. There was one he'd seen in Partridge's grocery called green mango. He could just imagine what that tasted like.

In dismal weather, the cottage presented a cheering sight. Built of rosy brick and flint, with leaded casement windows and dark gray thatch, Kingston pegged it as mid nineteenth century. He was reminded of a quote from the influential gardener of that time, William Robinson: "Among the things made by man, nothing is prettier than an English cottage garden."

The narrow strip of front garden was well cared for, with the typical higgledy-piggledy of colorful perennials and annuals. A canopy of honeysuckle blanketed the arched entrance. Alongside, spread-eagling the wall, the climbing rose Alchymist was putting on quite a show with its copper-colored old-garden-form blooms and dark, glossy leaves. He got out of the TR4 and stretched his legs, running his fingers through his tousled ivory hair, knowing that it would have little or no effect. He took his carefully

folded double-breasted navy blazer from behind the seat
and slipped it on. Using the puny side-view mirror—which
required squatting in an ungainly position—he checked his
appearance. With a yellow hanky dangling from the blazer
pocket, Tattersall-check shirt and tan gabardine slacks, he
was beginning to think he might be a trifle overdressed
for the occasion.

He stepped up to the powder-blue front door, dropped
the bronze dolphin knocker, and waited.

The door was opened by a petite woman with glossy
dark hair cut in pageboy style with not a hair out of place,
no makeup—maybe lip gloss—and unusually blue eyes.
She was smartly dressed in a Jaeger look: pale blue cardigan over a white blouse and black skirt. At first glance,
Kingston figured her to be fortyish, but as she moved into
the band of light from the open door, he noticed the laugh
wrinkles on the sides of her eyes and the faint creasing at
the edge of her mouth. He upgraded her—or was it down-
graded—to mid-fifties.

"I'm Alison," she said, taking Kingston's large hand in
hers in what served as a handshake.

"A pleasure meeting you," said Kingston. "Your cottage is lovely, by the way."

"Thank you. I'm so glad you could come, Doctor." It
was the same disarming voice he'd heard over the phone.
She let go of his hand and looked him up and down without attempting to disguise it. "You're—well, somehow as
I pictured."

Kingston smiled. "Lawrence, please. No need for the
professor stuff—it makes me feel like I'm back in the class-
room. Old before my time."

Smiling back, dimples appeared on each cheek. "Well,
we can't stay on the doorstep. Come on in," she said.

He nodded and stooped to clear the black beam above the door.

Kingston glanced around the living room with an approving eye. Based on the TLC put into the garden, it was as he expected: tastefully furnished in scale to suit the small room, with sofa and chairs alongside and facing the stone fireplace, mostly antique furniture, and cinnamon-color sisal carpeting. Atop a mahogany Pembroke table by the window, mixed in with a gilt carriage clock, a few porcelain figures, and some silver pieces, was a framed photo of what he assumed was a pre-teen Alison with an older woman—probably her mother. Alongside it was another photo of her, clearly more recent. A third picture of her was perched on the fireplace mantel. The walls were painted in a wash of pale yellow, the wood trim white enamel. Everything was neat and tidy, with not a mote of dust in sight.

"Please," said Alison, gesturing to the chintz sofa.

Kingston sat and crossed his long legs, careful not to kick the coffee table.

She sat facing him. "The kettle's on, so any time you want tea, let me know."

"Perhaps a little later." Kingston undid the brass buttons on his blazer and got as comfortable as the pillowed sofa would allow. "So, you knew Stewart?" he asked.

"Yes, a nice man. I'd met him—oh, two or three times—at Adrian Walsh's house in Upper Woodford." She plucked a stray hair that had fallen across her eye and put it back in place. She was a neat one all right, thought Kingston. He was about to ask what her relationship with Walsh was but there was no need.

"I should explain. I'm—I should say, *was,* I suppose—Adrian's private secretary."

"I see," said Kingston, leaning forward. "Then Walsh's death must have been an awful shock?"

"It was and still is. I still can't get over it—or understand why it happened." She reached into her cardigan sleeve, pulled out a small handkerchief, and dabbed her nose.

Kingston could tell that she was trying hard to keep her composure. She seemed the type who would rather leave the room than betray any kind of emotion or show even the slightest signs of vulnerability.

"Do you have any idea why Stewart was visiting Walsh?"

She hesitated, placing a finger across her lower lip, looking away for a moment. "I'm not sure. I used to take things to Adrian when he wasn't at the office in Farnborough. It was usually just a case of dropping off or picking up. There was the odd occasion, though, when I'd stay for a cup of tea or sometimes—if it was toward the end of the day—a drink. Adrian was a bit of a loner, not to say that he didn't enjoy company once in a while, but mostly if it was someone he knew and was comfortable with. He didn't suffer fools gladly and let it be known."

Kingston noted that she used his first name. She had on the phone, too, he recalled. Did that suggest that there might have been more familiarity than she was implying? She was certainly attractive and it would be no surprise if that were the case. "Was Adrian Walsh married?"

"He *was*—some years ago. His wife was an alcoholic. She was in and out of rehab and treatment centers for years. It finally caught up with her. There were no children, which Adrian deeply regretted. She was too sick to raise a family, of course, so in some ways it was for the best, I suppose." She shrugged and continued. "Not long after his wife's death, Adrian's only brother, Malcolm, was killed in a car accident. It was in all the papers at the time. To make matters worse, the accident was Malcolm's fault—drunk driving. Adrian used to talk about him all the time. 'My kid brother,' he called him. They were very close. Adrian was devastated, as you can imagine." She thought for a long moment then looked directly at him, making a brave but hapless effort to smile. "I have no idea what's going to happen to the estate—well, we didn't discuss those matters, of course—but I'm sure Adrian had it all taken care of. A will."

"That's all very sad" was all Kingston could think of saying.

"I'm sorry, I didn't mean to rattle on like that." She gave a tight-lipped smile and folded her hands in her lap.

Kingston had her attention again—or so it seemed. "Getting back to Stewart. You said you weren't quite sure of the reason he was seeing Walsh?"

"Yes. I knew that Stewart Halliday was a botanist and that he and Adrian shared an interest in gardening. The garden was a huge part of Adrian's life, by the way. He wasn't what they call a checkbook gardener—paying other people to do all the work and taking all the credit. Mind you, he could have afforded an army of gardeners if he had wanted, but he was a hands-on person. Spent his every spare moment in the garden. It was beautiful." She looked away again, a habit he'd come to accept.

Kingston was hoping she wasn't off on another trip down memory lane.

"You never saw it, I take it," she said, looking back at him.

"No. Sadly, I arrived the day of the fire."

His answer seemed to have taken her by surprise. She had pulled out her handkerchief again and was twisting it, nervously, in her lap. There was a moment of silence then she said, "You were at Swallowfield?"

He nodded. "Yes, I was."

"What were you doing there?"

"A chap called Oswald suggested I go there. He was an acquaintance of Adrian Walsh's. They belonged to the same garden club in Salisbury, as did Stewart. Oswald told me that Walsh was a bit of an expert with water plants and I wanted to know if he and Stewart had been working together—you know, swapping stuff, hybridizing, that sort of thing. From what you've told me, it appears that he might have been."

"Probably…yes." She nodded, as if her mind was elsewhere. "You said you arrived the day of the fire?"

"Yes. By the time I got there, the fire had obviously been going for some time. The police had the house cordoned off. So, sadly, I never got to meet your boss."

Alison sighed and rubbed the center of her forehead between her eyebrows. "I'm sorry," she said. "I still can't believe this has all happened. What was your last question? About wanting to know if Adrian and Stewart were what?"

"I was curious to know if the two of them had been working on any projects together—breeding new plants, hybridizing, designing anything?"

"I can't be absolutely sure of it, but, yes, I believe Adrian and Stewart were doing something of that sort. I overheard them talking in the garden one evening. They were talking about water lilies, come to think of it. I remember thinking about Monet's garden at the time. Have you been there?"

"Here we go again," Kingston said under his breath. "I have. It's wonderful. Please, tell me more about Walsh's garden."

"Well, to start with, it's big—several acres. Old yew hedges, lawns, a rose garden, Italian garden, a big fountain." She rested her chin on her forefinger. "Let me see, what else? Oh, the pond—more of a lake, really. It's filled with those beautiful Japanese fish—the red-and-white ones."

"Koi."

"Yes."

"And water lilies, I take it?"

"Right. Large ones. I didn't know they grew so big."

Kingston leaned back in the sofa. One of the casement windows was open and the room was getting quite cool. "You know," he said, "that cup of tea would be good now, if it's not too much bother."

"Oh, no. Not at all," In an instant, she was out of the chair, smoothing her skirt, as if she'd been waiting for the opportunity. "It'll only take a minute or so. There are some magazines over there in the rack," she said, leaving the room.

Kingston got up, took a *BBC Homes & Antiques* magazine from the rack, went back to the sofa, and opened it on his lap. Best to have her think he'd been reading while she was gone. He needed time to think.

Meeting with Alison Greer was starting to look like a wasted trip. Why in heaven's name had she dragged him all the way down to Hampshire? Surely not to tell him what little she had thus far. Was there something she had forgotten? Something that may seem insignificant to her but could, at the least, give him a lead to pursue? He was out of ideas. On the phone, she had said, "Stewart and Walsh were friends or in business together." What made her think it might have been business? Five minutes ago, she'd been vague about Stewart and Walsh. Was she holding something back? And if so, why? Another thing—though it might be immaterial—was her relationship with Walsh. Was it more than she had led him to believe? When she came back he would try to find the answers. He glanced down at the magazine and started leafing through the pages.

Hearing the rattle of china, he looked up see Alison carrying a tray with tea and what looked like a plate of chocolate-covered digestive biscuits—his favorites. As a small boy he'd called them "suggestives." She placed the tray on the coffee table and sat down. Right away, he spotted the Twinings Assam teabag label dangling from the white teapot, relieved that it wasn't mint or herbal.

"If you like it strong you may want to wait a minute," she said, picking up the teapot and swirling it.

"Now is fine," said Kingston, shifting forward on the sofa.

"Milk and sugar?"

He thought about asking for lemon but let it pass. "Please," he said, waiting while she did the honors.

Kingston broke off a piece of biscuit and popped it into his mouth. "On the phone, you said that you thought Stewart and Walsh might be in business. What made you think that?"

She took a sip of tea, looking at him over the gold rim of her teacup. Kingston couldn't recall having seen anyone with eyes as blue as hers. "Yes," she said. "I should have explained the reason for my saying that. If it were just the two of them, it would be reasonable to assume that they met purely for gardening's sake—as you said, to exchange plants and ideas. But a third person was involved."

Kingston wanted to say, *Why the hell didn't you mention this earlier, woman?* What he said was "A third person?"

She nodded, putting down her cup. "I was going to mention it earlier but we seem to have got sidetracked."

The editorial "we" didn't escape his attention. He was tempted to remind Alison of the old catchphrase that "we" should only be used by poets, kings, and people with tape-worm, but chose to remain silent.

She continued. "Yes, another man, somewhat younger than Adrian. We were introduced the first time he was there."

"How did you know it was his first visit?"

"Adrian was pointing things out in the house and in the garden. He was taken with Adrian's art collection, particularly the pre-Raphaelite paintings—the Rossetti, Burne-Jones, and Waterhouse. They discussed them for some time."

"Sounds like they both had good taste in art. What was he like, this man?"

"He was tall and thin—not quite as tall as you—and intimidating. I don't often say that of people, but he made me feel uneasy. Frankly, I didn't take to him at all."

"Why was that?"

"The way he stared at me when we were talking, as if he were sizing me up. I don't think he smiled the whole time he was there. I found that very strange." She sighed, closed her eyes briefly, and massaged her forehead again, as if she'd rather not think about their meeting. Regaining her composure, she continued, "And when he shook my hand, he squeezed so hard it hurt. He knew it, too. I could read it in his eyes."

"Sounds like a misogynist. Did you tell Adrian about your dislike for him?"

"I didn't." She shrugged. "I couldn't, really—not if he and Adrian were about to join forces in a new business venture, which is what I took the meetings to be all about. It's not my place to like or dislike the people he does business with."

"I can understand. What's this fellow's name?"

"Everard."

"Is that the first or last?"

"The last. His first name is Miles."

"What kind of business is he in?"

"Also construction. There hasn't been much correspondence between them—not that's crossed my desk, anyway. I know only what Adrian has mentioned, and that's not much."

"Do you know his company's name?"

"Yes, it's called Paramus—Paramus Partners International. The company's much bigger than Adrian's—engineering, project development and management, that sort of thing."

"So, they would subcontract construction work to Adrian's company."

She nodded. "That's how I read it—specialized projects, jobs that were too small for Paramus."

"But as far as you know, a deal has not yet been struck between Walsh's company and Everard's?"

"Not that I know of, unless it was all conducted strictly between the two of them. Adrian had an office at Swallowfield and he spent a lot of time there, so I couldn't rule that out."

In the pause that followed, Kingston was pulling on his earlobe. "Tell me something, Alison. In recent months, has the subject of desalination come up in connection with any of Adrian's dealings?"

She frowned while thinking. "You mean converting salt water into fresh water? I can't say that it has, no. Why do you ask?"

"It's nothing," Kingston replied, with a shrug. "Just a thought, that's all."

"More tea?" she asked. "I can make a new pot if you'd like."

"No thanks. That was excellent," he replied, getting up

slowly. "You've been a wonderful host, Alison. I've taken far too much of your time already."

After taking Kingston's card and giving him her phone number, she walked him to the front door. Outside, it had just started to spit rain.

"You will let me know if you find out more about Adrian or your friend?" she said.

"It's a promise."

"Safe drive home, then."

"Thanks, Alison," he said, starting up the path. He'd taken a few steps when he stopped and turned. "I forgot to ask you, are Paramus's offices in London?"

"Yes. Bakers Landing. It's in the East End."

"Thanks." Kingston closed the picket gate behind him and got into his car. With the TR4's windscreen wipers squeaking noisily, he waved to Alison, still at the door, and drove off.

ELEVEN

THE MORNING AFTER his visit with Alison Greer, Kingston had received a call back from an apologetic Inspector Carmichael, who admitted to being swamped with a greater than usual number of cases and problems. Kingston's request to visit Swallowfield was granted right away, as if it were the easiest decision Carmichael had had to make all morning—not even as much as a "Why do you want to see it?" Someone from the station would call the security company that was now in charge of Swallowfield, he said, and tell them of Kingston's impending visit and to allow him entry to the gardens but not the house.

Three days later, checked in by the uniformed guard at the gate, Kingston drove between the brick pillars and up the gravel drive to Swallowfield. The sloping greens edging the drive could have shamed St. Andrew's. At the back of the lawns on both sides, tall conifers formed a dark backdrop to a harmonious landscaping of shrubs, mostly huge rhododendrons. After a left curve, the house came into sight—or what was left of it. The damage caused by the fire came as a shock. One entire wing was a charred skeleton. A red brick chimney was the only thing standing that wasn't entirely black; few of the shrubs or trees bordering that part of the house had escaped the intensity of the blaze. Inside, a half-dozen workmen wearing safety masks were at work with power saws and sledgehammers, clearing the blackened lumber and debris, loading it into two dump trucks.

Kingston sized up the undamaged part of the house. He guessed it to be not more than twenty years old, a well-executed takeoff of a traditional Georgian country house. Its mantle of Virginia creeper and several years of weathering on the pale-colored stone facade would further deceive the untrained eye. Kevin's "nouveau riche" description was obviously based on his paperboy days, when the house was new.

Kingston parked by the house, away from the trucks, and stepped from the car. The reek of smoke was still in the air. As instructed by the guard, he headed toward the main entrance to the garden—a scrolled wrought-iron gate set between brick pillars, centered in an eight-foot-high yew hedge. Once inside, he stopped to take in the sight. For a moment, he imagined he was at Sissinghurst, the scene facing him was so moving. A dozen or so low box hedges corralled deep beds chock-a-block with old roses, delphinium, penstemon, euphorbia, hardy geraniums, and other herbaceous perennials, all in full bloom. The air was perfumed and alive with the industrious drone of pollinating bees.

A central stone-and-worn-brick path led to another opening in the surrounding yew hedge, through which Kingston could see wide stone steps leading up to a lawn. Beyond the lawn, his eye was led to an antique white statue—a goddess of some sort—on a plinth, artfully positioned against a dark hedge that looked like holly. Walking slowly up the path, letting the sights and smells sink in, he entered another disciplined enclosure, this one larger. It was surrounded by old brick walls—at least, they looked old—all hosts to rambling roses and vines. In the center of the lawn, the dolphin-mouth jet of an octagonal-based Portland stone fountain sent plumes of water high in the air, misting the sleeve of Kingston's jacket as he passed.

Off to his right was a small orchard. Under the trees, the grass had been left to grow tall, the paths formed by mowing. Up another shallow flight of steps and there it was—the lake, tranquil and idyllic. Instantly, he could see why Alison had likened it to Monet's garden at Giverny. Encircled by lawns and sandy gravel paths, the shore closest to him was edged with random-sized stone slabs separated by clumps of white iris. A long Japanese-style bridge with a high rail spanned a stretch of water from the shore to a small island, on which clumps of bamboo and grasses undulated in the soft breeze like graceful Hawaiian dancers. Water lilies of varying sizes were concentrated in colonies here and there.

Kingston walked to the water's edge and looked down into the lake. Not much to see other than the expected. He walked farther along the shore. Still nothing. No evidence that Walsh's lake had anything to do with Stewart's experiments. He kept walking and was soon around the far side of the lake, hidden from view from anyone standing on the lawn. He spotted a narrow path. As he approached it, he could see that it led to a separate lake, somewhat smaller than the first. Walking thirty or so paces down the muddy path, he reached the water's edge. At first glance, nothing appeared unusual about it. Then, as he looked beyond the lake to the dense stand of bamboo in the background, he saw something that looked out of place. Circling the lake, walking faster now, he came to the place he had spotted. On the ground was a pile of curved metal rods, each at least twenty feet long. Several paces off to one side, a tarpaulin staked to the ground concealed a rectilinear mound. Kingston walked over and with effort pulled out one of the iron stakes. Lifting the corner of the tarp, he bent to see what was underneath. It was as he expected: neat stacks of folded clear plastic sheets.

He stood and looked around. Now he could see the heavy circular anchor bolts buried in the ground at the precise angle to clamp on to the cross members that would span the lake. Each was set in concrete piers about eight feet apart to support the framework for the greenhouse that would cover the lake. Now there was virtually no doubt about it—this was where Stewart had started his aquatic-plant experiments. It was Kingston's educated guess that once Stewart had proven it possible to hybridize his water lily in a small, primitive environment such as this, the next logical step would be to graduate to a much larger and more sophisticated facility, using seawater. So how did Stewart salinate the water? Kingston was sure that if he looked around more closely, he would find empty drums or containers of salt, pumps, and other equipment. Either that or Stewart had insisted on using seawater. But that would have posed cumbersome logistical hurdles, not the least of which would be draining the lake and shipping thousands of gallons of seawater forty miles from the coast. Not likely.

He knelt by the lake and looked into the water. It looked remarkably clear. Cupping his hand, he scooped out some water and took a sip. There was no trace of salt.

DRIVING BACK TO LONDON, Kingston was pleased with the morning's visit to Swallowfield. Now all doubt was removed about what Stewart and Walsh had been up to. When he got home, he would call Desmond and tell him what he'd found.

He turned down the volume of the Boccherini concerto on the radio and thought about tomorrow and another trip he planned, this one much closer to home. It was his hope that it could be equally revealing—though he doubted it. He was going to Bakers Landing in the East End of London to visit the offices of the enigmatic Miles Everard.

TWELVE

AT TEN-THIRTY IN THE MORNING, there were few passengers on the Jubilee Line train as it pulled out of Westminster station heading toward Waterloo and Stratford, in East London.

Sitting opposite Kingston was a young woman—no more than seventeen, he figured—with scarlet hair, black-lashed eyes, and lips the color of aubergine, the lower one pierced by a silver ring. Her complexion was unearthly, as if her face had been dusted with flour in a vain attempt to hide the pimples. He imagined her to be some nocturnal creature, venturing into daylight only when absolutely necessary, slithering back into her subterranean haunts at the soonest chance. Tapping a boot with five-inch soles, she stared at Kingston as she had since he sat down. Avoiding her vacant gaze, he found something less distracting in the band of adverts above her: the picture of a tooth-some blonde promoting, of all things, a secretarial school.

After his visit with Alison Greer, Kingston had decided to pay Miles Everard a surprise visit. Knowing corporate mentality, he knew that trying to break through the protective wall of receptionists, secretaries, and personal assistants, by phone or writing, would not be easy. Most of all, it would require sound justification, and if a request were made by letter, the process would squander several days. Neither was he naïve enough to think that showing up on the doorstep would be any more successful. But at least he would see Paramus's headquarters close up and get an idea of what kind of league Walsh, Stewart—and now he—were playing in. If it went well and he managed to meet Everard, he would have to play it by ear. He was adept at doing that. Earlier, he'd pondered how he would answer what would surely be Everard's first question: "What is it you want to see me about?" He would simply tell the truth: that he was helping the police find his friend Stewart Halliday. "Helping the police" might be stretching it a bit but having been interviewed by two police inspectors—one having asked for his advice—he didn't see why he shouldn't use it as an opening gambit. The word "police" always got people's attention.

The girl got off at Bermondsey station. Watching her clip-clop out onto the platform, Kingston couldn't help thinking of Longfellow's lines: "How beautiful is youth! How bright it gleams / With its illusions, aspirations, dreams!" As the doors slid shut, Kingston muttered under his breath, "Bloody hell, so much for aspirations and dreams."

The next stop was his. He put thoughts of the adolescent Vampira and Miles Everard aside for the time being.

Kingston arrived at Bakers Landing after a five-minute walk from the Underground station. He'd learned a lot about the parklike development from the Internet search he'd done the day before but wasn't prepared for the size, scope, and grandeur of what he saw. Standing at the top of the sweeping entrance steps, gazing around the main plaza, he stood for a minute and took it all in.

Bakers Landing, he'd found, was a 50-acre business estate, opened in 1995. In addition to a dozen high-rise office buildings, the sprawling center featured retail shops, restaurants, pubs, a conference center, and an entertainment complex, all set in a landscaped environment.

Checking and orienting the site map in the brochure

he'd picked up at the station, he headed up the central path. All around were public parks with full-grown shade trees, gardens, fountains, and colorful plantings. After five minutes he arrived at Devon Place, the building that housed Paramus Partners. Devon Place was one of the smallest office buildings in Bakers Landing and one of the earliest. Unlike most of the other high-rise buildings, which had glass-and-steel exteriors, it had a gracefully curving ivory-colored stone fascia. Kingston entered the lobby to find that it echoed the outside curve. He approached the security desk and signed in, telling the guard who and which office he was visiting and the purpose of his visit, making sure that his title "Doctor" was repeated more than once. After a brief call to Paramus's office, the guard gave Kingston a visitor's badge. "Wear this at all times. Paramus is on the ninth floor," he said. Kingston clipped the badge on his lapel and strode to the bank of lifts where he pressed one of the buttons and waited. Seconds later, at the ninth floor, he stepped out of the elevator into a spacious, Berber-carpeted reception area.

Modern paintings in the manner of Rothko and Diebenkorn all but covered the walls—walls that looked remarkably like gray suede. Kingston stopped to study one of the abstracts. The Rothko signature was clear. A long oriental runner that Kingston pegged as a tribal Serapi led down the center of the vestibule ending at a massive ebony-colored desk. There sat an attractive platinum-haired woman of indeterminate age, wearing a silky black blazer with lilac-colored blouse. As he approached, she looked up over her rimless glasses and gave him a thin smile. "Good morning. How may I help you?" she asked, a little too haughtily for Kingston's liking.

"I'm here to see Miles Everard."

She reached for a black book, one of the few things on the desktop. "Do you have an appointment? I don't recall—"

"I don't. No. I didn't think it necessary, given the circumstances."

"And can you tell me what those 'circumstances' might be, Mr.—"

"Kingston, Doctor Lawrence Kingston." He let his name and title sink in, then said, "I'm helping the police with a missing-persons case."

His answer had the required effect. The supercilious look vanished. She was clearly muddled and trying to think of an appropriate response.

"Mr. Everard is familiar with the person in question," said Kingston, pressing the point, articulating the words for effect.

She gestured with an open hand to several black-leather-and-chrome Corbusier-style chairs placed around a low, round, glass-topped table. "Why don't you sign our guest book and take a seat, Doctor, and I'll see what I can do?" Her tone was now much more deferential.

Kingston thanked her, signed in, and then sat down. Out of the corner of his eye, he saw her talking on the phone. Retro chairs were not his style but this one was surprisingly comfortable. He picked up a magazine from the neatly fanned stack that lay alongside a crystal bowl containing a white flower arrangement. Not silk, he noticed.

He'd been reading for a few minutes when she called his name. "Mr. Blake, one of our vice presidents, will be out to see you shortly," she said.

"Here comes the next 'wall,'" he said to himself. "Thank you," He nodded.

A few minutes later, the door across from Kingston opened and a tallish man walked into the reception area—

mid to late forties, Kingston guessed. He was wearing a navy pinstriped double-breasted suit with a red polka-dot tie and had a spare physique, the kind on which clothes hang well. As he approached, Kingston stood to meet him. His face went with the clothes: dark, neatly combed hair, angular features, and a square jaw. He looked like a man one could trust. They shook hands and sat facing each other. Blake crossed his legs, careful not to rumple his sharp trouser creases. "Gavin Blake," he said with a wide smile, crossing his arms. "Mr. Everard is not here today. Perhaps I can be of help? A missing person, Eve said?"

"Yes. A friend of mine, actually—Stewart Halliday."

"And what brings you here? Does Miles Everard know your friend?"

"That's what I'm told. They were working on a project together."

"A Paramus project?"

"That I can't say. It could have been."

Blake unfolded his arms, rested his chin on his closed fist, and looked aside, frowning. "Halliday?" he said, looking back at Kingston again. "Sorry, the name's not familiar. If he were involved with one of our projects in any way, I would almost certainly know about it. Perhaps their relationship was of a personal nature."

"That's a possibility," said Kingston, knowing that further questions about Everard would be pointless. "When is he expected back?"

"Not until next Monday."

"Well," said Kingston, standing, "there's not much point in taking up any more of your time." He reached inside his jacket and produced a card, which he handed to Blake. "Perhaps you'd be good enough to tell Mr. Everard about my inquiry and have him give me a call when he returns."

Blake smiled again. "I'll make sure he does."

"Thanks for seeing me," said Kingston as they shook hands again.

"No problem at all. I'm sure Miles will be of more help, Doctor." Blake turned and headed for the door.

Kingston thanked the receptionist and walked back to the lift.

He got off on the ground floor and headed past the row of lifts into the lobby. Why he turned at that moment to glance at the last lift, he would never know. The doors were closing as he did. But it was not too late to see the woman standing alone in the lift. It was Alison Greer.

He watched the floor numbers light up as the lift ascended. He knew what the first stop would be. He was right—the ninth floor.

THIRTEEN

THE TWENTY-MINUTE Underground journey back to Sloane Square was taken up with Kingston's trying to figure out why Alison Greer would be visiting Paramus. If Everard was not at the office, whom would she be visiting? More important, why? Perhaps she knew more about Everard than she had implied and had other business there. Furthermore, if he had misread her and she was hand in glove with Everard, why would she have phoned and dragged him all the way down to Hampshire? Why would she expose Everard as one of the players—maybe a key one—in a possible deal involving Walsh and possibly Stewart? It made no sense.

Though nothing could be seen outside the train compartment except a dark wall flashing by, he stared abstractedly at the window opposite, oblivious to the monotonous clickety-clack of the wheels. Perhaps she knew more than she was telling about Walsh's death. Come to think of it, she had hardly talked about it.

Harking back to their conversation, neither had she sounded like the grieving girlfriend, either—if indeed she was. Then again, perhaps it was all speculation on his part and she was really nothing more than Walsh's secretary. If so, her reaction to his death would be much as expected.

The train was slowing and Kingston grabbed the handrail next to him and got up. It was all too confusing. He'd think about it later. It was past noon and he was getting a little peckish. Like Jonathan Swift, his stomach served him as a clock. Walking out of Sloane Square station, he headed for Partridge's, one of London's best delis. Like a smaller version of the Harrods food halls, it was yet one more good reason for living in Belgravia. What would hit the spot? A Cornish pasty or a bacon, egg, and sausage pie sounded awfully good.

Back at his flat, the light on the answerphone was flashing, registering one message. He put the Partridge's bag on the kitchen table, went back to the living room, and pushed the PLAY button. It was Detective Inspector Chisholm. He had a declassified copy of the aerial footage at Lymington Police Station and was asking Kingston to call to set up a viewing time. Kingston reflected for a moment. The timing was good—he had nothing planned for the next couple of days. If he went down to Lymington early tomorrow, he should have time to drive up to Fordingbridge to see Becky on the way home. He would call her when he got down to Lymington to make sure she was home. Between the hospital auxiliary and her bopping off to Sarah's, it made no sense to drive the twenty-five miles or so all the way up to The Willows on the off chance she might be home.

At eleven thirty the next morning, Kingston sat at a desktop computer in a back room at Lymington Police Station. He was watching the Air Support footage that, according to Chisholm, had been taken with a Sony high-definition camera with a 32x zoom capability. This, he had said, allowed the operator to identify a vehicle number plate from at least a 500-foot altitude in good daylight. To show Chisholm he was impressed, Kingston had faked incredulity. On his photo shoot, he'd been using a comparable camera.

Rubbing his eyes, he slipped another tape into the videocassette recorder and pressed PLAY. This was the fifth and last tape and he was tiring quickly. When he'd arrived at the station, Chisholm had also told him that Air Support had reviewed the tapes and had found nothing on them that they felt warranted further investigation.

So far Kingston had sat through two hours of police video surveillance covering roughly fifty square miles of the Hampshire countryside on the west side of the New Forest, from Fordingbridge in the north to Christchurch and Milford on Sea on the south coast. Most of the footage was of open fields and farmland. Not familiar with the area, he recognized none of the towns or villages, not that it would have made any difference. All he was looking for was any inland expanse of water that might serve, or have served, as a site for larger-scale experimentation with botanical desalination.

Hearing a knock on the door, Kingston stopped the tape and turned around. The door opened and a young policeman entered, carrying a tray with tea and biscuits. "Thought you might like to take a break, guv," he said, smiling. He put the tray down on the table next to Kingston. "Any joy with that lot?" he asked, nodding to the tapes.

Kingston sighed and shook his head. "So far, not a damned thing. Only twenty minutes left, though. So I'll be out of your hair soon."

"Don't worry on our account, sir," he said, about to leave. He stopped by the door and looked back. "By the way, the sergeant's missus made the biscuits," he said, closing the door behind him.

Kingston poured a cup of tea and restarted the tape. More fields, more farms, nothing but bloody countryside. Now he was giving up hope of finding anything. He broke off a piece of biscuit and munched on it. It was remarkably good. He took another sip of tea, taking his eyes off the screen for a few seconds. When he looked back, he caught the tail end of what resembled the edge of a berm, a level mound of grass-covered earth that appeared to be about five feet high. He rewound the tape ten seconds and restarted it in the frame-by-frame mode. A second or so, and there it was again—the berm and next a sweep of a large rectilinear reservoir. He reversed the tape and played it again. From the altitude the video was taken, it was impossible to tell whether there was anything in the water. Pity the operator hadn't zoomed in, he thought. The reservoir was only on the screen for a few seconds but it was sufficient time to also show several quasi-industrial buildings and what could easily be a pump house. With no signs of people or vehicles, the area looked deserted. As the tape continued to run in the jog mode, Kingston saw an unpaved lane leading away from the reservoir that ran for what looked like about a half mile and eventually joined a road lined with a row of tall conifers. He made a written note of the time-codes on the bottom of the screen. This way he or the police could select the relevant frames when rerunning the tape. He wasn't to know that if he were viewing the original tape, the screen would have shown all kinds of data and symbols: GPS positioning, latitude and longitude, date and time, camera angles, camera settings, and more. For security reasons, these had been deleted.

Kingston let the tape run to see if he could spot a landmark—a building, pub, or church—anything that could help pinpoint the approximate location of the reservoir on an Ordnance Survey map. About twenty seconds further into the tape, he saw a small village with a Norman church that had an unusual bell-turret. That might help, he thought. He made a note of that time-code also. He needed to talk to Chisholm and have him ask the Air Support police if they were able to correlate the time-code with map coordinates. If so, it would save him a lot of time making local inquiries and running around trying to locate the reservoir. The rest of the tape showed nothing of further interest. Kingston rewound and ejected it, then placed it neatly on top of the others. Then he turned off the computer.

Kingston went to the front desk to let Chisholm know that he was leaving. The constable on duty—the one who had brought the tea—said that Chisholm had left some time ago and that he would pass on Kingston's question regarding the time-code and map coordinates when Chisholm returned. Kingston thanked him again for the tea, saying that the biscuits were exceptional—"worthy of Harrods."

The constable smiled. "I'll tell the sergeant. His wife'll be right chuffed," he said.

In the car, Kingston called Becky at The Willows but there was no reply.

TWO DAYS LATER, with the top down, Kingston drove through the New Forest headed toward the village of Woolstead on its southwest edge. This was the village with the Norman church that he'd seen on the videotape.

Much to his surprise, he'd received an e-mail from Inspector Chisholm the day after he'd viewed the tape. Air Support had come up with answers to Kingston's questions. The Sony 3-chip digital camera, they said in their forwarded e-mail, was linked to an onboard GPS tracking system that interfaced with all the other data on the tape, including the time-code. This meant that Air Support had been able to provide latitude and longitude and GPS coordinates for the two time-codes Kingston had given to Chisholm. He now knew exactly where on the Ordnance Survey map sitting beside him on the passenger seat the reservoir and the church were located.

It was a day that sports-car owners lust after: blue skies

with Constable-like clouds, not a breath of wind, and a steady 22 degrees. With the balmy weather and no need for haste, he had chosen a leisurely route to get to Woolstead. The small roads of the New Forest crossed great stretches of heath, covered with gorse, purple-flowered heather, hawthorn, and blackthorn; winding their way through grazing lands and farms, past bogs and ponds, thatched cottages, and little old churches. The forest was home to several varieties of deer, wild ponies, and donkeys, and it was a rare pleasure having to stop now and then to watch the native ponies amble across the road in front of him. Here the animals had the right of way.

Just before leaving home, he'd called Becky but there was no answer. He would try a little later after he'd checked out the reservoir. Being in that part of Hampshire made him think about the garden at Cranborne Manor, which in turn reminded him about the aerial videotape they'd shot of the other two gardens, Leven's Hall and Powis Castle. That was some time ago, and he was surprised that he hadn't heard from Martin at New Eden. There was obviously some explanation for it. Perhaps it was a good sign. If the video had been bad, he would have undoubtedly heard about it right away. He made a mental note to give Martin a call in the morning.

Fifteen minutes later, he was out of the forest passing through Woolstead. The village was remarkably pretty, a mixture of Norman and Early English architecture. Kingston had found out that the church, named St. Andrew's, was the oldest documented building thereabouts—mentioned in the *Domesday Book* of 1086. It also had "pretty gardens," according to one of the guidebooks. Kingston decided that he would stop on the way back for a pit stop and a cup of tea. Afterward, time permitting, he would take a walk around the village and visit the church.

Once out of Woolstead, he pulled over to check the map again. If his map reading was right, the reservoir was only six miles away.

A few minutes later, he spied the row of conifers he'd seen on the tape. He slowed down, aware that the lane leading to the reservoir was small and it would be easy for him to overshoot it. He couldn't remember from the tape if it was gated or not. With no cars behind him, he stopped alongside the lane. There was a gate. It was metal and looked new. He pulled over onto the grass verge, left the engine running, got out of the car, and walked across to the gate, which he fully expected to be padlocked. To his surprise, it wasn't. Lifting the iron strap, he opened the gate, went back to the car, and drove through. Remembering the countryside code—leave gates as you found them—he stopped, got out again, and closed the gate behind him. After he passed a sign warning against trespassing, the reservoir came into view. The site was bigger than it appeared from the air, with five buildings of varying size, the largest a double-door, barnlike structure of galvanized metal. Farther along, he could see the pumping station. He pulled up alongside one of the buildings and got out, standing for a moment, sizing the place up. No vehicles in sight, which he assumed meant that there was nobody around. It certainly looked deserted. He walked toward the bank of the reservoir. The long side facing him was at least the length of a football field. Looking around, he could appreciate even more why it would be the ideal place for Stewart and his partners to conduct their experiments at industrial-strength level.

The sky was now clouding and a slight wind was picking up. For the first time, he sensed an eerie silence about the place. He headed toward a flight of steps cut into the reservoir bank. Gripping the rail on one side, he climbed the eight or so metal steps and reached the top. What he saw made him smile.

Two feet above the surface of the water, metal tracks spanned the reservoir about every twenty feet. On closer inspection of the inside wall, Kingston could see the edges of glass-covered frames that were designed to run on the tracks. Without question, they were operated electrically, much like a garage-door opener, turning the reservoir into a huge retractable greenhouse. Just below the water level, gauges set in the wall measured the water temperature. He kneeled to get a closer look into the water. There they were, approximately a foot beneath the surface: the spent leaves of *Victoria* hybrid water lilies.

Curious to see if the pumping system did indeed import seawater, he walked past the outbuildings and the barn to the pump house. Built of breeze blocks with a heavy pad-locked door and galvanized roof, it was not much to look at—nothing more than a few large- and small-gauge pipes projecting from the structure. What Kingston was looking for was evidence of new pipes: a pipeline from the pumps all the way to a source of seawater. He found it quickly. A few yards from the pump house, a new eight-inch pipe made a right-angled turn and headed south, across the end of the reservoir and out of sight. There was not much point in his following its path any farther; it couldn't serve any other purpose that he could think of.

He retraced his steps past the barn to check the out-buildings. The first door he tried was locked, as were the second and third. The fourth and smallest of the buildings also had a padlock but it was open. Lifting the padlock off the latch, he pushed the metal door open and entered. Enough light came from the high clerestory windows for him to see the interior. He took a few paces and looked around at the makeshift living quarters. A full kitchen took up one corner. Next to it was a rectangular table covered with a red-and-white-checked tablecloth and surrounded by four chairs. On the table, several upturned glasses and cups were set alongside condiment containers. Two single beds, one unmade, were pushed up against one wall. The facing wall was the "entertainment" center: crudely fashioned shelves with the usual VCR, DVD player, tape deck, et cetera, and a large TV as the centerpiece. A partly open, hinged dartboard case with three darts stuck in the center of the board was positioned on the last wall, alongside a couple of cheap art prints in frames but with no glass.

He sensed, rather than heard, somebody behind him. The blow to his head was excruciating but only for an instant. He slumped to the ground, unconscious.

KINGSTON GOT UP, easing himself into a half-sitting position, leaning on one arm. The headache came in waves, each one more intense than the last. He put a hand up and touched his scalp. The hair was matted with congealed blood where he'd been struck and the bump was a snorter. Thank God, he thought to himself, his vision wasn't blurred and he wasn't vomiting. Then he noticed his wallet on the floor, a few feet away. Surely robbery couldn't have been the motive, he asked himself. After resting for a couple of minutes, fighting back the nausea, he got slowly to his feet, picked up his wallet, and made his way to the sink. He pulled a clean handkerchief from his pocket and soaked it under the cold tap for a compress. Applying it over the next few minutes helped ease the pain. He checked his watch, wondering how long he'd been out. It was not quite noon. Guessing that he'd arrived at the reservoir about 11:45 meant that he'd been unconscious for ten minutes or so.

Wanting to be sure he was okay to drive, he sat at the table for about five minutes nursing his injury, staring around the room. If Stewart had been living here at any time or even if he had simply been using the room while supervising the experiments, there was certainly no evidence of it. Not that Kingston was expecting a note pinned to the wall with his name on it. If Stewart had left any clue, it would be subtle, yet evident right away to Kingston or anyone who was adept at solving cryptic messages; something along the lines of the one he'd left in his stapler. But as far as Kingston could tell, there was nothing. On top of being in considerable pain, he was disappointed.

He'd been through his wallet and nothing appeared missing. The sixty-five pounds was still there, as were his license and credit cards. He could only think that whoever had taken the wallet out of his back pocket must have done so to establish his identity. He was loath to call 999 as he no longer considered his condition an emergency. He would seek medical treatment, though—just in case. One never knew with head trauma. He didn't know the area at all but remembered that New Milton on the coast was close by. It was quite a large town and he was sure to find someone there to look at his injury. There was no point in dwelling on *who* it was that had knocked him out. *Why* was rather obvious. Desmond's words came back to him again: "They're not people you want to mess with." He would also have to report the assault to the police. He would wait on that until after he'd had his injury examined.

Hand resting on the table, Kingston stood, took a deep breath, and walked gingerly to the door. As he passed the dartboard, still a bit wobbly, his shoulder caught the edge of the case. It swung back to reveal a black chalk scoreboard inside. He had no idea what prompted him but he opened the other side of the case. He stepped back a couple of paces and looked at the two chalkboards, now flat against the wall with the dartboard in the center. The result of the last game was still on the board: the vertical rows of chalk scores for each player crossed out as they were deducted from the beginning score of 301. The name Keith was scrawled at the top of the left board. The name of the player on the right side was Hal. Kingston stared at the right-hand board. Hal had won the game by going out with a double 19. "Good going, Stewart," he muttered, smiling. "Damned good score, too." He turned away from the dartboard, his pain and sullen mood gone for a fleeting moment. Hal was Stewart's nickname when they were at university together. It was hard to abbreviate Stewart— "Stew" was unacceptable—so someone, somewhere along the way, had shortened his second name instead.

Outside, Kingston stopped and took a deep breath. A drizzle had set in, dampening all sound; it was so still that he could hear himself breathing. He walked to the car, cursing that he hadn't put the top up when it had started clouding over. In a minute, he had the vinyl soft top up and had wiped the seats dry with an old towel kept in the boot. Checking that everything was locked down, he slipped behind the wheel. Propped up on the hub of the three-spoke steering wheel was one of his business cards, He picked it up and turned it over. On the back was written in capital letters: STOP INTERFERING *NOW*—OR ELSE!

FOURTEEN

AFTER LEAVING THE RESERVOIR, Kingston went straight to New Milton, where he found a sports-injury clinic and a doctor who examined and cleaned his wound and gave him some medication to ease the pain. The diagnosis: nothing more serious than a mild concussion. When he had been asked by the office nurse upon arrival how he sustained the wound, he gave a more or less accurate account of what happened, omitting the fact that he had been trespassing on private property and searching for giant water lilies that consumed salt. Before leaving the clinic, head still throbbing, he called Ringwood Police Station on his mobile, to learn that Carmichael was not in the office. Kingston told the sergeant on duty that he was helping Inspector Carmichael in connection with a missing-persons case and reported what had happened at the reservoir. When finished, Kingston was told that the report would be filed and that a patrol car would be sent to investigate, albeit it was "rather late in the day," as the sergeant put it. Ending the conversation, he took Kingston's address and phone numbers and told him that Inspector Carmichael would be given a copy of the report as soon as he returned.

Next, he called Becky. This time the phone rang a half-dozen times before she picked it up. "This is Rebecca," she said, panting.

"It's Lawrence," he said. "Were you in the garden? You sound out of breath."

"No, I was upstairs, sorry. How are you, Lawrence?"

"I'm fine," he lied. "Never mind about me. How are you?"

"Coping as best as I can. You know—stiff upper lip and all that."

"Any more from the police?"

"They called once when I was with Sarah. But no news, really. Nothing's changed, I'm afraid."

He was tempted to tell her that he was in New Milton, but that would mean having to tell quite a few white lies or do an awful lot of explaining. There was really no point in telling her what he'd been up to, about his probing into Walsh's death and the other unexplained incidents, until he had some tangible proof or solid evidence. The very last thing he wanted was for Becky to have to start worrying about him, too. "I have a question," he said before she could ask him where he was or what he had been doing while she was gone.

"What's that?"

"A few days ago, I got a phone call from a woman named Alison Greer. She said that she'd spoken to you about Stewart."

"Alison Greer? Oh, that's right. She did, yes. We had quite a long chat on the phone."

"She said that you referred her to me."

"No. Why would I? I might have mentioned you, told her you were helping me. I really don't recall now."

"Hmm, that's odd. What did you talk about?"

"As I recall, she said that she'd met Stewart at another man's house—his name escapes me right now. He'd recently died in a fire at his home. She wanted to know if I had met him or knew him."

"Adrian Walsh."

"Walsh, that's right."

"According to her you hadn't."

"That's true. I've no idea who he is—or was, I suppose."

"Why call you?"

"Apparently she'd read about Stewart's disappearance in the papers and wondered if the two events were connected in any way."

"It all seems rather odd. I'm surprised you didn't mention it at the time."

"I'm sorry. If I'd thought for one moment it might be important, I certainly would have. At the time, it seemed innocent enough."

Kingston sighed. "It probably is, Becky. Don't worry about it."

The conversation ended with his promising to call her on the weekend to arrange for another visit to The Willows.

Tired and still hurting after the drive back to London, made interminable by roadworks on the M3, he got back to his flat around six.

Sitting on the sofa, he sorted the mail, a glass of Macallan at his side. Separating the bills from the junk mail, he was glad to find a postcard from his friend Andrew, who was holidaying in New Zealand. Kingston was beginning to wish he'd taken up Andrew's offer to accompany him. "Wish you were here," Andrew had written in jest.

Putting the postcard aside, Kingston leaned back, thinking back on his conversation with Becky and on Alison Greer's lie about Becky having suggested calling him. What was the woman up to? he wondered. The medication had helped his headache, but the occasional dull throbbing reminded him about his trip to the reservoir and the warning—not that he would ever forget it. On the drive home he'd concluded that whoever attacked him must have been at the reservoir when he'd arrived and had been watching him all that time. No cars in sight probably meant that a motorcycle was tucked away somewhere on the grounds. It seemed the most logical explanation. The circumstances—particularly the more-dead-than-alive water lilies—led him to believe that the reservoir trials were finished and the place was now being put to other use. Despite having paid very painfully for it, the visit was not wasted. He was convinced that the "Hal" written on the chalkboard was no coincidence, meaning that Stewart could have been living there all or part of that time. He wished he could go back and see if there was any further evidence or clues that would confirm his suspicion.

Assuming that the trials—or experiments, or whatever they should be called—had been successful, what would Everard's next step be, if indeed he were the mastermind behind the scheme? Logical reasoning suggested that if Everard was selling the water-lily hybrid or setting up a joint venture to build a more sophisticated desalination plant, he'd have to prove that the process not only worked but would function efficiently when scaled up. To achieve that, interested parties would have to have seen a demonstration of the system at work to make such a consequential decision. Documentation, statistics, charts, photographic examples, and samples of purified water would not be enough.

So if the results had been positive and the project was near completion, where did that leave Stewart? And where was he now? Kingston picked up Andrew's postcard and looked at the photograph of the mirror-like surface of an azure lake with a backdrop of snow-dusted mountains— one of the National Parks. It was all so tranquil and far removed from everything that was happening in Kingston's world. He sighed, wishing he *were* there.

Since that very first phone message from Becky's daughter—it seemed so long ago now—Kingston's life had been upended. Now he had become a target: that changed everything. At his time of life, self-preservation trumped heroism every time. He swirled the amber liquid in his glass, inhaling the peat-smoky aroma. Fitzgerald had it right, he mused, when he penned: "Show me a hero and I'll write you a tragedy." Stewart's disappearance and Walsh's murder had brought tragedy enough already. How did he manage to get entangled in these unlikely situations, and why was he always the one singled out to help solve other people's problems? Of course, he knew why. He took another sip of the single malt and reached for the phone. He'd call Desmond and tell him about the latest episode. Kingston could hear him now, when he told Desmond he'd been mugged: "Can't say I didn't warn you, Lawrence. I told you not to mess with those people."

Kingston was about to hang up when Desmond answered after the umpteenth ring.

"It's Lawrence. How are you?"

"Fine. Looks like the Finchley nursery will happen. Nip and tuck for a while but I finally managed to convince the bank that there really was gold in goldfish."

"Not to mention water lilies."

"Right. How's all that going?"

"That's why I'm calling. Not too well, I'm afraid."

Kingston went on to tell Desmond everything that had happened since they last met, ending with the incident at the reservoir.

"Jesus! You can't say I didn't warn you, Lawrence. I told you not to mess with those people."

Kingston smiled. "You were right, Desmond. I still have the lump on my head to prove it. The rotten thing is that I'm nowhere nearer to finding Stewart than I was on day one. I'm starting to get a sickening feeling that we may never see him again."

"What about the police?"

"Zip. Nothing. In fact, I got a call from the inspector at Ringwood who's handling the case asking *me* if I had any further ideas. That says it all. I've done the best I can, Desmond. I don't know what more I can do."

"For God's sake, just let it go, Lawrence," Desmond yelled. "How many times do I have to tell you?"

Kingston heard a sigh, then a calmer voice. "Tell Stewart's wife—what's her name?"

"Becky."

"Tell Becky what you just told me and I'm sure she'll understand. If the truth be known, by now she no longer has her hopes up too high, anyway."

"We're not going to give up hope, Desmond, if that's what you're saying."

"That's not what I'm saying at all. I'm saying knock off the detective work."

"All right, all right. I hear you."

"By the way, I'm coming into town next Monday. Want to do lunch? My treat this time."

"Monday's fine."

"Great. I'll call you over the weekend and we'll set it up. No more nice guy, okay?"

Kingston put the phone down. Desmond was right. It was time to end his investigation. However, he hadn't told Desmond that, before closing the book on his search, he was about to do one more thing: check on Google Earth, the Internet satellite imagery and mapping site, to see if he might be able to obtain an aerial view of the reservoir.

IF THE PHONE WERE TO RING only once a day, Sod's Law would have it that the call would be in the middle of either lunch or dinner. In this case Kingston had just sat down at the kitchen table with a bowl of last night's leftover fettuccine al pesto and a glass of Chianti Classico Riserva—

also from the previous night. At first, he considered letting the answering machine take the message but instead he took a quick sip of wine, got up, and picked up the phone.

"Doctor Kingston?"

The man's voice was cultivated and unfamiliar.

"It is," Kingston replied, looking across to his cooling pasta.

"This is Miles Everard. I understand you were in our offices last week, asking for me."

Caught off guard, Kingston hesitated. "Yes—yes, I was," he said. "Thank you for getting back to me."

"I understand that you talked to Gavin Blake, one of our vice presidents—he usually subs for me when I'm gone. My secretary was out that day."

"That's right," said Kingston, playing for time, figuring how he should broach the question of Stewart's disappearance. Everard saved him the trouble.

"Blake said you wanted to talk to me about a friend of yours who's gone missing. He said that you felt sure I knew him and thought that I might be working with him on a project of some kind." Everard's tone was cordial, not at all businesslike.

"In a nutshell, that was the purpose of my visit, yes."

"What's your friend's name?"

"Halliday. Stewart Halliday. He was a colleague of Adrian Walsh's, whom I'm told you also knew."

A lengthy pause was followed by Everard's answer: "I'm sorry, Doctor, I'm not familiar with either of those names."

This was not at all what Kingston had been expecting. The idea of Everard's denying knowledge of Stewart and Walsh had never crossed his mind. Before he could reply, Everard spoke again.

"May I ask what made you think I knew these people?"

"The information came from a woman named Alison

Greer. She maintained that you, Halliday, and Walsh were involved in a project to develop a new type of desalination process. She believed you were partners and had met at Walsh's house in Hampshire." Kingston was about to tell him that Walsh had been murdered but thought better of it—for the moment, anyway.

Everard laughed politely. "First I've heard of it," he said. "If it works and it's more cost-efficient than conventional methods, I might like to know more about it. But it's not really our kind of business. Essentially, we're an engineering and construction company. So if we *were* to be involved in such a project, it would most likely be as a subcontractor."

Kingston was getting a sinking feeling that Everard was telling the truth. Nothing in his answers, or the straightforward manner in which he had phrased them, gave Kingston any reasons to think otherwise. He had run out of questions—almost.

"You're saying you don't know Alison Greer, either? You've never met her?" he asked.

"Absolutely not."

"Well—"

"Sounds like she's led you up the garden path, Doctor."

Kingston wanted to say, You don't know how true that is, but instead replied, "It rather looks that way."

"Sorry I couldn't help," Everard said as if he meant it.

"Thanks for taking the time to call. I appreciate the courtesy, Mr. Everard—rare these days."

"No problem."

"This is going to sound like an odd question, but would you mind if I asked you your height?"

"My height?"

"Yes."

"That *is* a strange question."

"I know."

There was a pause, after which Everard replied, "Five-nine."

"Thanks," said Kingston. "Thanks very much."

They said good-bye and Kingston put down the phone.

ALISON GREER WAS LYING. What other explanation was there? Why would she concoct such a story to mislead him so duplicitously? She had been so convincing. Not only convincing, he had even taken a liking to her. He laughed to himself. On the drive home from her cottage he had toyed with the idea of finagling a way to see her again under more sociable terms. Such stirrings had been rare, almost nonexistent, during his many years as a widower.

Oddly, he wasn't furious about what she had done. He was more at a loss as to her motivation to have gone to such lengths to deceive him. In a perverse way, it was an admirable performance. Nevertheless, he'd made up his mind, regardless of Desmond's admonitions, that he would confront Alison Greer to find out who had put her up to it and what was going on. He wasn't going to let her get away with it. Now was as good a time as any. He picked up the phone and punched in the number she had given him.

It rang for some time before he heard the message: *"Sorry we missed your call..."* Kingston put the phone down, none too gently, and looked up at the ceiling. "That's odd," he said under his breath. "*We* missed your call." Was someone living with her? Wouldn't she have said so? Or was it the editorial "we" again?

Kingston lay awake half that night, thoughts and visions of Alison Greer coming and going as he tried to rehash their conversation of that morning at the cottage. By the time first light sliced through the shutters, projecting an abstract light show on the wall, his mind had long since been made up. Today was Saturday, and if the weather was half decent, he would take a spin down to Hartley Wintney with the intent of surprising Miss Greer and having it out with her.

Dressed in his navy terry robe, he went into the kitchen and put the kettle on. Waiting for it to boil, he called her again, just in case he had mistakenly dialed the wrong number yesterday. He heard the same message.

Several minutes later, a cup of tea and a bowl of steaming Scott's Porridge Oats on the table, and Alison Greer off his mind for a while, he cast his eyes over *The Times* crossword and read a few clues. Cleverly concealed anagrams—some eleven- and twelve-letter words or longer—often appeared. He had become a whiz at ferreting out and solving them. Now and then, just for fun, with nothing better to do, he would look at words in magazines, on packages, in waiting rooms— wherever—and make anagrams of them. By shuffling the letters of "Alec Guinness" he'd made *Genuine Class*. "Marriage" became *A Grim Era*. One of his all-time favorites, though not of his making: "Eleven Plus Two" translated to *Twelve Plus One*. He'd been staring at the Scott's Porridge Oats package for many years before thinking of turning it into an anagram: *Go stir paste, doctors* was the best he'd been able to come up with. Other clues in *The Times* were even more difficult. One that he'd finally solved yesterday was particularly ingenious. The clue read: *Try to measure speed of arrow? You must be patient (4,4,4).* The answer was three words, each four letters.**

Two hours later, under a mackerel sky and with the top down, Kingston turned left off the A30 to the village

---

** Answer is: Time will tell (William Tell)

green at Hartley Wintney. He stopped outside Pennyroyal Cottage, looking at the leaded windows as he got out of the TR4 and stretched. They were all closed—unusual for such a warm day, he thought. He knocked on the door and waited, wondering how Alison would react, what she would say, when she opened the door and saw him. After a minute or so he knocked again, this time harder. He knew it had been a gamble to drive down unannounced, but, it being Saturday, he'd figured there was a greater than fifty-fifty chance of her being home. Now he was beginning to think he might have acted too impulsively, blinded by the slap in the face he'd received—and it still stung. The damned woman was probably away—that was why he'd got the answering machine. He was about to give it one last try when he heard a voice calling. He turned to see a stumpy white-haired lady wearing an apron approaching the gate. She had busybody written all over her.

"You looking for the Wilsons?" she asked, wiping her hands on the apron, stopping at the garden gate.

"I was actually looking for a woman named Alison Greer," Kingston replied as he walked toward her.

The woman looked perplexed. "I don't know anyone by that name. This is Peggy and Edgar Wilson's cottage. I'm their neighbor. That's my place," she said, nodding in the direction of the whitewashed cottage next door.

Now it was Kingston's turn to be perplexed. "The Wilsons own it?"

The little lady stiffened. "May I ask who you are?"

Kingston cranked up his best smile, crinkling the laugh lines at his blue eyes. "I'm terribly sorry. I should have introduced myself. Doctor Kingston," he said with a slight emphasis on "Doctor."

It worked every time. Her tenseness and the quizzical look disappeared like thistledown in the wind. "Well, nice to meet you, I'm sure, Doctor. I'm Millie—Millie Watkins." She smiled at last and looked suitably impressed, so Kingston continued.

"I was here about a week ago, visiting the lady I mentioned—Alison Greer. She led me to believe it was her cottage."

"Well, the Wilsons have lived here for about—" She looked up, creasing her already deeply wrinkled brow. "Oh, at least five years, I would say."

"They own it?"

She paused, obviously wondering whether she should be divulging all this to a complete stranger. "No, they rent."

"Forgive me," said Kingston. "I'm sorry to be asking so many questions but how would she—the woman whom I mentioned— have been able to entertain me for several hours in this very cottage?" The instant the words were out of his mouth, he realized how they must have sounded. He felt his face flush and tried to cover his tracks. "When I said 'entertain,' I meant that we just chatted and had tea and biscuits, that sort of thing. I had every reason to believe it was her house." As he talked, he realized how easy it would have been for Alison Greer to pull it off. A few strategically placed photographs, making tea in the kitchen, it would have been all so easy if she knew she had the place to herself for a few hours.

"This lady—what did she look like?"

"About your height—petite, I guess you'd describe her. Dark hair, on the short side, and blue eyes—very blue."

Millie looked off to the side, thinking for a moment, then turned back to Kingston. "Now you mention it, there was a lady here once. I chatted briefly with her. Oh, months ago it was. I was coming back from the shops and it looked like she was letting herself in. The Wilsons were away that time, too. I asked, from across the front lawn, who she was and what she was doing. She said not to worry, that she worked for the leasing agent who looked after the property. She held up the key for me to see and mentioned the agent's name but my memory's not what it used to be, I'm afraid. She wasn't what you'd call talkative but she was well dressed and seemed quite nice, so I took her at her word."

"Do you recall if she had dark hair?"

"I believe so but I wouldn't be certain. I never saw her close up so I don't know about the eyes. I only saw her that one time." She shrugged. "Could have been her, I suppose."

"If it was, it would certainly explain how was she was able to let herself in." Kingston looked back at the cottage. "Where are the Wilsons now, may I ask?"

"I shouldn't be telling you all this, but they're on holiday. Coming back this Wednesday, they are." She paused, frowning again, clearly trying to fathom what it all meant. "They're retired and travel quite a lot. I always keep an eye on the cottage while they're gone." She shrugged and took on a defensive air. "I can assure you it's all been very normal since they left—nothing out of the ordinary. I would have noticed if there had been."

"Do you know who owns the cottage?"

"Now? I'm not really sure. The lady who used to own it passed away."

"Did she live here?"

"Yes, for a long time. Dear old soul she was. Marjorie." Millie looked melancholy, her eyes downcast. "Poor thing died of pneumonia, always ailing, she was. She was in her late eighties, so she'd had a good innings. I never knew any of her family, though I know she had a son. She was real proud of him. She must have left the cottage to somebody, I suppose."

"Do you recall Marjorie's name? Her surname?"

Millie put a finger up to her lower lip. "Let me see—I believe it was Walsh. Yes, that's right, Marjorie Walsh."

Kingston nodded. "It makes sense—yes, it makes sense," he muttered. It was supposition, of course, but Marjorie Walsh was most likely Adrian's mother and it was he who had bought the cottage for her. After she died, he got it back. Being privy to Walsh's affairs, Alison knew about the cottage and where the key was kept. Most likely, one was kept in the office, too.

"Well, you've been very helpful, Millie. Thanks for answering my questions." He flashed the Kingston smile again. "I have one request before leaving. Would it be impertinent of me to ask if I could see inside the cottage? Only for a minute—there's something I want to check."

He knew from the look on her face that he was pushing his luck. Reading her mind wasn't hard: being outside in the relative safety of the village green was one thing, but being alone in a house with a total stranger twice her size was another matter entirely. He could see that she was struggling to find a suitable answer, not wanting to give the impression that she didn't trust him.

"You don't have to come in with me," he said. "You can watch from the door if you like. I'll stay in the living room. It'll only take a minute."

She had knotted the corner of the apron and was twisting it nervously.

"Promise I won't nick anything," he said, smiling.

"All right," she said at last. "Let me go get the key."

In a minute she was back. She opened the door and let him in.

Kingston looked around the living room. Everything was the same except for one thing: the photographs of Alison Greer were gone. In their place: framed family photos of what he took to be two or three generations of Wilsons.

Outside on the front porch Kingston thanked Millie, got in the TR4, and drove off. First, before heading for home, he was going to make a pit stop at a nearby pub that came highly recommended by Andrew: the Shoulder of Mutton. He needed a pint and then some lunch. He had a lot of thinking to do.

FIFTEEN

SETTLED AT A CORNER TABLE in the dark-paneled lounge of the Shoulder of Mutton at Hazely Heath, Kingston took a sip of beer while studying the lunch menu. The decision made, he leaned back and thought about Alison Greer's deception. Why would she go to all that trouble just to tell him about Everard? Come to think of it, she'd lied about her conversation with Becky, too. He'd rehashed their conversation that day at the cottage more than once and was still unable to come up with another reason for her wanting to see him personally. If it was only about Everard, she could as easily have told him on the phone.

After a minute or so, he gave up trying to figure out her motive. Regardless of what or who put her up to it, he was convinced of one thing: she knew much more than she was telling about Stewart, Walsh, and Everard. However, it was now immaterial. If she had done a vanishing act—and it looked that way—he might as well forget about her; too bad, because she was the only link to the three men. Once again, it was stalemate.

A waitress arrived and took his order for lunch plus another half pint of best bitter. Not yet noon, the pub was still relatively quiet, but Andrew was usually right; it looked like the kind of place that would fill up quickly. He smiled to himself and thought about Andrew eating and drinking his way through New Zealand. He gulped down the remainder of his beer and took stock of the situation. His search for Stewart was all but over and he knew it. The chilling message was no idle threat and he wasn't out to prove otherwise. It had crossed his mind, too, that they—whoever *they* were—might be keeping tabs on him. It wouldn't surprise him, with so much at stake. Now that he thought about it, there had been little discussion, with the police or anyone else, about the billions of dollars to be made if the biological desalination process was proven industrially viable and cost-efficient. When announced—if that day came—it would get international media coverage and governments in arid regions of the world would be the first ones clamoring for it.

Kingston traced a question mark in the droplets of beer on the polished surface of the tabletop. Much as he tried to forget her, he couldn't get Alison Greer off his mind. It was something she had said. A moment later it came to him. Why hadn't he thought of it before? Why hadn't he called her place of work—Walsh's construction company? Surely there couldn't be many construction companies in Farnborough. A Google search would find it in a flash. As he was thinking about it, the waitress appeared with his lunch and another beer. Feeling a little more bucked up—at least he had one more avenue of investigation—he took a sip of beer and tucked into his Dover sole meunière.

By THE TIME KINGSTON had reached the Chiswick Flyover—ten minutes from home—it was raining stair rods and the TR4's aging windscreen wipers were chattering like false teeth on a frigid night. He'd best get them replaced in the next couple of days. At last he reached the garage. Locking the car inside, setting the alarm, he braced himself for the walk to his flat. In the few minutes it took, his umbrella blew inside out twice, and by the time he reached the front door, he was drenched. From the thighs down, it was as if he'd been wading in one of Desmond's pools.

In the living room, dressed in an Irish wool pullover and corduroy pants, he sat in front of a newly lit fire, PowerBook on his lap and a glass of whisky on the table at his side. A search had turned up nearly two dozen construction companies in Farnborough, none under the name Walsh. He ran the cursor down the list again and stopped at AW Construction. That had to be it. He glanced at his watch. It was near five. He picked up the phone and entered AW's number, hoping it wasn't going to be one of those infuriating "If you know the extension number of the person..." jobs.

"AW Construction, how may I help you?" A cheery woman's voice interrupted his thoughts.

"My name's Lawrence Kingston—Doctor Kingston. I'm calling about one of your employees, a Miss Alison Greer. I understand she was Adrian Walsh's secretary."

After a pause, the woman replied, "I'm sorry, Doctor, there's nobody by that name on our staff."

It was not the response he was hoping for. It looked as though his assumption was wrong and the AW initials had nothing to do with Adrian Walsh. "You're sure of that?" he asked. "Not even in the past?"

"Yes. I've been here for six years. I suppose she could have worked here before that." She paused again. "You say she was Mr. Walsh's secretary?"

"That's what I'm told, yes." Kingston was thinking about what she'd just said. "There is a Mr. Walsh, then?" he asked.

"Well, there was. He passed away recently, though. Were you aware?"

"I was, yes," he replied, trying to give the three words a sympathetic edge, at the same time trying to suppress a sigh of relief that he hadn't been wrong after all. "Most unfortunate," he added.

"His secretary left the company. We're trying to fill that position."

"May I ask what happened to her?"

"I'm sorry, I'm not permitted to give out information about our employees. It's a company policy."

"I fully understand," said Kingston, not about to give up. "I'm not asking for personal information or even a name, for that matter. I'm working with the police on a missing-persons case and Miss Greer's name came up in a recent inquiry. We're trying to locate her, that's all."

"Will you excuse me a moment, sir?" she asked.

"Of course," he replied.

In less than a minute she was back. "I'm going to have you speak with Mr. Gordon, our personnel director. I'll transfer you now."

A young-sounding Gordon came on the line. "Good afternoon, Doctor, I understand you were asking about Adrian's secretary."

"I was. I explained that it was in connection to a missing-persons case I've been working on—cooperating with the police."

"Yes, Cynthia mentioned that. What would you like to know?"

"You've no record of an Alison Greer ever having worked for your company?"

"Not in my time, no."

"Adrian Walsh's last secretary, what were the circumstances concerning her leaving?"

"It was a medical problem. I'm sure you can understand why I'm not able to give you details."

"Of course. How long ago was that?"

There was a pause while Gordon thought. "I would say about four or five months."

"Could I ask if she was married?"

"Not as far as we were concerned. Her employment records listed her as a single woman."

"Has anyone talked with her since?"

"I couldn't say for sure but I could ask around."

"Can you tell me her name?"

"I see no reason why not. It was Marian Taylor."

"Hmm. Petite, dark hair, blue eyes?"

"Smallish, blue eyes, yes—but I would've said lighter hair, more brownish. But that would describe her adequately, I suppose."

Kingston knew what the answer would be, but he asked the question anyway. "You wouldn't have an address by any chance, would you?"

Gordon's answer was emphatic. "No, I wouldn't."

"Well, you've been very helpful, Mr. Gordon. If I have further questions, perhaps I could call you back?"

"Anytime. Well, good luck with your inquiry, Doctor."

Kingston put the phone down and looked up at the ceiling. "Quite a chameleon, our Alison," he mumbled to himself.

He picked up his drink, got up, and walked over to the window. Outside, the rain was showing no signs of letting up, spattering off the shiny pavement as pedestrians slanted their umbrellas against the wind. Absently, he found himself looking for anybody who might be watching the flat. He was thinking that in the movies, it was always a shadowy figure that slipped away into the night. Daft idea, he decided. Anyone keeping an eye on him would have seen him come in and would have given up watching long ago, particularly on a night like this. He took one last glance but everybody appeared to be hurrying and nobody loitering.

Back at the fireplace, he stoked it and added more anthracite briquettes. He was about to sit down when the phone rang. It could be Desmond, he thought; he'd said he would call over the weekend about Monday's lunch. Kingston picked up the phone. It was Desmond.

"I'm calling about Monday, Lawrence."

"Still okay for lunch?"

"I'm not, unfortunately. I was supposed to meet a contractor in Finchley—you know, the new nursery—to go over some construction plans, but he can't make it. So I won't be coming into town until next week."

"Not a problem. Next week's wide open."

"I'll let you know what day. Any news of your friend, Stewart?"

"Not a word."

"No more sleuthing, I hope?"

"No. Not really."

"Not really? What the hell does that mean?"

"Just a couple of loose ends, that's all." Having given Desmond his word of honor that he was aborting his investigation, he would rather not tell him about his trip to the cottage and the phone call to AW Construction.

"Loose ends, my foot. I know you better than that, Lawrence."

Kingston didn't respond quickly enough.

"Come on. What's going on? Tell your uncle Desmond."

"All right. It's no big deal. I found out that Alison Greer, Adrian Walsh's former secretary, is not who she says she is. Her real name is Marian Taylor and she left AW Construction—Walsh's company—on sick leave before Walsh was murdered."

"Which means?"

"I wish I knew."

"Have you talked with the police again?"

"I haven't, no. And if they'd turned up anything, I'm sure they would have called me."

Desmond's next words were lost on Kingston, who was distracted by the doorbell ringing. "Can you hold on for a moment, Desmond? Someone's at the front door."

Kingston put the phone down, went to the hall door, and opened it part way. Facing him were two men: the older white-haired, wearing a tan raincoat with the collar up, the other in a black waxed jacket. Both looked as if they'd just walked through a car wash.

"Doctor Kingston? Lawrence Kingston?" the older man inquired.

"Yes."

"I'm Detective Inspector Crosbie. This is DS Phillips," he said, nodding to the sergeant, brushing a raindrop off the end of his nose. "May we have a word?"

"Of course," Kingston replied, opening the door and standing aside to let them in. "You'd…you'd better come in."

The three stood in the narrow hallway, Kingston watching with barely concealed displeasure at the steady drip of water from their sopping coats that was forming a puddle on the hardwood floor that he had slavishly cleaned and polished only yesterday. "Come on in," he said. "You'd better give me those coats. I'll put them in the back and get a mop."

Discombobulated by the arrival of the two policemen, he'd forgotten all about Desmond. "Excuse me—I've got someone on the phone." He ushered the policemen into the living room and went to dispose of their coats. Back in the living room, he picked up the phone off the table, half expecting Desmond to have hung up. "Desmond?" he asked.

"Yeah, I'm still here. Do you want me to call you back?"

"If you would, old chap. Right now I have to talk to two policemen who just showed up."

"Policemen?"

"Right."

"Dammit, Lawrence, can't you stay out of trouble for five minutes?"

Kingston glanced at the detective inspector, whose eyes were roaming around the room, appraising the many antiques, bibelots, and artifacts.

"Don't worry, they haven't read me my rights yet, Desmond. Look, I have to go. I'll call you later, okay?"

Kingston put the phone down and faced the two policemen. "Please, sit down," he said. "How can I help you?"

Crosbie sat on the edge of the sofa, hands clasped between his legs. "We're investigating the death, the day before yesterday, of a Mr. Miles Everard." He pursed his lips, clearly waiting to see what effect his announcement would have. Despite the perturbing news, Kingston managed to rein in his surprise.

"I'm sorry to hear that," he said.

Sergeant Phillips spoke for the first time. "You knew the man, then?"

"I wouldn't say 'knew' him, no. As a matter of fact I'd never met him."

"What was your relationship, then?" asked Crosbie.

"I was told that he might have been in partnership with Stewart Halliday, a friend of mine. I wanted to find out more about him." He was about to add that Stewart had gone missing, when Crosbie interrupted.

"We're informed that you were at Everard's offices in Bakers Landing approximately two weeks ago. I believe you told the receptionist and one of his executives that you wanted to speak to Everard about a missing-persons case you were working on with the—police?" Crosbie paused, eyeing Kingston. "Would that be an accurate statement, sir?"

Kingston hesitated before replying. This didn't seem to concern Crosbie, who sat rubbing his thumbs together, seemingly nonchalant.

"It would," Kingston replied, nodding.

"So, Doctor, who is this missing person and which police authority are you working with, might I ask?" His tone was calculated, stopping just short of doubt and of... accusation.

"The missing person is a friend and former colleague named Stewart Halliday. The case is under the jurisdiction of the Hampshire Constabulary. Detective Inspector Carmichael at Ringwood Police Station is the officer in charge of the case."

The sergeant pulled a small pad from his pocket and wrote something down—doubtless the names.

Kingston thought his concise answer to Crosbie's question would have a positive effect but the inspector remained as phlegmatic as before. "Has your friend been found?" he asked.

"Not yet, and I'm afraid it doesn't bode well. It's been too long now."

The sergeant cut in. "You never got to see Everard that day and you said you'd never met him."

"That's correct."

"Was there any other communication between the two of you? Letters, phone conversations, e-mails?"

"There was, actually. He called me only a few days ago, apologizing for not having seen me when I visited his offices. Frankly, I was surprised. I thought it was considerate of him—unusual for someone in his position. I asked him if he knew my friend and if he'd had any business dealings with him."

"And what was his response?"

"He denied having any knowledge whatsoever of Stewart."

"You believed him?"

"I did, yes. I had no reason not to."

A moment of silence followed, neither policeman showing any signs that the interview was over. Kingston seized the opportunity to pop the question he'd wanted to ask ever since they'd sat down. "Can you tell me how Everard died?"

Crosbie glanced at the sergeant then back to Kingston. "No harm in your knowing, I suppose. It'll probably be in the papers anyway. He fell from a ninth-floor balcony—his office."

"Good God! An accident?"

"We don't know yet, sir."

Kingston was tempted to tell them more but decided that now was not a good time. Moreover, if he did he would have to explain about giant water lilies that could desalinate water. He wasn't about to give them even the slightest impression that he was some crackpot professor type. If and when he was ready to talk to the police, Inspector Carmichael would be the person he would go to. And that, he was now realizing, should be as soon as possible.

Crosbie stood. Taking his cue, so did the sergeant. "Well, thanks, Doctor Kingston. If we have further questions, we'll be in touch."

"Let me get your coats," said Kingston, already halfway out the door, happy that the interview was over.

Returning with the soggy, though no longer dripping, coats, he handed them over. Crosbie gave Kingston his card and started to leave. At the hall entrance, he stopped and looked around the room one more time. "Nice place you have here, Doctor. Impressive antiques. I particularly like the two Sepik River, New Guinea, masks. And that oil painting above the chest—it's almost good enough to be a Constable."

"It is," said Kingston with a smile.

SIXTEEN

KINGSTON SAT at the pine breakfast table working on his second cup of tea. Finding it hard to concentrate, he pushed the newspaper aside, still unable to dispel from his thoughts the news of Everard's inauspicious demise. Yesterday, after the policemen had left, he had thought back to his and Everard's brief phone conversation. Nothing Everard had said had given Kingston cause to think he might have been involved with Stewart and Walsh in any way. To further bolster Everard's claim of innocence, there was the matter of his height. He'd said he was five foot nine, but Kingston distinctly remembered Alison Greer describing him as being tall, "not quite as tall" as Kingston. There was always the possibility that, being diminutive, Alison had misjudged Everard's height, but Kingston was convinced that wasn't the case. He was six-three, a six-inch difference from five-nine.

Kingston took a sip of tea, wiping a stray tea leaf from his lower lip. He always used loose tea—another one of his pet preferences. Loose leaves, he insisted, brewed a superior cup of tea, and he would never be convinced otherwise. Many blends of tea were not available in teabags, and with the loose leaves he purchased from the venerable Drury Tea & Coffee Company, he knew exactly what he was getting. Plus, with loose leaves he was free to experiment with his own blends. He placed the china cup on its saucer and fiddled with his propelling pencil, thinking.

Assuming that the man he had talked with on the phone

had been the real Everard, then the man Alison Greer had described was an imposter. Either that or the woman had lied, which wouldn't be at all surprising given her track record. Trusting his first-impression judgment, Kingston had concluded that Everard was who he had claimed to be and had absolutely nothing to do with the desalination project. Why, then, had his name been introduced by Alison Greer? The only logical reason he could come up with was that it was intended as a red herring, to steer Kingston in the wrong direction.

He got up from the table, taking his cup and saucer to the sink and rinsing it. Drying his hands, he glanced at his small leather-bound calendar standing on the granite countertop. Thursday was only two days away. Martin at New Eden Productions would be back from his holiday then and would be anxious to know the status of the aerial photography. Kingston had already spoken with Henley Air Services and had booked a tentative date, one week hence, to shoot the remaining two gardens, those at Sissinghurst Castle in Kent and Hatfield House in Hertfordshire.

After taking his daily calcium and vitamin pills, he went into his office, where he took down a book from the top shelf of the floor-to-ceiling bookcase. The title: *Sissinghurst, Portrait of a Garden.* It had been several years since Kingston had visited the legendary garden, and he thought it might be a good idea to take a quick refresher course on its content and layout. He settled back into his chair, put on his glasses, and opened the book and started to leaf through its pages. Quickly, he found himself once again under the spell of this storied garden and its two gifted and charismatic creators.

Sissinghurst was originally a great Tudor and Elizabethan mansion. It acquired its "Castle" cachet in the mid-1700s, when it was used to detain French prisoners of war and the name stuck. In 1930, when it was purchased by the writer Vita Sackville-West and her diplomat husband, Harold Nicolson, it was a fraction of its former size, and a partially demolished ruin. Undaunted, the Nicolsons went about restoring the great house and shaping the beginnings of what would come to be considered by many the most famous garden in the world.

Today, the six-acre garden at Sissinghurst is divided into ten separate gardens, or "rooms" as they are called. These include the Rose Garden, with its collection of old roses and perennials; the Cottage Garden, with an exuberance of colorful flowers; the Herb Garden; the Spring Garden and Lime Walk; and the fabled White Garden. This small garden has been replicated by gardeners all over the world, in some cases right down to the last daisy. As the author, Jane Brown, put it, "The White Garden is more than part of garden legend; it has transcended into general folklore, to be celebrated by painters, poets, photographers, and essayists."

The design of the garden was the achievement of Harold Nicolson. He created the stage on which his wife, Vita, assembled a star-studded cast of plants, shrubs, and trees to create one of the most extraordinary masterpieces in the annals of gardening.

Kingston put the book down and stared at its cover, caught up in Sissinghurst's subtle witchery. His last visit had been almost ten years ago, yet it was as vivid and touching in his mind as if it had been yesterday. Nicolson's and Sackville-West's son Nigel had been there that day to personally escort him through the gardens. Regrettably, Nigel Nicolson had since passed away, but Kingston would be forever thankful that the kind and courteous man had given up almost his entire day, indulging Kingston with a behind-the-scenes tour of the garden, reminiscing about the garden's early days and growing up at Sissinghurst as a child, and offering intimate recollections of his celebrated parents, about whom he had written several books.

The last property to be featured in New Eden's one-hour program was Hatfield House and its historic gardens. In this case Kingston had no need to go to his bookshelf. He had visited the gardens, located just north of London, less than an hour from his flat, many times and knew them well.

Hatfield House is perhaps the finest example of Jacobean architecture in Britain. Centered in its own 4,000 acres of parkland, it was built at the beginning of the seventeenth century. Throughout four centuries, the gardens at Hatfield have undergone many changes, particularly over the past thirty years, during which the present Dowager Marchioness of Salisbury has imbued them with new life. Next to the house, a rambling extravaganza of red brick, are formal gardens, the origins of which go back more than three hundred years. These large gardens retain their ancient ancestry with designs sympathetic to the house: formal in nature, with avenues of clipped trees, Italianate statuary, symmetrical box-edged flower beds, fountains, lawns, and gravel walks.

The garden on the west side of the house is less formal. The center feature is a large circular lily pool with an elaborate fountain. In the summer, the beds that are cut out of the grass walks are crammed with a hodge-podge of multicolored perennials.

Flanking the Privy Garden is the Old Palace, the childhood home of Elizabeth I. In front of the medieval brick façade is the Knot Garden, planted with three knots of low box and a foot maze around a central fountain. Such gardens were designed for viewing from the upper windows of the house, from which position a greater appreciation of the patterns is possible.

Hatfield also boasts a scented garden, a kitchen garden, an orchard, a pool garden, and a wilderness garden.

Kingston was looking forward to seeing and capturing it all from the air. He sat for a moment, thinking back to the day he'd been at Hatfield to interview Lady Salisbury for a story in *The English Garden* magazine. It was yet another day he had tucked away in his memory bank, for keeps.

KINGSTON'S IDEA OF DOING an aerial search for the reservoir on Google Earth—not that he knew what it would prove—had been unsuccessful. He had mentioned this to Desmond—telling a white lie as to why he had been doing it—who had suggested an alternative: to try Land Registry. He said that he had used the government department's Web site, Land Register Online, on one occasion and was confident that Kingston would find it helpful.

Forsaking thoughts of gardens, Kinston turned on his computer and quickly located the site. It was as Desmond described it, and looked promising. He found that, for a modest fee, the service enabled the general public to obtain and download the title register and title plan of registered properties in England and Wales, simply by providing a postal address. The title register would show who owns the land and/or property, price-paid information, and any rights of way or restrictions. There was only one problem: he had no address.

Further searching provided an alternative. In the absence of an address, a scaled Ordnance Survey plan could be submitted by mail, showing the extent of the property outlined in color with its position in relation to nearby roads and other landmarks.

Fifteen minutes later, Kingston walked out of his local

copy shop with a same-sized copy of the page in question from his large-scale Ordnance Survey map. Taking it home, he had inked in make-believe boundaries of what he guessed would be those of the land on which the reservoir was located. Sealing the map inside an envelope along with a copy of the completed application form he'd downloaded from the Web site, plus a check to cover the fee, he walked to the post office in the Kings Road and mailed it.

THE NEXT FEW DAYS were remarkably quiet. After the string of unsettling events of the past several weeks and now, to cap it all, the news of Everard's death, Kingston looked upon this time as a blessing of sorts. For the first time since he undertaken his search for Stewart, he was finding the opportunity to devote himself enthusiastically to the vicissitudes of daily life as a bachelor. There were numerous things that had been neglected while he had been tooling around the Hampshire countryside and traipsing to East London on what now had all the earmarks of a futile exercise.

Mrs. Tripp, the lady who came in once a week to house-clean, do his laundry, and iron, was on holiday in Spain, so a few hours of each day were taken up with housekeeping. The laundry, changing the bed, and ironing could wait, but Kingston could not abide a house that was unclean and disorderly. The days went by unnoticed and soon he found himself back in his old routine, reading, renting movies, lunching at the Antelope, and cooking proper meals in the evening.

Thursday had come and gone with no word from Martin Davis about the video. Lord knew what had happened to Desmond. Kingston had called him several times, leaving messages, but with no response. That surprised him. Knowing Desmond, Kingston thought he would be itching to know what the police were doing at Kingston's flat the day they'd last spoken.

Tomorrow, he was taking a much-anticipated visit to see Becky. When he had called her to confirm, there was a noticeable change in her voice and mood. For the first time since Stewart's disappearance, she sounded almost upbeat. He even detected a hint of optimism as they talked—so much so that he wondered if anything had triggered the change. She assured him nothing had and that she was simply following Sarah's and his earlier advice: to think positively and not waste time dwelling on what might or might not have happened. The answers she was seeking would not come any sooner with her continually fretting. It would only result in making her more despondent, at the risk of impairing her health. As if to underscore her newfound attitude, she said that she was planning to cook dinner for him. "Nothing fancy, mind you," she said, "but it'll save us going out again. The restaurants are so expensive these days."

"Nothing could please me more," Kingston said, ending the conversation.

After he had put the phone down, he contemplated whether the time had come to tell Becky about his investigation. Should he do so, it would mean, among other things, having to tell her that Stewart was involved with some extremely dangerous people. That was out of the question. Frightening her and dashing what little hope was left would almost certainly send her into another tailspin.

On the more cheerful side, he had got a call from Andrew, who was back from his New Zealand trip and couldn't wait to tell Kingston all about it over dinner at a "brilliant" new restaurant he'd just discovered in Westbourne Grove. Kingston made a mental note to call him later. At this moment, he couldn't deal with such mundane matters as new restaurants. He could only think of one thing: Where the hell was Stewart?

The morning's post contained a surprise: a reply from the Land Registry. He opened the manila envelope and withdrew the contents. He read the cover letter followed by the report. The land on which the reservoir was located was owned by Conway-Anderson Ltd., 384 Neville Street, London, E14. The date purchased was November 1992 and the price paid for the fifteen-acre parcel: £1,250,000. There were no restrictive covenants or easements of any kind, and no mortgage lender.

As he looked at the accompanying Title Plan and Ordnance Survey detail, a smile spread slowly over his face. In addition to the reservoir and the outbuildings, it showed the existence of a house. This was more than he'd hoped for.

With the letter in his hand, Kingston walked over to the window and gazed out at the square below. He watched absently as a meter maid made her way up the street checking the parked cars for permits. His mind wasn't on her, though. It was on two things: first, the postal code of Conway-Anderson's address, E14. He was willing to bet that was the same code as Bakers Landing. Was that just a coincidence? The second disclosure was the existence of a house. Presumably, but not necessarily, it was also owned by Conway-Anderson. He didn't quite know what to make of that. After the episode at the reservoir, he'd speculated that Stewart might have been living in the building at the reservoir. Now he was starting to wonder if it wasn't a much more likely scenario that Stewart would have been held captive at the house and not the makeshift living quarters where Kingston had been bashed on the head. As he thought about it, that building more likely served as a home away from home for others involved in the project.

The house was certainly well hidden. He couldn't recall

having seen a driveway or even a path to suggest the existence of a house. It must be accessible from farther down the main road.

Still watching from the window, the meter maid had got into an argy-bargy with an arm-waving motorist who had arrived at his parked BMW the very second she had slipped a ticket under the windscreen wiper. Kingston smiled, knowing who would have the last word. He turned away from the window, crossed the room, put the letter on the coffee table, and picked up the phone. Desmond's line was busy. At least it indicated that he was back in circulation, thought Kingston.

SEVENTEEN

KINGSTON'S PRELIMINARY SEARCH of Conway-Anderson revealed little. He was surprised to find that the company had no Web site. Not only that, but he found only two mentions of the company after scrolling through a dozen pages containing more than a hundred references. Neither provided a clear understanding of what the company did or specified exactly what kind of services Conway-Anderson performed. In one case the company's role was articulated vaguely as "Developing management, project organization, and people skills to increase productivity and profits." Another description positioned them in the role of problem solvers, equipping companies with the tools to resolve manufacturing, productivity, management, and labor issues. No mention of history, clients, personnel, or contact numbers. To Kingston it was all business-speak. Conway-Anderson appeared to be a management firm that sought anonymity—most unusual. Six more pages and still no further mentions.

Kingston sat back and rocked in his chair. Earlier, he'd thought about visiting Conway-Anderson's offices but he'd dismissed the idea—for the time being, anyway. His last corporate-office visit and its grisly outcome—the word "fallout" was inappropriate, he decided—was still very much on his mind.

What next? Give "Conway" a try? He typed in the single name in the search bar and tapped RETURN. He scrolled through a dozen pages of miscellaneous

"Conway" sites and references without success. He was about to give up when he decided that thirteen might bring him luck. And it did. The result read:

Robert Conway 1914–1990. (Conway-Anderson Ltd.)
Reigate, Surrey

Robert Conway, surviving founder of Conway-Anderson Ltd., a London-based management and consulting company, died last month at his home in Surrey. Conway and his partner, Nathaniel Anderson, who died in 1987, started the company in 1942. During the war years, Anderson, who was partially disabled, ran the company while Conway enlisted in the Middlesex Regiment and fought in North Africa, and later in the European campaign. As a lieutenant, Conway was awarded several medals, including a Military Cross. Conway later served two terms as a Reigate town counsilor and was active in several community organizations, including the Arts Council and the Rotary Club. Prior to Conway's death, negotiations had been under way to sell Conway-Anderson. The prospective buyer is Viktor Zander, a Russian-born businessman with interests in Britain and Asia.

Reigate Times© August 2, 2001

Kingston read the article twice. The question was: Did the sale go through? Did Viktor Zander now own Conway-Anderson? Without thinking, Kingston typed Zander's name in the search bar. For ten minutes he scoured the results, reading page after page, line by line. Nothing. For a man who had bought a management company—if indeed he had—Zander had certainly kept a low profile.

Why? Kingston wondered. It was certainly an unorthodox way to run a business. Close to accepting defeat, he continued through four more pages. Then, finally, Zander's name came up, not in a headline but buried in the middle of a five-page article titled "American banks linked to Russian 'Mafia' money laundering."

The story reported that two American banks were under investigation for their involvement in a massive money-laundering scheme operated by Russian organized crime. Involving as much as $8 billion, the case was being handled by the FBI and the U.S. Attorney's Office in collaboration with British, Swiss, and Russian authorities. Later in the story, it was stated that British inquiries had focused on a Russian businessman named Vasily Banovich. Banovich had reportedly been involved in racketeering, extortion, and selling weaponry looted from the Russian army. For several years, Banovich spent his time moving between Britain and Bulgaria, eventually returning to Russia, where he disappeared, evading prosecution. The story went on to reveal that as much as $2 billion was thought to have passed through Sentinel World Marketing, an import-export company headquartered in a three-room office in London's East End. From there, the trail led to a network of other shell companies implicated in the sting.

The story went on to describe how the U.S. investigations started with suspicions and tips about a manufacturing company, ALM Partco in Scranton, Pennsylvania. ALM had registered the company in the Channel Islands in 1989. The subsequent circuitous search that followed led investigators on an international treasure hunt involving companies, financial institutions, law firms, and private individuals in six European and Asian countries.

On the fourth page, Zander's name came up in a list of people under investigation at the time. He and several other persons had been questioned by U.S., British, and Russian authorities but, for reasons that were not quoted, had never been indicted. It was also stated that one of Zander's companies based in England did business worldwide, specifically in Russia and former Soviet Republic countries. No wonder Zander and Conway-Anderson stayed under the radar, Kingston thought as he waited for the pages to print.

He turned off the printer, got up, and stretched, pleased with his research, awed once again at the avalanche of information accessible through the Internet at the click of a mouse. Carmichael was certainly going to be impressed with this development. The equation was simple: Conway-Anderson owned the house and reservoir; Zander owned Conway-Anderson; Stewart had been working at the reservoir and was possibly being held captive at the house. Ergo: Zander was the individual they should be looking for, and in all probability, he was the man directly or indirectly responsible for Stewart's kidnapping.

UNDER GRAY SKIES, Kingston drove out of London headed for Fordingbridge. Merging onto the M4, gradually working his way over to the fast lane, he was trying to recall the number of times during the past several weeks that he had made the same journey to Hampshire: Becky, Alison Greer, Inspector Carmichael, the reservoir. Thinking back on them, the cavalcade of incidents, conversations, highs, and mostly lows were becoming blurred. But now, for the first time since that fateful day Stewart went missing, he had what appeared to be the makings of a huge break. Finding out about Zander was one thing, but knowing that he once had ties to organized crime made him even more suspect.

For a change, he'd made good time from London. Motorway construction workers must be on holiday or strike, he mused. Crossing the top corner of the New Forest, he was approaching Fordingbridge. Five minutes and he would be there. This time, when he arrived at The Willows, he would be the bearer of positive news for a change.

Except for the empty chair at the head of the table—a solemn reminder of Stewart's absence—Becky's dinner reminded Kingston of the old days at The Willows. Despite her assurance that it wouldn't be fancy, he couldn't help smiling when she entered the dining room carrying their main course: plates of roasted local guinea fowl with port and orange sauce.

Earlier that afternoon, in the garden, he had told her about Zander and the house without mentioning Zander's mob connections. The news had brought the expected reaction: an initial rush of elation that gradually turned to anxiety as she weighed the implications. For five minutes, with eloquent logic buffed with the occasional white lie, he tried to convince Becky that the news could only be seen as positive. He knew, though, by her sentient look and reticence, that despite all his efforts, she was also weighing the downside. She'd known him too long.

Kingston stayed overnight again, rising early to work in the garden, deadheading, pruning, and tidying up. At lunchtime he brought in a bouquet of roses, arranging them in a vase and placing it on the kitchen table as a surprise for Becky, who had gone to the post office. Later that afternoon, after a hearty lunch of Cornish pasties and raspberries with clotted cream, Kingston left The Willows to return to London.

By EIGHT-THIRTY the next morning, Kingston had showered, dressed, and finished his breakfast of cereal and yogurt while leafing through *The Times*. He'd also called Becky, thanking her again for the "simple" meal and lodging. A solid seven hours of sleep had been made more restful by the decision he'd made the previous night after a third glass of Côtes du Rhone: not only to tell Inspector Carmichael about Viktor Zander, but also to divulge everything he had learned about Stewart's activities in the weeks and months prior to his disappearance.

The night before, he had jotted down a summary of the events of his search and inquiries. He would have it on hand when he called Carmichael. It surprised him just how much explaining he would have to do.

That raised yet another concern: with so much to divulge, Carmichael could rightly accuse Kingston of withholding critical information in the police investigation, not only into Stewart's disappearance, but also of a homicide and, with Everard's death, of a suspected homicide, too. Coming up with an acceptable explanation of why he hadn't long ago told the police about his involvement presented a real problem. He couldn't think why he hadn't done so a lot earlier. It had been damned foolish of him. He was supposed to be helping the police, not withholding information. There was no rational answer; he would simply have to take his lumps if and when Carmichael chose to press the issue.

The more Kingston thought about it, there was simply too much to discuss over the phone. Once the inspector heard what Kingston had to say, there would be no question that he would want Kingston to make an appearance at the station. Kingston wasn't keen on the idea of driving down to the New Forest again, and even less enthusiastic about the confrontation that could leave him with a bloodied nose. But now he needed Carmichael in his corner because a plan had been swimming round in his head whereby he might be able to persuade the inspector to enlist Kingston's help, physically. Be on the case officially.

He picked up the phone and punched in the direct number that Carmichael had given him. While the phone was ringing, he was reminded that their last conversation had been weeks ago. It wouldn't surprise him if Carmichael had forgotten about him. His apprehension was groundless. Carmichael was on the line immediately.

"Doctor, an unexpected surprise. Nice to hear from you again."

Kingston didn't wait to be asked why he was calling. He was wondering how long Carmichael's affable demeanor would last once he learned what Kingston had been up to.

"I'll come right to the point, Inspector. Since we last talked, I've been carrying on—well, I suppose you'd call it an investigation of sorts, trying to find Stewart Halliday."

"Yes, I remember you were close friends. How's his wife doing? Rebecca. I haven't spoken with her for some time. I wish I had encouraging news to report, something that would give her some hope. We've published appeals in just about every newspaper and TV news program in the country and gotten not one damned lead."

"Holding up remarkably well. She's been staying with her daughter on and off but she's back home now. As a matter of fact, I just got back from visiting with her. She's in a much more positive frame of mind." Kingston was about to get to the point of his call when Carmichael interrupted.

"Investigation of sorts, eh? That reminds me, you never got back to me after your visit to Walsh's garden. Did you go there?"

Kingston was surprised that Carmichael remembered the call, his being so overloaded at the time. "I did, and it proved worthwhile." Kingston paused, waiting for Carmichael's response while he searched for the right words to launch into his "confession."

"So, why exactly are you calling, Doctor?"

"I have a lot to tell you, not only concerning Stewart's disappearance but also about Adrian Walsh's murder and the death of a City businessman named Miles Everard and—" He paused, debating whether he should tell Carmichael about Zander now or wait until he had a better sense of the inspector's mood. He opted to hold off, for the moment, anyway.

After a long pause, Carmichael responded. "You *have* been busy," he said.

"I've every reason to believe the three are connected—but there's more. Too much to discuss on the phone."

Kingston's words had hit their mark and Carmichael's attitude suddenly changed. "When can you come down here?" he asked bluntly.

"Tomorrow, if it suits you."

"It does suit me. The sooner the better, I might add."

In the pause that followed, Kingston was wondering if this was where he was about to get a royal wigging. The sober-voiced inspector continued as though he'd had occasion to use the words many times before.

"If what you've been saying has relevance, you must be aware that withholding information in a police homicide investigation is serious business. I suggest you arrive tomorrow fully prepared and ready to come clean."

"That is my intention," Kingston replied, knowing that the less he said from now on, the better. "What time?"

"Let me check," said Carmichael. Kingston waited. "How about eleven o'clock?"

"All right. Where do I find you?"

"Large white building with red chimneys, Christchurch Road. Hard to miss."

"I'll see you tomorrow, Inspector."

Kingston put the phone down and sighed. It had gone as well as expected. At least Carmichael hadn't read him the riot act.

KINGSTON GOT UP to make a pot of coffee. Sitting in the kitchen while waiting for it to percolate, he leafed through the current issue of *Country Life*. The subscription had been a Christmas gift from Andrew. Turning a page, his eyes went immediately to a picture of a thatched, flint-and-brick cottage. It looked exactly like Pennyroyal Cottage, where he'd met the so-called Alison Greer. He read the caption, disappointed to discover that it wasn't Pennyroyal. Now that he thought about it, Pennyroyal's front door had been a lighter blue with a dolphin knocker, and the door of the cottage in the picture had no knocker.

He sat drinking his coffee staring into space, thinking of Marian Taylor. What a fool he'd been. Suckered into believing her. Infatuated by her fastidious looks and seemingly ingenuous nature. And all the time she had been lying through her teeth. She was a clever one all right, using the cottage that couldn't be traced back to her, staging it with photographs of herself. He was about to take a sip of his coffee but left the cup suspended inches from his lips. Those photographs? He tried to think back to when he had first entered the room. How many were there? He recalled two on the mahogany table, the larger taken when she was in her teens. An older woman was with her in that photo. The one next to it was a smiling close-up. He remembered thinking at the time that it resembled a film-star fan photo. She looked uncharacteristically glamorous. A third photo had been on the mantelpiece. How did that one portray her? Just as he was congratulating himself on his excellent memory, he drew a blank. "Come on... think," he muttered.

He stared out of the window, across to leafy Cadogan Square, neatly skirted with black railings, its familiar shrubs, and mature trees. Watching the usual parade of pedestrians, schoolchildren, and pram-pushing nannies, a yellow-jacketed mounted policeman on a gray horse came trotting into view. Kingston's eyes followed him as he rode, straight-backed, out of sight.

"That's it!" he said, slapping his knee. In the third picture, she was with a horse. It was an almost-full-figure pose: a smiling Alison, wearing a riding jacket, holding the bridle of a chestnut horse. Her hair, tied in a ponytail, was brown, much lighter than when they had met. Was there anything in the background? Damned if he could remember. He tried harder to visualize the photo. Now it was coming back to him. Her traditional riding jacket was black, with high buttons and nipped in at the waist. Yes. And he remembered the jodhpurs being tan. He smiled. She hadn't struck him at the time as being the horsy type.

He sipped his coffee, oblivious to its tepidity. Maybe, just maybe, he'd found a way to track down the elusive Marian Taylor and thrash it out with her. It was the riding jacket. It suggested only one thing: Marian Taylor was serious about matters equestrian. Chances were that she belonged to a riding stables or a hunt club—more likely the former.

In his office at the iMac, he did a search for "Hampshire riding stables." Expecting a dozen or so, he was surprised to find that there were forty-plus in the county. He printed the list. Next, he took a four-miles-to-the-inch *AA Road Atlas* off a nearby bookshelf and turned to the Hampshire page. His logic: Marian Taylor had worked in Farnborough and used Walsh's cottage in Hartley Wintney, little more than ten miles away. This suggested that most likely she lived—or had lived—within an arbitrary twenty-mile radius of Farnborough.

After a five-minute search, Kingston located a compass and with a pencil inscribed a five-inch-radius circle around Farnborough. Putting the map aside, he started down the list of riding clubs, checking off those that fell inside or close to the penciled line. Within a couple of minutes he had narrowed the list to eight. He intended to call each stable and equestrian center, asking if they knew of Marian Taylor. Fifteen minutes and five calls later, he came up empty-handed. By this time, he had established a pat introduction and line of questioning.

Next on the list was Rookshill Farm Stables. He dialed the number and waited. As he anticipated, the phone rang for some time. This he'd found was the norm, and understandable, considering that stables' workers are outdoors ninety percent of the time. Waiting for an answer, he read Rookshill's Web site printout: SMALL RIDING SCHOOL AND LIVERY YARD SET IN THE HEART OF THE COUNTRYSIDE NEAR THE VILLAGE OF ABBOT'S CROSS, HAMPSHIRE.

"Rookshill, Peggy speaking." She sounded like a teenager.

"Yes, good morning. My name's Kingston, Doctor Kingston. I'd like to speak with the stables' owner or manager."

"That would be Jill Merryweather." A horse whinnied in the background. "You're in luck. She's just leaving but I think I can catch her. Hold on a jiffy."

Kingston waited, wondering if he was really clutching at straws, calling the stables. He smiled at the unintended play on words.

"Jill Merryweather here. How may I help you?"

Even though she'd uttered only a few words, she sounded as if she were from central casting. Her clipped "county" accent and stereotypical verbal mannerisms were spot on. Kingston went into his routine. "I'm helping the police find a woman named Marian Taylor. She's also been known to use the name Alison Greer. We know that she is a keen horsewoman and may have belonged to a stables or equestrian center. Any chance she might have had an affiliation with Rookshill?"

"Marian Taylor, yes. She was with us for quite a while. I remember her quite well."

Kingston tried to hold back his jubilation. "How long ago was it?"

"Perhaps a year, thereabouts."

"And you haven't seen her since that time?"

"I haven't, no. What's this about, Doctor? Has she done something wrong?"

"No, not at all. It's just that she may have knowledge of a person who's gone missing. A friend of mine, actually."

"I see. I'm afraid I'm not going to be of much help, then."

"Do you happen to know if she lived near Abbot's Cross?"

"I don't. Even if I did, I can't divulge personal information about our clients. I'm sure you understand, Doctor."

"Yes, I do," Kingston mumbled.

"There is the possibility, of course, that I could provide her with your phone number—if I can contact her, that is."

"I'd appreciate that," he said, giving her his number.

"If I'm unable to reach Marian, I'll let you know."

Disappointed that his bright idea hadn't resulted in establishing Marian Taylor's whereabouts, Kingston put the phone down. He glanced at the clock on the kitchen wall. It was still early. For the remainder of the day, he would try to shut Marian Taylor, Zander, and Inspector Carmichael out of his mind.

THE MEETING, WHICH STARTED the following morning at eleven sharp, was held in Detective Inspector Carmichael's office at Ringwood Police Station, an older two-story building that could easily be mistaken for a pub by a passing motorist. A young policeman, introduced as Constable

Marsh, was also in attendance. His job, as evidenced by the tape recorder in front of him, was to take notes and record the conversation.

Kingston was well prepared. The night before, he had spent the best part of an hour going over his first summary, adding notes, listing all his conversations, meetings, and the incidents of the past several weeks, each appended with as-best-he-could-remember dates.

With Kingston and the inspector seated on opposite sides of the desk, each with a mug of coffee, and the constable to one side with the tape recorder turned on, the meeting commenced. Kingston took a sip of the hot, milky coffee, placed his notes in an orderly stack on the desk, leaned back, and started to relate how he became involved with Stewart's disappearance, beginning with the phone call from Rebecca Halliday's daughter. During a brief break, when Carmichael left the room to answer a personal phone call, Kingston glanced at his watch, surprised to see the time. He'd been talking, almost nonstop, for close to forty minutes. Five minutes after the inspector returned, the meeting was adjourned and the constable dismissed, leaving Kingston facing a stern-looking Carmichael.

The inspector folded his arms, swiveling his chair to and fro. "Dammit, Kingston. Why on earth did you keep all this to yourself? I don't know if you're aware of it, but should I decide to press the issue, you could face legal proceedings for jeopardizing a police investigation. Withholding information the likes of which you just reported is a chargeable offence." He stopped abruptly and so did his chair as he looked straight at Kingston. "Not only that, but by the sounds of it, you have placed yourself in considerable danger. You were damned lucky. You could easily have suffered serious bodily harm or even been killed," he said, cracking his knuckles, which made Kingston wince.

"You got my message about the incident at the reservoir, then?"

"I did, yes. Lymington station followed up on that. They found nothing out of the ordinary, apparently."

"That doesn't surprise me."

Carmichael scowled. "What *were* you thinking of, man? Getting mixed up in all this?"

Kingston straightened up in the wooden chair, trying to put on a good face before choosing to answer. He knew that he had no defense whatsoever and could only throw himself on the mercy of the policeman with the best apology he could summon.

"I have no excuse," he said, purposely leaving the four words hanging longer than necessary. "In doing what I thought best for Rebecca—trying to find her husband—I simply deluded myself into thinking I could solve the case alone. I now realize—and I have for a while now—that this was a terrible mistake. After I got whacked on the head and received the warning, I knew it was far too risky to go on." He made an effort to smile and added, "I recognized I wouldn't be much help to Becky propped up in a hospital bed or in the morgue."

Carmichael leaned back, a look of exasperation on his face, and sighed. "Look, I'm letting you off the hook this time. Despite the seriousness of your actions, I don't want to see someone as intelligent as you made an example of. From now on, if you want to help or you receive any information that may be germane to the case, you call *me*. Is that clearly understood, Doctor?"

Kingston nodded. "It is. And thank you for understanding—if you'll excuse the cliché—and for giving me the benefit of the doubt." As he spoke, he was wondering whether this was the right time to introduce the matter of Viktor Zander and the house. If he did, he ran the risk of getting Carmichael even angrier, after everything he'd said in the past minute or so.

As he was debating the point, there was a knock on the door. "Come in," Carmichael shouted. The door opened part way and Constable Marsh poked his head in, coffee pot in one hand. "Fresh coffee?" he inquired. Kingston and the inspector both nodded.

After taking a sip of the fresh coffee and almost burning his tongue, Kingston spoke. "There's one more thing you need to know before I leave," he said. "It just struck me that I hadn't mentioned it before." He smiled apologetically. "A senior moment."

"Oh," Carmichael said, swiveling his chair and giving Kingston a stony look. "And what is that?"

"There's also a house on the property where the reservoir is located. It's well hidden from the road."

Carmichael was still eyeing him as if he'd had enough for one day and just wanted Kingston out of his sight. *"And,"* he said.

"I've reason to believe that that's where Stewart Halliday is or was being held."

"You do, do you? What makes you think that? And why didn't you bring this up while we were taping?"

"As I said, I had every intention of doing so. I believe it's a huge break."

Carmichael still looked irritated but said nothing.

"It belongs to a man named Viktor Zander, a businessman and a dodgy one, to say the least. Owns a company in the East End named Conway-Anderson. I think it's a front."

"Go on."

"It's a known fact that he has or had ties to the Russian 'Mafia.'"

The inspector's eyebrows shot up. "Are you serious, Doctor?"

"Very."

"What are you proposing?"

"As I mentioned, he also owns the land on which the reservoir is located. So if Stewart Halliday was supervising the desalination experiments from there, Zander has to be involved, wouldn't you think? It's doubtful any of this could have taken place without his knowledge. It's a guess, but I think Zander knew Everard. I can't be certain, but the odds are good."

"But a half an hour ago you went to great lengths to explain that Everard was not involved in Halliday's or Walsh's affairs. Tell me, how did you find out that Zander owned the house and the reservoir buildings and has mob connections?"

"It was remarkably easy: Land Register Online and the Internet."

Carmichael shook his head. "I don't know what do with you, Kingston. You want me to march up to that house and ask if they're holding a missing person hostage? Is that what you're getting at?"

Kingston pulled on his earlobe—to those who knew him, a sign that he was thinking hard, choosing his words carefully before opening his mouth. Carmichael sat back, holding his coffee mug in both hands, waiting for Kingston to reply.

"What I'd like to propose is that when you go to search the house I be allowed to go with you."

By the look on the inspector's face, Kingston knew immediately that Carmichael didn't think it a brilliant idea. This was borne out when he spoke.

"Doctor, if we're to follow your suggestion and check out this house—which we certainly will, by the way—

we will have to do it without your presence, I'm afraid.
We can't run the risk of allowing civilians to accompany
the police on a warrant of this sort." He shook his head.
"We can't assume the liability. It's simply not allowed. It's
out of the question."

"I understand," Kingston replied. "However, let me explain my reason for asking."

Carmichael nodded with a half smile. "Go ahead," he
said, his expression and body language indicating that it
wouldn't make any difference anyway.

Kingston ignored the poorly disguised inference and
continued, "Well, you see, there may well be things in
the house that I would recognize and you might not. The
same goes for certain people who might be in residence,
too. So, your going in—the police, that is—would, in all
probability, be a wasted effort. A missed opportunity that
could have blown the case wide open, as the saying goes.
Make sense?"

Carmichael interrupted, the smile gone. "If you're talking about identifying Stewart Halliday, that's a non-issue.
We have recent photographs provided by the family." He
paused, cracking his knuckles again. "And what are these
'other things' that might be in the house that you would
spot and we wouldn't?"

This was where Kingston was walking on eggs. Carmichael was already aware of Stewart's cryptic messages.
Now introducing the idea that Stewart could have left more
messages in the house could give Carmichael the impression that Kingston had read *The Da Vinci Code* one time
too many.

"Signs," said Kingston. "A sign or clue of some kind
that would prove beyond doubt that Stewart had been there.
If there were, wouldn't that be more than sufficient reason

to undertake a full investigation and bring in the owner for questioning?"

Carmichael was shaking his head again. "You and I live in different worlds, Doctor. Nevertheless, if I were not to take some sort of action based on the information you've just provided, I wouldn't be doing my job." He took a last sip of coffee and put the mug on the table with a thump that also served as a punctuation mark. "Here's what I'm willing to do. I'll make up an affidavit showing probable cause and see if I can convince a magistrate to grant what's known as an s8 PACE warrant, one that will permit you to accompany us as reasonable and necessary, given the circumstances we've discussed. I'm not promising it'll happen but I'll do my best." He got up and came round to shake hands with Kingston. "If you ever decide to give up what it is you're doing, Kingston, maybe there's a place for you in law enforcement." He grinned. "Only one thing—don't look for employment in Hampshire, please."

Kingston chuckled and thanked him. He was beginning to like the inspector.

Two days later, Kingston got a phone call from Carmichael saying that he had the search warrant and asking Kingston to meet him and another policemen at ten o'clock the following morning at Ringwood station. They would drive together from there to Viktor Zander's house. Kingston would receive further instructions about the warrant and procedure at that time.

EIGHTEEN

AT THIRTY-FIVE MINUTES past ten, under sullen skies and light rain, an unmarked Rover 45 police car made a left turn a half mile past the small road that led to the reservoir and proceeded up the gravel lane leading to Foxwood House, the property of Viktor Zander. Detective Inspector Carmichael sat next to the driver, a burly, leather-jacketed DS named Winters. Kingston sat in the backseat, the legroom appreciated. At the outset of the journey, Carmichael had briefed Kingston on how the search warrant would be conducted, stressing that he, and only he, would ask questions and do the talking. Kingston would be introduced as a private citizen helping in their inquiries. He was, Carmichael emphasized, to remain a silent observer throughout.

The sergeant parked in the curved drive in front of the house, and the three got out to a loud slamming of doors. No need for a doorbell or knocker, Kingston mused. Facing them, Foxwood House loomed large and gray in the drizzle. Built of weathered brick with stone quoins, it was three stories, rectangular, and unpretentious. A row of seven symmetrically placed windows looked out from the first-floor rooms mirrored by seven on the second floor. Four dormer windows were set in the gray slate mansard roof. A wide, shallow flight of steps led to the shiny, painted black door, sheltered under a substantial portico supported by quadripartite square pillars. A dense canopy of wisteria spilled over the porch, the gnarly, twisting vines braiding the outermost pillars. Except for patches of lawn and box hedging, Kingston could see no signs of garden interest. On a sunny day, the house and its surroundings were no doubt pleasant but unremarkable. In the shroud of drizzle, the prospect came across as a trifle forbidding. Carmichael pressed the buzzer on the doorjamb and they waited.

Before long, the large, paneled door swung open part way. Facing them was a tall woman with high cheekbones and sharp features. She had graying hair tied up in a braided bun and a no-nonsense air about her. A plain black dress, white blouse, and mouse-gray cardigan gave her a semblance of severity. Kingston's first thought was that she matched the weather. Her darting eyes looked the three men up and down.

"May I help you?" she asked as if they were door-to-door salesmen.

Carmichael offered his card. "I'm Detective Inspector Carmichael, Hampshire Constabulary. This is Sergeant Winters," he said, nodding, "and Doctor Lawrence Kingston, who is assisting us in our inquiry." He reached in his inside pocket and pulled out the folded warrant. "We have a warrant to search this house and would like to speak with everybody present at this time. Particularly Mr. Viktor Zander, who, I'm given to understand, is the owner of the property." He paused. "By the way, that includes all staff: cooks, maids, gardeners—everyone."

The woman showed not the slightest sign of surprise. She took Carmichael's card without even looking at it and opened the door wide with a curt "You'd better come in, then." As they passed her, she closed the door and said, "I'm Mrs. Murdoch, by the way—the housekeeper. Please follow me."

She led them into a spacious, high-ceilinged room lined with book-filled shelves on three walls. In the center of the fourth wall, handsome floor-to-ceiling French doors looked out to a long garden. Kingston went to the doors to take a closer look. Unlike the front of the house, the plantings here were plentiful and had been chosen with skillfully planned harmony in the restrained use of color. The design—a series of terraces flanked by high hedges— was orderly and pleasing to the eye. It was certainly not the work of an amateur. Kingston could see quite a few roses, all in full bloom. Some of the old climbers and ramblers were trained over curved pergolas and treillage, others spread across rust-colored brick walls. Close to the house he recognized one of his favorite roses, Albertine, unmistakable with its coral buds and blowsy, old-fashioned dusky-pink blossoms curling at the edges. The sight cheered him. For a fleeting moment he forgot where he was and why he was there.

"If you'll be seated, gentlemen, I'll fetch Gavin. He'll be the one you'll want to talk to."

"What about Mr. Zander?" Carmichael inquired.

Hearing the conversation, Kingston walked over to join them.

"Oh, Mr. Zander. He's hardly ever here, sir. Only a half-dozen times a year at most."

"I see," said Carmichael. "Other than you and this other fellow you mentioned, are any other people present or staying in the house?"

"No. It's just the two of us at this time."

"I see. When you find this fellow, would you return with him, please?"

"Yes." She nodded then turned and left.

Winters plopped down on the sofa, and Carmichael settled into a leather wingback. Kingston wandered over to one of the bookcases and studied the volumes on the shelf. The books offered no definitive clues about the reading

tastes or interests of whoever had amassed the collection.
Mixed in with more contemporary works, there were many
old volumes: an eclectic mix of classic English literature,
poetry, historical tomes, and novels. Kingston's eye came
to rest on the spine of C. S. Lewis's *The Silver Chair.* He
pulled it out and studied the cover. It was in remarkably
good condition, He opened it and leafed to the title page,
astonished to see that it was a 1953 edition, illustrated by
Pauline Baynes, the most rare of British first editions of
The Chronicles of Narnia. He had read somewhere, recently, that a similar copy had sold at auction for several
thousand pounds. It made him wonder what other treasures
might be among the countless books in the room. If Zander
had amassed the collection, he was not only wealthy but
had impeccable literary taste. He slipped the book back
into place and was about to pull out another when a man
spoke. The accent was Estuary English. "Good morning,"
he said. Kingston turned to see a dark-haired man who
had entered the room. He was casually but immaculately
dressed in a black polo shirt and tan slacks, a thin gold
chain on one wrist. He glanced at the two policemen first,
with a polite smile, then fixed his hazel eyes on Kingston. Mrs. Murdoch was standing a few paces behind him
by the door.

"And who are you?" asked Carmichael, standing.

"Good Lord!" Kingston exclaimed before the man could
answer. He stared at the newcomer. "You're—"

"Yes, Doctor—Gavin Blake."

"You know him?" asked Carmichael.

"I know *who* he is," Kingston replied. "We met at the
Paramus Partners offices. He's one of Everard's vice presidents."

Blake nodded. "We did meet there, and yes, I am. Nice
to see you again, Doctor." His pleasant expression clouded.

"I take it you know about Miles?" he said, shaking his head. "Dreadful business."

"I do. The police told me. They wanted to know why I'd visited your offices."

"I know. They questioned all of us, too."

Carmichael glared at Kingston. "You're forgetting what we agreed on," he said caustically. "*I* do the talking."

Kingston nodded. "Sorry," he said.

Blake looked at the inspector. "Mrs. Murdoch tells me you're here to search the house?"

"That is correct, sir. We have a warrant to search these premises based on information we've received in connection with a missing-persons case. That would be the disappearance of a Mr. Stewart Halliday. Before we conduct our search, would you tell me if you have any knowledge of Mr. Halliday or his whereabouts or if you know of any other persons who might be in a position to provide such information?"

"The missing friend you came to see Everard about, I take it?" said Blake, glancing at Kingston.

Kingston nodded.

"Sorry," said Blake, answering Carmichael's question. "No, I don't know anyone by that name."

"How about you, Mrs. Murdoch? Ever heard of or seen Stewart Halliday?"

She shook her head emphatically. "No, I haven't."

Carmichael glanced at Sergeant Winters, who was perched on the arm of the sofa, notepad in hand but not writing, then looked back at Blake. "Viktor Zander. He owns this property, is that correct?"

"He does, yes."

"Are you in his employ?"

"No, I'm not. I'm just a guest."

"Would you mind telling me why you're here?"

"As I said, I'm a guest of Mr. Zander's. He uses the house infrequently and often invites people to stay for a few days. It's nice to get out of London once in a while." He glanced sideways at Mrs. Murdoch, who was rooted to the spot, her face expressionless. "Not to mention Mrs. Murdoch's cooking—well worth the drive down any day."

Mrs. Murdoch eked out a thin smile.

Carmichael continued, "And what does Mr. Zander do, might I ask? What line of business is he in?"

Blake was slow to answer. He was clearly tiring of Carmichael's abrasive attitude. Kingston, too, felt that the inspector's bluntness was not helping his cause.

"I can't see why it's relevant, but if it helps, he runs a management consulting business."

"Here in Hampshire?"

Now Kingston knew Carmichael was trying to rattle Blake. He knew damned well where Zander's offices were located.

"No, in London."

"Are you a client of his?"

Blake smiled. "No. As I said, I'm just a guest."

Carmichael sighed, seemingly satisfied with Blake's answers. "Very well," he said, looking at DS Winters. "Let's get this thing under way. Kingston, you go with Winters."

"I have to leave for London soon," Blake interjected. "I was packing when you arrived. If I can be of further help, let me know. I'm easy to reach."

"Right," said Carmichael. "The sergeant here will take down your address and contact numbers." He looked past Blake to the housekeeper. "Now, Mrs. Murdoch," he said more calmly, "perhaps you would be kind enough to show us through the house. We want to see everything: cupboards, closets, cabinets, drawers—all of it."

The search commenced shortly after eleven, starting in

the basement rooms. Well organized, painfully efficient, and with few words, Mrs. Murdoch pointed out the not-so-obvious places to look as the two policemen and Kingston went to work. An hour later, the search of the basement and half the ground-floor rooms was complete. Carmichael called a break, partly because Winters was desperate for a smoke, plus he thought a breath of fresh air would do them good, though it was still drizzling.

Kingston and Carmichael pulled up a couple of wicker chairs under the shelter of the stone-paved loggia that faced the garden and settled back, despite the chill. It was colder now and the skies were even darker than when they'd arrived. The dismal weather looked as though it had set in for the rest of the day. They sat in silence for a moment, each with their own thoughts, Carmichael picking at his nails.

Kingston was disillusioned; things weren't going at all as he'd expected. Being the "glass half full" type, he reminded himself that a few more rooms still remained to be searched and that if Stewart had been staying there, he would have occupied one of the bedrooms. It was the most likely place where Stewart would have left a clue: a room frequented only by him and probably Mrs. Murdoch or a maid, if there was one.

"Nice-looking euphorbia."

Kingston's thoughts were interrupted by Carmichael's off-the-wall comment. "*Griffithii* 'Fireglow,' isn't it?" he added.

Kingston looked at the clump of brick-red plants to their left. "You're right," he said.

Carmichael looked pleased and said no more.

"I never figured you for a gardener," said Kingston.

"Neither did my wife, ten years ago. She used to say I had the brownest thumb in Verwood."

Kingston looked at him and smiled.

"Now she complains that every waking moment I get, I'm off in the garden. You can never satisfy them, you know," he said with a grin. "Wives or plants."

"Come spring and summer, I'm sure she appreciates it, though."

Carmichael nodded. "Yes, she does, bless her heart. She's nuts about hydrangeas—and roses, of course."

The conversation turned back to their search.

"What do you think?" asked Carmichael. "So far."

"I must admit that it's not too encouraging."

Carmichael sniffed, got up, and walked to the stone balustrade that enclosed the terrace, staring into the distance where giant chestnut and copper beech trees demarcated the garden from the farmland beyond. "Bit of a coincidence, wouldn't you think?" he said, his back to Kingston.

"What's that?"

"That fellow Blake. Working for Everard and knowing Zander, on a first-name basis by the sound of it."

"That's what I told you. I'm convinced that Everard and Zander knew each other."

"Right."

Kingston thought for a moment. "If they did, how does that help us, though? We should ask Blake before he takes off."

"What did you think of him?"

"Blake?"

"Yes."

Kingston shrugged. "Nice enough chap, I suppose. Didn't seem like he had anything to hide."

"Probably not." Carmichael sniffed again and walked over to join Kingston. "I guess we'd better go back and wrap things up before it gets dark." He buttoned up his herringbone sport coat, faking a shiver. "Getting bloody nippy our here," he said.

About then, Winters showed up after his cigarette fix and the three went back into the house to resume the search.

Another twenty-five minutes passed and still not a single piece of evidence to suggest that Stewart Halliday had ever set foot in the house. All that remained to inspect now, according to Mrs. Murdoch, were two more bedrooms on the second floor and three smaller ones in the dormer. Kingston was now finding it hard to conceal his disappointment. He was conscious of being less thorough than he had been at the start of the search. Whether Carmichael sensed it or not, it was to his credit that he hadn't made one mention or barbed comment about Kingston's having brought them on a wild-goose chase.

Ten minutes later, Kingston and Sergeant Winters were going through the last of the three small dormer bedrooms. Carmichael had given up and gone downstairs to see if he could cadge a pot of tea for them from Mrs. Murdoch.

"Well, sir," said Winters deferentially, "looks like we were mistaken after all."

Kingston had already reached that rather obvious conclusion. Nevertheless he appreciated the sergeant's use of "we." Perhaps Carmichael, who had also chosen not to point a finger, had put a word in his ear. It would have been so easy for the two policemen to pin the wasted journey on him. After all, it *was* his idea in the first place.

Kingston and the sergeant descended the stairs and entered the living room where they'd first convened. Carmichael had already made himself at home, ensconced on the sofa, a cup of tea in his hand and a plate of biscuits on the coffee table in front of him. "Come sit down," he said. "Mrs. Murdoch just brought the tea in. It's still hot." Kingston and the sergeant did as suggested, choosing the two upholstered chairs facing Carmichael. There were no signs of Gavin Blake.

It seemed that none of them wanted to talk about the abortive search. What conversation there was concerned only two topics: the best route for Kingston to take back to London—given traffic works on the M4—and Viktor Zander's excellent taste in furniture and antiques. Kingston had already told Carmichael about the books and how he figured there was a small fortune in first editions on the bookshelves.

Mrs. Murdoch returned with hot water for the teapot. While she was engaged in a brief conversation with Carmichael, Kingston looked around the room one more time, knowing with some certainty that this was the last time he would visit Viktor Zander's house.

His eyes passed over two handsome nineteenth-century landscape paintings on the wall to the left of the fireplace. John Clayton Adams's work, he guessed. Scanning to his right, he studied the gilt-framed Victorian oil portrait of a young woman, which filled the space over the fireplace mantel. It was exquisite, her sad eyes never leaving the viewer. His gaze dropped down to the ebonized bracket clock that held center stage on the mantel. He'd studied it earlier, admiring the elegant scroll-engraved back plate with the signature "John Ellicot, London," dating it as mid-eighteenth century, and worth plenty. Alongside the clock on one side was a pair of Staffordshire pottery figures of dogs. Quite rare, Kingston knew. On the other side of the clock...

"It can't be," he muttered to himself.

Kingston got up abruptly and strode to the fireplace. Carmichael, cup poised in midair, watched with mild curiosity. The sergeant was busy deciding which biscuit to eat next.

Reaching the mantel, Kingston picked up a small porcelain figure of a drummer boy. The charming little soldier was wearing a maroon jacket and lace cravat. It looked familiar. He turned it over and saw the stamped serial number and blue crossed swords, the maker's mark of Meissen, Europe's oldest porcelain manufactory. Could it possibly be the one he had given Stewart and Becky all those years ago? No doubt many had been made. He stood holding and admiring it for a moment, thinking that if it was indeed the same one and Stewart had planted it on the mantel, why would he have brought the figurine with him to the conference? Nothing made sense. It had to be another copy.

NINETEEN

THE PORCELAIN DRUMMER BOY stood alone on the coffee table.

Exquisitely painted and no more than five inches high, it had suddenly become the centerpiece of a criminal investigation.

Kingston put the phone down, watched by Carmichael and the sergeant. "Nobody home, I'm afraid," he said, shaking his head. "She might be at the hospital."

"The hospital?"

"Women's auxiliary."

"Good for her," said Carmichael. "She's a strong woman, that one."

A few minutes earlier, Kingston had told the inspector the significance of the figurine and how he'd given it—or one that was identical—as an anniversary gift to Becky and Stewart. If Becky could be certain that it was no longer in its customary place in the living room, where Kingston had last seen it—or elsewhere in the house—it would suggest that it could have been in Stewart's possession when he was abducted. That would mean that he had kept it all this time, waiting until he could find the right place to display it, with the slimmest hope that someone- -most likely Kingston—would spot it.

"Too much of a damned long shot, if you ask me," said Carmichael. "My money says it's a duplicate. The Jerries probably knocked out hundreds of these things—even back in those days. What year did you say it was made?"

"Late 1800s would be my guess," Kingston replied.

Carmichael shrugged. "We could easily find out, I suppose."

Kingston nodded. "Yes. Meissen would have records, I'm sure. All I can tell you is that it's the real thing, all right—authentic, first quality, that is. If it were a reject there would be an incised mark across the swords. If the defects were bad, more incised crosses. Meissen insisted on perfection."

Carmichael sniffed. "How come you know all this stuff?"

"Love of old china and selective memory, I guess."

Carmichael raised his eyebrows and did not deign reply.

All this time, Sergeant Winters had been silent, quietly examining the porcelain figure. He looked up. "There's a bit of problem, though, isn't there, boss?"

"And what's that?" asked Carmichael, a trifle too condescendingly for Kingston's liking.

"Stewart Halliday wasn't abducted from the house, was he?"

"Oh, come on, Winters, we know that," Carmichael said with a dismissive wave of his hand.

The sergeant wasn't going to be put off that easily. "What I'm trying to say is, if he *had* been, I could see him grabbing the drummer boy, knowing that it might be associated with him, his wife, and the doctor here. But he hadn't been kidnapped from the house, so why on earth would he have had the figurine in his possession that day? It's not like he *knew* he was going to be kidnapped."

Carmichael nodded begrudgingly, knowing that Winters was right.

Kingston had already figured the same and remained silent, thinking of other possibilities.

"Well," said Carmichael, "we'll know the answer when

we get word from Becky Halliday, won't we? No point in our staying here any longer. Wrap the damned thing up, Sergeant," he said, nodding at the drummer boy. "And try not to drop it."

A few minutes later, Carmichael thanked Mrs. Murdoch for her cooperation and bade her farewell at the front door. When the inspector inquired after Gavin Blake, she said that he had left for London soon after he had provided Sergeant Winters with his contact information.

Fifty minutes later, the three arrived at Ringwood Police Station. After a brief chat in the parking lot, they parted, with Kingston promising to call the minute he heard from Becky.

With the wipers on full speed and the inside of the windscreen fogging up, he headed up the A31 on his way home and to a steaming-hot bath. It would be a couple more miles before the TR4's heater could demist the windscreen. In the meantime, he had to make do with a dustcloth, which was always in the glove compartment.

KINGSTON CALLED BECKY the minute he got back to his flat. He was on tenterhooks waiting to find out about the drummer boy. Getting no reply, he tried her daughter Sarah's number. He got her answerphone, leaving a message saying it was urgent that Becky call him as soon as possible.

On the drive home, he'd decided it was time to tell Becky about his investigation and that he was now working hand in hand with the police on Stewart's case. He knew that informing her would give her plenty of reasons for consternation but he saw no further point in keeping her in the dark. He was going to have to ask her about the figurine anyway, which would undoubtedly open a floodgate of questions.

He poured a stiff Macallan and flipped through the

mail: as usual, mostly bills and junk mail. He took off his sweater and went to the bathroom to run his bath. As the water was running, he heard the phone ringing. He turned the taps off, hurried back to the living room, and grabbed the phone. He breathed a sigh of relief and took another sip of whisky. Good, he thought to himself, Sarah must have reached Becky. "Hello, Becky?"

"This is Marian Taylor."

For an unbalanced moment, the name didn't register. His grip on the phone tightened.

"About time," he said, surprised that he was still moved by the sound of her voice.

"You called Rookshill about me."

"Yes, you know I did. The Merryweather woman told me you used to go riding there."

"You remembered my photo?"

"Yes."

"Smart of you, Lawrence. A mistake on my part."

"Why are you doing all this?"

"I can't tell you. I'm calling to tell you to stop searching for me. It'll do you no good."

"It looks like I've found you."

Her voice took on a sudden urgency. "You haven't. And I'm asking you—begging you—to stop what you're doing."

Kingston told himself to remain calm. Getting her riled up wouldn't help. She could easily hang up on him. "You have a lot of explaining to do," he said evenly. "You've been lying to me since the day you first called."

"I know that's what it looks like but you must believe me, I had no choice. I only wish I *could* tell you the truth."

"The truth?" Kingston wanted to raise his voice but held his resentment in check. "I suppose the charade at your cottage—which we both know wasn't your cottage at all—wasn't a lie? Is that what you're telling me? And

Alison Greer—what's that all about? Another lie, isn't it, Marian?"

Kingston waited for her answer, too long in coming. "I think you owe me an apology and an explanation," he said calmly.

"You're right," she said finally. "And you've every reason to be angry. But now you must forget me. Forget I ever existed. If you don't, it could prove to be disastrous for both of us."

"This is all about Stewart Halliday, isn't it?"

"Lawrence," she said, followed by a lengthy silence.

Kingston detected a trace of tenderness in the way she had spoken his name—a subtle slip that she was probably regretting. He sensed she really wanted to confide in him, disclose her true feelings, what it was that she was holding back so desperately.

"You *must* believe me," she said, taking a breath. Her voice was now subdued and controlled, as though she were about to say something that she didn't want anyone else to hear. "I'm taking a big risk phoning you as it is—I'm calling from a phone box, by the way." She paused again. "I don't want to sound melodramatic, but if these people find out I'm talking to you, you may not hear from me again."

"Who are 'these people'? If your life is in danger—which I assume is what you're suggesting—why don't you call the police?"

"I can't do that and I can't tell you why."

"All very convenient. Just like the lie about Everard."

He heard her inhale quickly. He must have struck a nerve.

"It was the truth. Unfortunately for him, he became involved, too."

"That's not what he told me."

"You spoke with him?"

"I did. And he flatly denied knowing anything about Stewart or Walsh—or *you*."

She waited a few seconds. "He would have said that."

"You just said 'unfortunately for him.' You know he's dead, then?"

"Yes, I do," she replied in an almost whisper.

"Good God."

"I'm going to hang up, Lawrence. How I wish you'd never become involved. That things could have been different."

"Very well, I'll do as you say, Marian. But you must call the police."

"I told you, that's out of the question," she exclaimed. Then her voice softened, quavering slightly. "Whatever you do, don't try to find me—please."

Kingston heard the phone go dead.

EARLY THE NEXT MORNING, while he was shaving, Kingston received the much-awaited call from Becky.

"Thanks for returning my call, Becky. Are you at home or still with Sarah?" he asked. He dearly wanted to inquire about the Meissen figurine right away but told himself to be patient and let her establish the ebb and flow of the conversation until the right moment presented itself.

"I'm at Sarah's but I really do have to get back home soon. Sarah and Jim, her husband, have been simply wonderful. I don't know what I would have done without them. But I can't lump myself on them forever. I'm sure they're getting a bit fed up with me by now." She paused. "They never say anything, of course. But I really do have to get back down to Hampshire and pick up the pieces."

"When do you think that might be?"

"Next week, I think."

"I'll come down again, if you want. It looks as if I'm

going to have some time on my hands for a change. I could give you a hand with the garden. I would imagine it needs some more attention by now."

"I'm sure it docs—but how about you? Sarah told me you said it was urgent. Is everything all right, Lawrence?"

He noted that she hadn't mentioned Stewart. Was that intentional? "I've been quite busy," he replied, knowing that he would quickly run out of small talk. Now was as good a time as any to tell Becky about his investigation, but not before he asked about the figurine. "You remember that little Meissen drummer-boy figurine I gave you for your anniversary a few years ago?" In the silence that followed, he could almost hear her thinking.

"What an odd question. Why, yes. What about it?"

"Do you still have it?"

"Of course we do. We love it. Why on earth do you ask?"

"Well, one just like it has shown up in a house near New Milton."

"Surely they made more than one of them, wouldn't you think?"

"Yes, there's little doubt about that. But it seemed such a coincidence. Tell me, Becky, I want you to think hard. Is it possible—even remotely—that Stewart could have had it with him the day he went missing?"

She paused again then said, "No, that's not possible."

"You're sure?"

"Of course."

"You still have it, then?"

"Not right now, no. It's at an antiques shop being repaired." After a moment's hesitation, as if she were tiring of his questions, she blurted, "For heaven's sake, Lawrence, what's this all about?"

"Repaired, you said?"

"Yes. Unfortunately it was broken. The little chap's hand got knocked off when I was dusting—"

"Did you take it in or did Stewart?"

"You haven't answered my question, Lawrence."

"Bear with me. I will. Did *you* take it to be repaired?"

"I did."

"Did they say how long it would take?"

"No. The man just said they were frightfully busy and it would be some time before he could get to it. He'd call when it was ready."

"And he hasn't, I take it?"

"Not yet, no."

As he was about to ask his next question, she interrupted, "Do you mind telling me what all this is about, Lawrence? Can you get to the point?"

"I'm sorry. I apologize. It could be very crucial."

"I'm confused, Lawrence. Why is it so important?"

"If I can be sure that Stewart had the drummer boy in his possession when he went missing, it would prove—or certainly suggest—that he was at the house I mentioned. It all depends whether your figurine is the one that was at the house."

"Oh, my God!" she said, her voice trembling.

"Listen, Becky," Kingston interjected in the most avuncular tone he could muster. "This might or might not lead us to Stewart. It's an important break but there's still a lot we don't know. I can't explain it all to you right now. It would take far too long. Why don't you call me when you get back to The Willows next week? We'll set aside a couple of days when I can come down and tell you the whole story—that's a promise. By then I hope to know a lot more."

"Lawrence, you can't expect me to wait that long. I

need to know now. Are you saying that Stewart could be all right...that he could still be...alive?"

"That's our hope, Becky." He was trying to sound as compassionate as he could. "I can't promise more than that, I'm afraid."

"I understand, Lawrence," she said in a halting voice that implied that she really didn't and was saying it just for him.

During the wait that followed, Kingston could visualize her trying to grasp the slender lifeline he had just thrown, struggling to make sense of what he had just told her. He heard the slightest sniffle and when she spoke her voice had brightened, as if she were making the effort for his sake.

"Who would have thought that a little statue would be so important?" she said softly.

"Let's just hope we're right, Becky. Where is this antiques shop? What's its name?"

"It's a funny little place on one of those little backstreets in Salisbury, near the cathedral gate—someone's Antiques Repairs. The man's surname, as I recall. I've still got the receipt. When I get home I'll phone you."

"If you would. In the meantime, I'll call a couple of antiques dealers in Salisbury. They'll know all the restorers in the area. The police will want to talk with whoever repaired it."

Less than five minutes after their conversation ended, Kingston had tracked down the Antiques Repairs shop in Salisbury and was speaking with the owner, a pleasant-sounding chap named Alistair. "Charming little piece. Remember it well," he had commented when Kingston inquired about the drummer boy. In less than a minute, Alistair had checked his record book and confirmed that restoration of Mrs. Halliday's Meissen figurine was completed on Tuesday, June 6 and had been picked up on Friday, June 9.

"Do you recall who picked it up?" asked Kingston.

"I do, yes. It was Mr. Halliday. Nice man. We talked about hellebores, as I recall."

"Was it Stewart Halliday you spoke to on the phone when you called to say the figurine was ready to be picked up?"

Kingston waited while Alistair was thinking. "Yes, that's right, I remember, it was Mr. Halliday."

Two minutes after they'd hung up, Kingston was talking to Carmichael. Trying hard not to sound too pleased with himself, he told the inspector what he'd learned from Becky and Alistair. If Carmichael was encouraged by the news, his tone of voice didn't show it. Kingston accepted his matter-of-fact attitude, assuming that it was standard procedure for the police officers not to get too optimistic about such matters, particularly when dealing with the public.

Carmichael thanked Kingston for calling, offering a modest apology for his earlier doubt, saying that an investigation was already under way into Viktor Zander's possible involvement in the disappearance of Stewart Halliday. This, he said, would most certainly involve the Metropolitan Police.

They said their good-byes and Kingston put down the phone. At last things were looking up, he said to himself as he went into the kitchen to make a fresh pot of tea.

TWENTY

THE CHELSEA PHYSIC GARDEN is a four-acre horticultural and botanical jewel, set on the Chelsea Embankment of the Thames, a fifteen-minute walk from Kingston's flat on Cadogan Square. It was founded in 1673 by the Society of Apothecaries to promote the study of botany in relation to medicine, at the time known as the "physic" or healing arts.

Whenever Kingston felt hemmed in by London's gray walls and jostling throngs, he knew that in Chelsea Physic's sensual embrace he would always find solace and time for purging inconsequential thoughts from his mind; a respite to focus on the problem at hand. In short, it had become "his" garden.

He had taken his customary stroll through the garden, his keen eye observing, admiring, and noting changes from his last visit three months ago. He was in no hurry—one never should be in a garden—and had reached the place on the pathway where it had become his custom to take a break. He sat on the wooden bench, crossed his legs, and gazed up at the imposing statue of Sir Hans Sloane. More than three hundred years ago, Sloane, a noted physician, scientist, and collector, had leased the garden and its land for the generous sum of £5 per year in perpetuity.

What would Sloane and all the other botanical trailblazers that followed say if they were told that a water lily had been discovered that could extract salt from the water in which it grew? On further thought, he decided that, compared to some of the wonders that they had encountered and discovered in remote parts of the world in the past several centuries, the water lily might not raise eyebrows that high.

He looked at his watch: almost four. He got up and headed along the path toward the exit. Walking with a lighter step and a smile in his heart, he passed the perfumery border, inhaling the bewitching fragrances, the murmuring and droning of the insects loud in the air. He recalled Thomas Hill's words, written more than four hundred years ago: "The garden is a ground plot for the mind." How true, he thought. Once again, Chelsea Physic had worked its magic.

TURNING THE KEY in his front door, Kingston could hear the faint ringing of the phone. Closing the door behind him, he hurried across the living room and picked it up. "Hello," he said, expecting it to be Andrew, whom he was meeting that evening.

"Mr. Kingston? Lawrence Kingston?"

"It is," Kingston replied, not recognizing the man's voice.

"This is Chelsea Police Station, Sergeant Jarvis."

Why on earth would the local police be calling? "Yes," he said uneasily.

"We just received a report from one of our patrol cars that a garage on Waverley Mews had been broken into. A neighbor discovered it and told us you park your car there, a Triumph TR4. Is that correct, sir?"

"It is, yes."

"We'd like you come down to the garage, if you would. We have a unit waiting there."

"What about my car? Has it been stolen?"

"It looks that way, I'm afraid, sir."

"I'm on my way," said Kingston, putting down the phone.

KINGSTON MANAGED the normal ten-minute walk to his garage in almost half the time. He'd already prepared himself for the worst, but when he turned the corner into the mews, perspiring and out of breath, seeing the gaping double doors and the empty garage, he had a hard time stifling his anger.

So much for the jimmy-proof deadbolt, he thought, examining the damaged lock. At least the alarm system had functioned—otherwise the police wouldn't have been called. Or had it? It suddenly struck him—where was the police patrol car?

Kingston looked around the dark, deserted mews. The only sound came from an unseen open window: the distant harmonies of Simon and Garfunkel's "Scarborough Fair." Four streetlights cast angular shadows on the narrow street as he stood, despondent, at a loss to know what to do next. Calling the police station would have been the obvious, but in his hurry to leave, he'd left his mobile on the coffee table. Clearly nothing could be achieved by waiting. Not much choice but to go back home, he decided.

As he turned to leave, the high beams of a passing car bounced off the rear reflectors of a car parked farther down the mews and lit up the NO PARKING sign next to him. The sudden illumination lasted barely a second or so but long enough for Kingston to see that it was his car. Either that or it was an extraordinary coincidence that another dark-colored Triumph would be parked illegally in Waverley Mews. With quickening steps, he took off down the mews, almost to its end, where the TR4 was parked flush against a brick building. "What in hell?" he muttered, looking the car over, fully expecting parts to be missing or other vandalism. It was untouched. He reached for the driver's-side door and opened it, glancing around the interior. It, too, was as he'd left it when he had parked it two days earlier. Instinctively, he looked up and down the mews, not knowing what he expected to see. A tabby cat skittered across the cobbles, up and over a wall in one graceful movement, the only sign of life.

He was already formulating a plan. He would get the TR out of there immediately, into a secure, monitored garage where it would be safe until such time as he could replace the garage lock with something more impregnable. He reached in his pocket, took out his car keys, slipped behind the wheel, inserted the key in the ignition, and turned it. To his relief, the engine started.

In first gear, handbrake off, about to let the clutch out, Kingston glanced up into the rearview mirror. "Damn," he muttered. A piece of newspaper was stuck to the rear window, obstructing his vision. He yanked the handbrake on, put the gearshift lever back into neutral, got out, walked to the back of the car, and started to remove the paper. It didn't look or feel right—almost as if it had been glued on. Out of the corner of his eye, he saw a sudden movement, a shadowy figure in the darkness. He turned—too late. The man had slipped behind the wheel, jammed the car in gear, and, with tires screeching like banshees, fishtailed out of the mews. Kingston stood there holding the scrap of newspaper, smelling burnt rubber. He took a deep breath, stamped hard on the cobbles, and yelled "Sonofabitch!"

Suddenly the mews was lit up like a stage set. Kingston turned to see the dazzling headlights of a car entering the mews from the opposite direction the carjacker had taken. He put a hand up to shield his eyes. If it was the police, it might not be too late to chase his car. The vehicle slowed to a stop in front of him. Stepping from the center of the mews, out of the glare of the headlights, Kingston could see now that it wasn't a patrol car. It looked like a Range Rover or one of the big Jeeps. The passenger-side window slid down and he looked in, meeting the driver's eyes.

"What was that all about?" the driver asked, leaning forward, one hand on the passenger seat. Though the man was in partial shade, Kingston could see he was clean-shaven, wearing a brown leather jacket and black turtleneck. "Left a lot of rubber, by the sound of it," he said.

"I've just been carjacked," said Kingston.

"Jesus. Hop in," the driver said, nodding, releasing the door lock. "Maybe it's not too late. Let's give it a go?"

"Thanks," said Kingston, as he got in, closed the door, and cinched his seat belt.

"What kind of car?"

"TR4, green, tan top."

The vehicle's big engine growled as they left the mews and slipped out onto the adjoining street in the direction the carjacker had taken. A few seconds later, Kingston glanced at the speedometer and was surprised to see that they were already doing fifty. The small green logo in the center of the steering wheel confirmed that it was a Range Rover. A newish one at that.

"I'll call 999," the man said, pulling a mobile from his inside jacket pocket. "We'll take Brompton to Cromwell Road, in the hope he'll be heading west. It's the nearest main road out of town," he added.

Buoyed by the man's confidence, Kingston was beginning to feel that there might be a sliver of hope after all, but he realized that in the minute or so since the carjacking, the TR4 could have put a lot of distance between them. It would depend on traffic lights and the long shot that they would be following the same route, toward the M4.

His eyes fixed mostly on the traffic ahead, glancing occasionally down side streets, Kingston caught snatches of the man's conversation with the emergency dispatcher. He was amazed at the driver's skill in handling the big car with one hand on the wheel, navigating the maze of streets to Brompton Road, dodging nimbly in and out of traffic, timing the lights. He'd always abhorred the use of mobiles while driving but this time he had to admit it had its advantages. The man was a damned good driver. They were now passing the Victoria and Albert Museum, heading west on Cromwell Road in heavy traffic.

Eyes peeled for any signs of his car, it took him a few seconds before he realized that they had turned right, off Cromwell Road onto Exhibition Road, running north toward Hyde Park. Why hadn't they continued on the main road, heading west out of London? he wondered. He saw why the minute the car slowed. Up ahead on the grass, inside the park, the TR4 was parked with no lights on.

Curious at this amazing stroke of luck or what could have been keen eyesight on the driver's part, Kingston unbuckled his seat belt and glanced at the driver. The driver turned to Kingston. "Wait a moment," he said. No sooner had the words left his mouth, Kingston watched dumbstruck as the TR4's door opened and a man got out. He slammed the door shut, walked the half-dozen paces to the Range Rover, opened the rear door, and climbed in. It had all happened in a matter of seconds.

As he reached for the door handle, Kingston heard the "thunk" of the automatic door lock. "Don't bother," the driver said.

"We're going for a little ride, Doctor," said an East End voice from the backseat.

THE DRIVER DID A U-TURN and headed back to Cromwell Road, made a right, and continued west heading out of

London. Kingston's first thought hadn't been for his own well-being but for the safety of his car. Leaving it unattended for long anywhere in London was asking for trouble—the park might prove to be one of the worst places. Vandals and thieves would get to it in short order. He decided that he didn't even want to think what might happen to it before the police or park officials discovered it had been abandoned. That could take days. His priority was here and now.

He realized now that the call from Chelsea Police Station was phony, just a device to get him to the mews. Zander's men—and it was a sure bet that was who they were—had been clever. Everything had obviously been well planned and executed. Nevertheless, it struck him as a hellishly complicated exercise just to get him into a car. The more he thought about it, the alternatives—grabbing him off the street or abducting him from the flat—invited failure or possible injury to any one of them. Despite his age, anyone confronting him would agree that, at six foot three and without an ounce of fat on him, he gave the impression of being physically powerful, a man who would not go down easily in a struggle.

Kingston sat in the passenger seat, watching the road. Not a word had been uttered since they'd left the park. He knew there was no point in asking questions. They were hardly going to tell him where they were taking him or what they were planning to do with him once they got there. Saying nothing was much more intimidating. Looking out the window, he saw they were now on the Great West Road, on the stretch just before it hooked up with the M4 motorway. He knew the factory-lined thoroughfare well, having traveled it often since moving to London, and more recently on his excursions to see the elusive woman who was indirectly responsible for the mess he was in right now. It also happened to be the quickest route to Heathrow airport. Surely they weren't going there?

His thoughts were interrupted by a low voice from behind. He didn't need to glance back to know that the man behind him was talking on a mobile.

"We have the passenger." A short pause followed. "Yes." Another pause. "Almost on the M4." Pause. "Right." The conversation ended. Now Kingston knew others were involved, no doubt awaiting his arrival.

Fifteen minutes later, they had passed the airport exits and were in the center lane, traveling a shade under the seventy-mile-per-hour speed limit. No way would the driver risk being pulled over by the police. Kingston had read in the paper last year that speed cameras were planned for stretches of the motorway in Wiltshire. If they were to go that far, and if the driver exceeded the speed limit, the Range Rover's license plate might be recorded. But that was miles away, and at this stage of the game, what would it amount to anyway? A speeding violation would hardly be associated in the minds of the police with an abduction. From the roadside exit signs, he knew they'd now left the M4 and were on the M3 motorway in Berkshire heading in the direction of Southampton.

After another half hour's driving, they left the motorway onto an "A" road heading south. Ten minutes later they were on a smaller road, crossing hilly countryside. Now it was much darker, and despite the occasional road sign, it was nigh on impossible for him to fathom their direction, let alone location. Before long, he gave up trying. Lulled by the Rover's smooth ride, he leaned back on the leather headrest and closed his eyes. What would the coming hours bring? he wondered. He preferred not to think about it. He'd already concluded—back in Hyde Park, when he had seen his cherished TR4 disappear from sight, perhaps forever—that whatever it was, would not be, pleasant. He thought back to Walsh and Everard—and what had happened to them—and broke into a cold sweat.

HE WAS JARRED INTO the present by the thud of the car's doors closing. His door opened and a voice in the darkness said, "Get out."

He did so, immediately feeling the stiffness in his knees, another reminder that of late he hadn't been exercising as much as he should. He zipped up his suede jacket, wishing that he'd put on a sweater before he left the house. It was damned cold and as black as soot.

The driver, no more than a dark silhouette, stood several paces from Kingston. "Follow me," he said, flicking on a foot-long black flashlight, aiming it at the ground and starting to walk.

Kingston followed, aware that the hefty flashlight could easily serve as a truncheon, if need be. Out of the corner of his eye, he saw that the other man—shorter but more muscular than his partner—had moved behind him as they started off.

With the bobbing pool of light ahead, he could see that they were on a cement path edged with mown grass. Where the light dissolved into blackness, he could make out tall, dark shapes on either side, but he couldn't distinguish whether they were hedges or small buildings. The silence was as brooding as the dark. He strained for sounds that might come in handy later as markers: trains, traffic noise, running water, farm sounds. But all was still.

Soon they stopped in front of a large building, a warehouse of sorts. Facing them was a solid door that had "security" written all over it. To the left, he could make out an industrial-sized roll-up steel door. Opening the smaller door, the driver stood aside to let Kingston and the other man enter, then followed them in. The door slammed shut and locked behind them, the sound echoing around the dark interior. In seconds, a single light came on, its source not visible. The meager light was barely sufficient for Kingston to see that it was a warehouse. They continued in file across an open space, flanked by floor-to-ceiling metal racks stacked high with containers, wooden crates, and other indistinguishable materials.

Reaching the other side of the cavernous room, they passed through another door and down a low-ceilinged corridor with closed doors on both sides. The lights in this area were also dimmed, leading Kingston to believe that it was prearranged—probably alerted by the mobile call from the car—to make it harder for him to get a good look at the two men. They stopped at what appeared to be the last door in the corridor. The driver, careful to avoid Kingston's gaze, took out a key and opened the door. He stepped aside, motioning with the flashlight for Kingston to enter. Kingston was a few paces into the room when he heard the door slam behind him and the key turn in the lock.

TWENTY-ONE

KINGSTON RUBBED HIS EYES and looked around the small room. It had obviously once been an office, now converted into living space. A single made-up bed was snug against the wall in one corner. A leather sofa and coffee table, piled with magazines, took up most of the space on the opposite wall. The only other items in the room were three black filing cabinets, an empty bookshelf, a steel desk, and a bottled-water cooler. Kingston was comforted to see another door, hoping it was a bathroom. He crossed the room and opened the door. It was as expected: a loo, a small sink, and a wall rack with two fresh towels. Two minutes later, relieved and refreshed, he was back in the room.

He hadn't noticed it when he had first looked around, but next to the bed, alongside a brass table lamp—the only light in the room—was a plate with a cling-film-wrapped bagel, a napkin, and a Mars bar. Next to it stood a bottle of water and, of all things, a small bottle of white wine, a glass, and a corkscrew. He went to the table and picked up the bottle: a Bordeaux Entre-Deux-Mers. How odd, he thought. Paradoxical.

He uncorked the wine, put it on the coffee table with the glass, and slumped onto the couch. Filling the glass part way, he took a healthy sip. A morbid thought crossed his mind. Was this akin to the prisoner's last meal? He dismissed the idea immediately, savoring the young, fruity wine. It wasn't chilled but went down well anyway.

Why bring him to a warehouse? he wondered, looking

up at the waffled ceiling panels. On the drive, he'd tried to construct a plausible explanation by connecting tonight's events to everything that had happened in the preceding weeks. Kingston was sure now that Viktor Zander was the man behind it all. Zander, Stewart, Walsh, Everard, Marian Taylor, alias Alison Greer—they were all intertwined in the conspiracy like a girdling of old wisteria vines. The more he tried to unravel the tangle, the more snarled it got and the more frustrated he became.

He went over it again, as he had on the bench at Chelsea Physic. Stewart enlisted Walsh's help, who in turn, according to Marian Taylor, brought in Everard as a partner. Gavin Blake worked for Everard and was also, as he claimed, a friend of Viktor Zander's. But how were Everard and Zander connected, or were they? Marian Taylor, an inveterate liar and imposter, had insisted that Everard was at Walsh's house, yet Everard—if that was who Kingston had talked to on the phone—swore that neither he nor Walsh nor Alison Greer knew anything about the desalination project. Yet Alison Greer's visit to Everard's office at Bakers Landing contradicted that. Was it just coincidence that both she and Kingston were there on the same day? And was it Everard she was meeting or someone else? If it turned out that Everard *was* murdered, what was the motive? And who had done it? Far too many questions.

It seemed so long ago now that Kingston had almost forgotten about the helicopter incident—not that he ever would. Given everything that had transpired since, speculation on how it happened wasn't hard to figure. The helicopter had merely been in the wrong place at the wrong time. It was just bad timing. If he hadn't made the snap decision to go back and videotape the village, it would never have happened. Seeing it circling at low altitude and then spotting the video camera suspended under the nose like a red flag, one of Zander's men had panicked and taken a pot shot at it from somewhere near the house. Kingston imagined the man getting all kinds of hell from Zander for doing something so senseless and dangerous that it could have shut down the whole operation right there and then. As if trying to down the helicopter hadn't been enough, Zander had to worry that revealing video footage might have been taken of the reservoir. If it had, and the videotape fell into the wrong hands—namely, the police—it could spell trouble. There was the chance that people on the ground might be identified, hence the phone call from "Patrick" and the video snatch in Hammersmith.

It was Marian Taylor who perplexed Kingston the most. He couldn't for the life of him figure out why she had stepped forward to help him in the first place, then gone purposely out of her way to deceive him in such a convoluted way. For reasons he couldn't explain, he couldn't see her mixed up in a kidnapping and a possible murder case. Then again, he'd never prided himself on being the greatest judge of character.

He took a long sip of wine and topped up the glass. Zander, or whoever had selected it, had good taste. It didn't come as much of a surprise, though, given the eclectic library and expensive furnishings at Foxwood House.

He kicked off his shoes and stretched out on the couch, arms folded. What about Stewart? Was he still alive? Kingston prayed he was. If so, how much did he know about what was going on? Was he aware of the kind of people he was dealing with? Kidnapping was one thing, but for the person kidnapped to be useful in one form or another—as with Stewart—all manner of round-the-clock care, support systems, constant surveillance, and security had to be enforced. Kingston couldn't help thinking of

Kate Sheppard, the young woman who had been kidnapped five years ago and held hostage for two weeks. She and her husband had discovered a rare and valuable blue rose in their garden and had asked Kingston to help them. In a series of bizarre incidents, the rose was stolen, her husband Alex became a murder suspect, and Kate was held ransom for the rose. In her case, her captors had taken good care of her and she had finally managed to escape, only to be recaptured by them. She had told Kingston, when he had last visited the Sheppards at their lovely home and garden in Wiltshire, that, to this day, she was still haunted by recurring nightmares of that experience. Thoughts back in the present, he reached over, picked up his wineglass, and drained the contents.

Escape had clearly been impossible for Stewart. One alternative that Kingston had mulled over earlier was that he might not want to escape. If so, why would he help Zander of his own volition? Had he been promised vast sums of money if the desalination process proved practical on a large scale and if he cooperated willingly? If that were the case, why would Stewart have gone to the trouble of leaving the clues? It didn't make sense. What else? Coercion seemed unlikely given the duration of his captivity. The only other explanation Kingston could think of, diabolical as it might be, was that Stewart could be sedated constantly, kept in a drugged state, yet still able to function for their purposes. On further thought, he dismissed that scenario as being far too "Hollywood."

Since being locked in, the only sound he had heard was the roll-up door being raised and lowered. He sat up and reached for the bagel, unwrapped it, and peeked at the filling: smoked salmon with cream cheese and capers. He devoured it along with half the water in less than a minute. He glanced at his watch: ten-thirty. Might as well try to get some kip, he thought to himself. He removed his jacket, switched off the light, pulled aside the sheet, and climbed into the small bed. Lying there, staring at the shadowy ceiling, he felt mummified between the snug blankets and head-to-toe fit of the bed.

He kept staring at the acoustic ceiling panels. Was this section of the warehouse the only part of the building with a false ceiling? From what he recalled, most of the warehouse was open-beamed. Was this a way of escape—crawling along ventilation ducts? He knew it was wishful thinking but he got up anyway and stood on the bed. He was tall enough to reach one of the panels easily and tried to push it up. At first, it didn't budge, but after a second try, it loosened and popped up. He slid it to one side and looked up into the empty space above. It was a typical T-bar frame installation, suspended from the existing roof, rigid and sturdy enough to support the tiles but by no means a man of his weight. Disappointed, he replaced the tile and crawled back into bed. It always looked so damned easy in the films, he thought.

He closed his eyes. Unable to sleep, his thoughts prowled back and forth like a caged animal searching for a way of escape. Until now he had been subconsciously avoiding it but he started to think about his own imprisonment and what the coming day might bring. Another fifteen minutes of tossing and turning produced not a glimmer of optimism. Eventually, he managed to steer his mind to more encouraging thoughts and finally dozed off.

The room was dark when Kingston woke. For a moment he couldn't recall where he was, then it all rushed back. He held his watch up close to his face and could just make out the luminescent hands: eight-fifteen. Surprisingly, he had slept quite well, and longer than he expected. He switched the light on, got out of bed, and went into the bathroom. With no razor or toothbrush, he did the best he could to make himself presentable for whatever was about to happen. He wasn't going to speculate on that, though. Right now his mind was on a pot of tea or at least a cup of coffee. Returning from the bathroom, he sat on the sofa and checked out the magazines on the coffee table, pleasantly surprised to find a recent issue of *Autosport*. Leafing through it, reading the Monaco Grand Prix results, he realized how out of touch he was with the sport. The only drivers' names he recognized were Michael Schumacher, Jacques Villeneuve, and Jenson Button. Back in the seventies and eighties, Kingston had followed the Grand Prix circuit, making annual trips to Europe. He and Megan had attended Monaco, the German, Spanish, and French races, and had been regulars at Silverstone for the British Grand Prix. He had owned more than a dozen sports cars and collector cars over the years, including a Jaguar, Bristol, Morgan, and his favorite, a 1934, 4.5 liter Lagonda Sports Tourer.

Kingston's mind flashed back to his prized TR4. Surely the police would have found it by now and would have tried to reach him. It might be too early for him to be considered a missing person but that would surely be the case in the coming hours. With luck, his car hadn't been vandalized and was now locked safely in a police garage. In turn, he thought about Carmichael, wondering whether the inspector had made any progress questioning Blake and Zander. Then he remembered that Carmichael had said the case would most certainly involve the Metropolitan Police. Perhaps Inspector Crosbie would be in charge. He was with the Met, and the connection with Kingston—the rainy-day interview—was already established, as he was the officer investigating Everard's death. Kingston put down the magazine, took a deep breath, and exhaled slowly. Why worry about all that now? he said to himself. He was in serious trouble and his prospects were dimming by the minute.

Another two hours dragged by, during which time Kingston had read all the magazines. He stretched out on the sofa, but his catnap was interrupted by the sound of a key being inserted into the door lock. He turned and reached for his shoes—one had found its way under the bed. He felt foolish standing in his socks, holding one shoe, about to confront one of his captors.

The door opened a few inches, enough for whoever opened it to place a cup of coffee and a napkin-wrapped pastry on the floor. As quickly as it had opened, the door closed. Kingston crossed the room and retrieved the coffee and pastry, returning to the sofa. Taking a bite of the pastry and washing it down with the hot coffee, he realized how ravenous he was. If this was breakfast, he hoped lunch would be more substantial.

The morning dragged on into afternoon. Kingston, with nothing left to read or amuse him, stretched out on the bed and soon dozed off again. He had no idea how long he had been napping when he was awakened by the sound of the key in the lock once again, and a surly voice. "Get dressed and come with me," the man said.

"I'll be right there," Kingston replied.

"Make it quick."

A few minutes later, Kingston was walking along the same corridor as the previous night, the man close behind. Reaching the door at the end, they passed into the warehouse. Kingston held a hand up to shield his eyes. After the dark room and corridor, the bright sunlight slanting through the skylights high above temporarily blinded him. It struck him as being incongruously cheerful, considering the gravity of things.

Moments later they left the warehouse and were headed

along a path toward another, smaller building about fifty yards away. Now in the open and considering a run for it, Kingston took a quick glance over his shoulder to size up his chances. As he did, the man spoke.

"If you're thinking of doing a runner, don't. You won't get more than ten feet and you'll have a hole in your back."

Kingston kept walking, his stomach churning as he sussed out the surroundings. The area was light industrial but the sight of cranes and ships' masts rising above the buildings to his left affirmed that it was also a shipyard. The snapping of nearby marine flags in the offshore breeze and the squeal of seagulls wheeling overhead left no doubt that they were near the sea. As they approached the low building where they were headed, he caught sight of the end of a quay and a row of iron bollards mooring an older boat. He recognized it as a navy tender, converted for private use. The bow of a motor yacht was visible behind it. Soon they reached the door of the whitewashed building over which the name JENSEN MARINE was affixed in gold painted, three-dimensional letters. The man opened the door and gestured for Kingston to enter.

As the door closed behind him, Kingston heard the lock click into place. He turned to see that the thug had left and he was on his own. The room was spacious, with a high ceiling crisscrossed with wooden trusses. Part living space and part workspace, it was surprisingly airy and light, decorated in shades of cream and beige, a confection that had the unmistakable stamp of an interior decorator. A bit twee for a marine business, he thought. Glancing around the room, his eyes came to rest on a large ship model in a mahogany-framed glass case. He walked over to the model and stood, admiring the exquisite craftsmanship. The sleek motor yacht was painted in dark blue and cream, every detail a miniature masterpiece. Kingston read the discreetly positioned plaque:

ALLEGRA

A converted "Baltic" tugboat built in Germany in 1990 and completely rebuilt and refitted in France in 2001. Welded steel hull and aluminum super-structure. Length O.A. 110.0 feet. Beam 27.5 feet. Draft 10.5 feet. Main engine: SKL 6-cylinder turbo-charged diesel engine. Range: 2,000 nautical miles. Various cabins (all with bathrooms and showers), accommodating up to 16 passengers. Fully equipped galley with dining area. Communication and navigation equipment, including Satcom C mobile earth stations satellite communications unit, a cellular system, VHF and SSB radiotelephones, radar, DGPS, magnetic and gyrocompasses, wind instruments, and echo depth sounder.

Kingston turned away from the model. For a blissful minute or so, his mind had been taken off the present and his fate in the coming hours. He was transported back to happier times. He had always been fascinated with boats, having learned to sail as a boy during summer holidays in Devon. In later years, he had bought a restored 1920s diesel-powered gaff-rigged cutter that he named *Old Gaffer*. Soon after, he joined the Cramond Boat Club, whose clubhouse and moorings were on the river Almond, only four miles from the center of Edinburgh. He, his wife, and daughter, Julie, had spent many memorable summers plying the waters of the Firth of Forth, picnicking on its numerous islands. It had been heartbreaking to have to let *Old Gaffer* go after his wife had died and he moved to London.

His reminiscing was broken by a man's voice. "So, you like boats, do you, Doctor?" The voice sounded familiar.

Kingston turned to see two men. He stared vacantly at the taller of the two for several seconds, numbed—as if he'd stubbed his toe on the furniture and was waiting for the throbbing to start.

He was looking at Gavin Blake.

It took no imagination to figure out that the other man was a bodyguard or minder. Alongside the tall Blake with his mannerly looks and stylish casual clothes, the man looked like a latter-day Bill Sykes. By his stocky build, Kingston pegged him as the man who had filched his TR4—the Range Rover driver's accomplice.

"You look surprised," said Blake. "Nice of you to join us." His expression showed mild contempt, as if he were saddled with an obnoxious guest at a cocktail party. "I trust the accommodations and snack met with your approval," he added.

Kingston decided to go along with the "nice guy" opening, knowing full well by the look on the bodyguard's face that it was merely a prelude to unpleasant news. "The Bordeaux was a nice touch, yes. Good taste," he replied. "Pity it wasn't chilled, though."

"Not my taste or my idea," Blake countered. "If it had been up to me, you wouldn't even be here now, Kingston. You'd have been taken care of long ago."

"You take your orders from Viktor Zander, then?"

Blake's eyes narrowed momentarily, then his expression became impenetrable.

Kingston knew he'd hit a nerve but could tell right away that Blake wasn't about to argue the toss. "You don't want to discuss your boss?" He paused, meeting Blake's icy stare. "How about Stewart Halliday, then?"

Still no answer, but Kingston noticed the muscles in Blake's jaw tighten.

"We know he was at the reservoir and at Zander's house. Where is he now?"

"*We?* Meaning you and the police?"

"You're damned right. And it's only a matter of time now before they catch up with you and Zander."

"Is that so?"

Recovered from his confusion at being suddenly confronted by Blake, Kingston was thinking how naïve he had been not having seen through Blake when he showed up at Foxwood House. He'd put on a bravura performance. Good enough to convince Carmichael, too, despite his earlier suspicions. "I must admit, Blake," he said, "you don't look like the sort to be mixed up with organized crime."

"I'm getting damned tired of you, Kingston," Blake snapped, his hazel eyes smoldering.

"Really? Perhaps you'd prefer to talk about Miles Everard—that poor sod."

"Just shut your bloody mouth and go over there and sit down." Blake turned to the bodyguard. "Go see if they're ready for us yet. Call me."

Kingston sat on the sofa and watched the bodyguard cross the room. He wondered who "they" were. At the door, the man reached for the doorknob. As he did, his jacket pulled aside, revealing the grip of a shoulder-holstered gun. The door closed behind him and a queasy tremor rumbled through Kingston's belly. Forcing it back, he looked at Blake, who was now perched on the edge of a table and studying his tank watch, seemingly content to wait. Judging by Blake's aplomb, Kingston figured he was armed, too. Clearly there would be no further conversation until the bodyguard called.

Several minutes passed before Blake's mobile rang. He

took it out, flipped it open, and held it to his ear, all the time avoiding Kingston's gaze. "Good," he said after a few seconds. "We'll meet you outside." He closed the mobile and returned it to his pocket. "All right, let's get this done with," he said with a long, chilling look at Kingston, then nodded toward the door. Kingston got up and, with Blake close behind, walked to the front door.

Outside, the sun was warm on their backs, the breeze tousling Kingston's already unruly hair as they headed toward the quay. A half minute later, they were joined by the bodyguard, who was waiting by the navy tender Kingston had seen earlier. Considering the number of boats moored alongside the quay, there were few, if any, people around. The innocuous-looking threesome passed an old racing sloop with a young couple, on their hands and knees, working on the deck, but they were too preoccupied with varnishing to notice them go by. When he'd first caught sight of the couple, Kingston considered making a scene, shouting for the couple to call the police. But knowing that the bodyguard was armed, he feared such action would put them all in harm's way.

Kingston saw the boat ahead. He recognized it from the model. This was the real thing and just as impressive. The name *Allegra* was on the stern. As they walked alongside the boat, Kingston made note of the telescopic boat cranes and davits with Zodiac life rafts and an inflatable tender with outboard engine—all the very latest and most impressive. At midpoint along the hull, the bodyguard motioned for Kingston to board across the gangway. Blake followed, leaving the bodyguard on the quay. On the deck, they were met by a shaven-headed crewmember in a spotless white T-shirt and jeans. Kingston caught snatches of the brief conversation, something to do with cabin locations. The man pointed toward the stern. "The captain should be here soon," he said as they made their way along the deck. Kingston noticed that the bodyguard had remained on the quay and was keeping pace with them, obviously making sure that Kingston didn't decide to jump off and make a run for it.

Blake paused at the second cabin they came to. No words were exchanged as the crewman opened the cabin door and Blake gestured for Kingston to enter. He stepped in, expecting to hear the door close behind him. It didn't. He turned to see Blake standing by the door, the sun backlighting him, his face a black shadow. "Well, Lawrence Kingston, your journey's almost at an end. Enjoy what's left of it." He closed the door with unnecessary force, and Kingston heard the lock slip into place with an ominous click.

TWENTY-TWO

KINGSTON SAT ON THE EDGE of the boxed double bed and surveyed the cabin, surprised by its spaciousness. The interior reflected everything else he'd observed about the yacht since boarding—first-class and no expense spared. The cabinetry wall facing him—rosewood, he figured— had an LCD television, DVD player, and AM/FM radio built into a center panel. On either side, two other panels recessed into the wood surround displayed gold-framed abstract paintings. Below, a row of custom-designed cabinets spanned the wall. Louvered shutters covered the long window next to the bed on his right. A built-in vanity with matching framed mirror filled most of the third wall. Through an open door, a mirror-walled corridor led to a bathroom. From where he sat, the counter appeared to be marble or granite, the fixtures, gold finish. Kingston was gaining new respect for Victor Zander—if indeed he owned the *Allegra*. Foxwood House, with its precious library and elegant trappings, had been impressive, but the yacht left no doubt that lack of cash flow was not keeping Zander awake at night. Kingston was starting to understand why he would be the sort to broker a deal for Stewart's desalination process. He visualized Zander as businesslike, polished, and erudite—the kind that could sell ice to Eskimos.

He stood, looked down at the Berber carpet, then glanced around the cabin again. The only escape was through the door or window. He went to the window to find that it was double-paned, apparently tempered glass—difficult or impossible to shatter—and that, not surprisingly, it would slide open only enough to provide ventilation. Though he knew the door was locked, he tried the handle anyway. As he had reckoned, there was no other way out of the cabin.

Trying to size up his predicament, attempting to second-guess what might come next, he was brought to his senses by the sudden hum of the big diesel engine starting. Even if he could get out of the cabin, there would be no escaping the *Allegra* at sea, save for the inflatable. "What a bloody mess," he mumbled to himself.

Kingston had often professed that some of his best ideas bubbled to the surface when he was horizontal. He had solved many a crossword clue or vexing problem in the moments before dozing off into the arms of Morpheus. Feeling powerless, while waiting for what he was coming to accept as his fate, he stretched out on the bed and closed his eyes, still wide awake, listening to the steady throb of the engine.

If escape was impossible, perhaps he could cause a disturbance, a diversion that would make someone open the door. Then what? He was unarmed. Smoke would get their attention but he quickly rejected that idea as ill advised. He could die of smoke inhalation before anyone noticed. Though he hadn't examined the cabin thoroughly, from what he'd seen so far, he hadn't found anything that might help his escape.

A mosquito or some kind of flying insect buzzed around his head. Swatting at it, he opened his eyes for a moment, looking up at the ceiling. Staring at the recessed lights and a smoke alarm, another idea started to form. The scheme was simple and could be carried out in seconds using things already in the cabin—guaranteed to cause a ruckus, if nothing else. First, he would set off one of the smoke alarms either by depressing the test button or, better yet, by using an inverted aerosol can that would emit HCF gas detectable by the alarm—if by luck the bathroom had spray toiletries or an air freshener. Then he would trip a breaker in one of the fuse boxes by shorting out one of the lights. This could be done easily by taking out a light bulb, putting a coin in the socket, and screwing the bulb back in. Whatever else was on that circuit—most likely other lighting—would also be shut off. In the hubbub that followed, they would quickly realize that the problem lay in his cabin. What then? If just one crewmember investigated, he might be able to overpower him. But a fire would likely bring the entire crew to his door. He sighed. So much for his 007 flight of fancy.

Frustrated by his impotence, Kingston got up, went to the window, and glanced out. The *Allegra* was in open water and he could see the quay receding in the distance, the sky blushed with the sun's last hurrah. They were headed southwest, it seemed. Where were they? he wondered. Yesterday, they'd driven west out of London onto the M3 toward Southampton, so surely he was looking at the south coast, meaning that the *Allegra* had to be in the English Channel. Until now, he hadn't given thought to where they might be headed. Did it matter anyway? Blake's last comment about Kingston's journey being almost at an end and to enjoy what was left of it left little doubt as to its meaning. Kingston could only hope that such a decision would be Zander's to make and not Blake's.

The fact that Blake was on board—if he still was— suggested that the boat had a specific destination requiring Blake's presence. Connecting the dots wasn't difficult. All along he had believed that a foreign country, in an arid region, would be the most likely first prospect for a biological breakthrough in water desalination. So, where were they headed? he wondered. Africa seemed an educated guess.

With the sun setting and clouds moving in, the sky was darkening. Through the window, Kingston could see the reflection of the starboard running lights blinking on the choppy water. He glanced at his watch. Two hours had passed since he'd stepped aboard, and he was starving. The measly pastry and coffee had been ages ago. He started to think again about the condemned prisoner and the proverbial last meal but banished that from his mind instantly. He stretched out on the bed again, wondering if anyone had discovered his absence yet. There was a remote chance that Andrew, his friend and neighbor, could have called or stopped by the flat uninvited, as he did occasionally. He had a key. Even if he had, there would be no reason for him to think anything was amiss. Kingston often took off for a couple of days at a time without telling him. In any case, it was barely twenty-four hours since Kingston had left his flat for the garage.

A knock on the cabin door woke him, followed by the sound of a key in the lock. The cabin was pitch-black; he must have dozed off. He rubbed his eyes and got off the bed. At last, he said to himself, food. Perhaps Zander would have been thoughtful enough to include another bottle of wine. Never mind the wine, he thought. Right now he'd give a mortgage payment for a double Macallan.

The door opened and the silhouette of large man appeared at the threshold. "Doctor Kingston?"

Kingston stood. "Who else?"

"Look, I don't have time for word games, Doctor. I have a medical emergency on my hands. I need your help— now. Let's go."

With little light coming through the door, Kingston

couldn't make out the man's features except that he was balding and had a trim beard and moustache. His voice was gruff, the almost imperceptible accent European.

"I'm Captain Becker," he said, stepping aside, motioning with his hand for Kingston to hurry. Outside, he closed the cabin door and took off along the deck. "Follow me." He glanced back to make sure Kingston was right behind him.

As they hurried along the deck, Kingston's mind was in fast forward. Obviously, the captain had assumed that Kingston was a medical doctor. Given the circumstances, he wasn't going to deny it. He'd go along with the pretense until it proved inexpedient or could risk harm or suffering to the patient—doubtless one of the crew. He just hoped it wasn't a grisly accident. Second, it suggested that Blake was not aboard. If he were, he certainly wouldn't have instructed the captain to ask for Kingston's help—unless Blake himself had the medical problem. Wouldn't that be an amusing irony? They stopped at another cabin door near the stern. The captain opened it and they went in.

In the dim light from a bedside table lamp, Kingston saw a man under the bedclothes. His face was ashen, his gray hair and bushy beard unkempt. As Kingston approached, the old man ignored him, staring vacantly at the ceiling.

"He's been like this for two days now," the captain said in a lowered voice. "Won't eat, doesn't talk. Nothing."

"And no accident, as far as you know? No unusual symptoms?" Kingston asked as he sat down on the edge of the bed, trying to sound like every doctor he'd ever known.

The captain shook his head. "No."

"Let's take a look, then." Kingston held the man's wrist, checking his pulse—uneven, rapid—then leaned forward and pulled one of the man's eyelids back, not knowing what he should be looking for. Next he opened the man's mouth and peered down his throat. "Hmm," he mumbled for effect.

"There's a thermometer on the table there," said the captain with a nod.

Kingston reached over and picked it up, relieved to see that it was digital, almost identical to the one he'd bought last year when he'd had the flu. He turned it on, checked to make sure it was operative, opened the man's mouth again, and slipped the sensor under his tongue.

"Fill me in," said Kingston, glancing up at the captain, who was standing beside him.

"Can't help you much, I'm afraid. One of the crew found him stretched out across the bed. Seems he was having a hard time moving. Been like this ever since."

Kingston nodded, staring at the man's pallid face framed in the grizzly beard, waiting for the thermometer to beep. Could it be…?

He kept staring.

"Good Lord," Kingston gasped.

He put a hand to his mouth, as if trying to stifle the words.

"What is it?"

"I'm not sure," Kingston replied. But the longer he gazed at the man's pitiful face, the more certain he was. He looked at the captain again. "Do you know who he is?"

"I don't. No. He came aboard the day before yesterday. The fellow who works for Mr. Zander was with him— Blake."

"Did he appear sick then?"

"A bit unsteady on his feet, that's all. I asked Blake if the old boy was all right. He said yes, he was fine, just needed a good rest. I was given the impression that he was important, and my instructions were to take good care of him, to give him anything he wanted, within reason."

"You didn't ask who he was or why he was on board?"

"Over the years, I've learned not to ask questions."

"You don't know why I'm aboard, then?"

"Other than you're to remain in detention and that I'm to hand you over to an agent in Sfax—no, I don't. It's better that way."

"This is Stewart Halliday."

"You *know* him?"

"I do. He's a friend of mine."

"A friend?"

"An old friend, yes."

The thermometer beeped. Kingston removed it and held it up to take a reading.

The captain was confused. His expression showed it. He was shaking his head. "It can't be a coincidence. No way."

"It's not, believe me." Kingston was thinking hard. Telling the captain that he and Stewart had both been kidnapped could only make matters worse. He had to keep up the masquerade and convince the captain beyond all doubt that Stewart's life rested in the captain's hands, to persuade him to return to shore and call the nearest hospital.

At any moment, the captain would expect Kingston's diagnosis, or at least a reasonable medical explanation for Stewart's condition. Stewart's temperature was high but not enough to cause concern. Kingston mind raced as he tapped the thermometer on his palm, buying a few seconds. Should he be vague in his diagnosis, or decisive and name a specific medical condition? He decided on the latter. That way, providing he could sound authoritative enough, there was a lesser chance that the captain would question his prognosis, giving him no reason to doubt that Kingston was a medical doctor. At this juncture, it was all or nothing. "We must get him to a hospital, Captain," he said soberly. "As quickly as possible."

"What's wrong with him?"

"A stroke, by the looks of it. Immediate treatment is crucial." He placed a hand on Stewart's cheek as if he knew what he was doing. "There're no signs of facial weakness," he said, leaning back. "I'd know more if we could get a speech pattern or find out if there's been any loss of movement in his limbs." He glanced up at the captain. "Didn't one of your men say he was having a hard time moving?"

"Correct."

Kingston expected the captain to make a move or at least say something, but he just stood, looking at Stewart, stroking his moustache as if deciding what to order from a dinner menu. "I think I'd better call Mr. Zander," he said finally.

"Dammit, man!" Kingston leaped to his feet. "This man could die. If he does, you'll be responsible. This is your boat. As captain, you have the final word. This is no time for a second opinion—certainly not from someone who's a hundred bloody miles away or more, on the other end of a phone. I'm not asking you anymore. I'm ordering you. Turn this boat around, Captain, or you'll be the next one locked up."

The captain pursed his lips and nodded. "You're right, Doctor. I didn't mean to question you. It's just that Mr. Zander—"

"Never mind, we can discuss that later. Right now we must get Stewart taken care of."

"You'd best come with me, then."

They left the cabin, headed toward the bow—probably to the bridge, Kingston assumed. Outside the cabin, Kingston exhaled a silent sigh of relief. It wasn't over yet, by any means, and Stewart was clearly sick. Whether he'd had a minor stroke or not was moot, but his not recognizing Kingston was troubling. A thought struck him: Could Stewart have been heavily sedated? Were that so, Kingston had little idea of what the symptoms might be, what to look for.

For the time being, he had to forget Stewart and focus on what could happen in the coming two hours or so, the time it would probably take the *Allegra* to reach a port somewhere on the south coast. There was no question that Captain Becker would try to reach Zander. Kingston couldn't stop him. He could only hope to delay the call somehow or that Zander couldn't be reached. He recalled reading that Zander's company did a lot of overseas work, so there was the long shot that he was out of the country. They reached the bridge, where Becker spoke briefly with the crewman in charge. The two went to a navigational workstation, where they studied a chart and the radar, presumably deciding in which port to dock and the quickest route. Kingston watched and waited as the *Allegra* commenced a wide turn and was soon on a reverse course headed north. Trying not to be too obvious about it, he attempted to sneak a peek at the chart and radar. The captain had a few more words with the crewman and rejoined Kingston.

Ten minutes later Kingston and Becker were sitting in directors' chairs at a small dining table on the rear deck. Kingston didn't know it, but Becker had told the crewman on the bridge to call the galley and ask for sandwiches, chips, a bowl of fresh fruit, and two cans of Pepsi. Over their meal, they talked about Stewart Halliday, the captain quizzing Kingston about his and Stewart's relationship, what Stewart did for a living, and his connection to Zander. It became clear that the captain and crew had been given little or no information as to their two passengers.

"So, why are you aboard, Doctor?" asked Becker. "Why does Viktor Zander want you dropped off in Sfax, of all places?"

Knowing that Becker would have a raft of questions, Kingston had cobbled together what he thought would be a plausible story. "First, I have no idea where Sfax is," he said.

"It's a seaport on the north coast of Africa. Tunisia," Becker replied, taking a sip of his Pepsi. "Not the most glamorous place in the world. I have difficulty believing that Zander does business there."

"He does, as a matter of fact—or plans to. I've invested a tidy sum with him on a construction project his company is heading up. Desalination," said Kingston. He was now thinking on his feet, hoping Becker would buy his story.

"Hmm. Makes sense, I suppose. Water's like gold in that part of the world."

Kingston nodded. "You're right." The less said the better, he figured.

"But why keep you under lock and key?"

"I'd like to know that myself. When we get back, Zander's got a lot of explaining to do."

"You didn't know we were headed to Africa?"

Kingston shook his head. "No. All I was told by Blake, who drove me to the boat, was that Zander would be aboard and wanted to talk to me. I didn't even know the man had a boat. Truth of the matter is that over the last few months, I've become highly suspicious about what's been going on with the damned project." He took a long sip of Pepsi, only to buy time and to keep his story straight. "*Not* been going on would be more accurate," he added, wanting to belch. He never could stand carbonated drinks.

There was nothing in Becker's expression to suggest

that he doubted Kingston's veracity. "Zander's a busy man" was all he said, with a shrug of his big shoulders.

Kingston carried on. "I've heard similar stories from two other investors. We were told that Zander had made a lucrative deal with a foreign, government-owned utility but we've yet to see any kind of agreement or contract. One of the investors has filed a complaint with the International Trade Commission, I believe."

Becker threw his head back and downed the last dregs of Pepsi. "Tell me more about your friend Stewart. Why is he aboard?"

It was clear from Becker's question and his tone that he wasn't completely satisfied with Kingston's earlier explanation. Kingston looked out to sea, but not long enough to make it appear that he was thinking up an answer. "Stewart?" he said, looking back into Becker's inquisitive gray eyes. "I wish I could answer you, Captain. Except that he's another investor, I haven't the faintest idea. That's why I was dumbfounded when I saw him."

They were interrupted by the loudspeaker system: a request for the captain to report to the bridge. Becker excused himself.

"Phew!" Kingston muttered, watching the big man lumber along the deck and disappear through a door to the bridge. A few more questions and Becker might have rumbled him. It was impossible to tell if Becker was buying his story or not, but at least he was sure of one thing—Becker hadn't reached Zander yet, thank God.

Within five minutes the captain returned, easing his bulk into the wobbly director's chair. "We're docking at Poole harbor," he said, pulling out a box of Swan Vestas and a pipe. He inspected the tobacco in the bowl, tamped it with a finger, then put the pipe in his mouth and lit it, shielding the match with his hands. "An ambulance will meet us when we dock, to take him to Poole General Hospital. They're expecting him." He glanced at his watch. "About two and a half hours, I'd say."

"I'll go with him, of course."

Becker nodded in agreement, then frowned. "Is he married?"

"Yes. He and his wife, Rebecca, live in Fordingbridge, not far from Poole, as it happens."

Becker took a long draw on his pipe. "I wonder if she knows where he is."

"You've got me. If she doesn't, she's probably worried sick. I'll call her from the hospital."

Kingston maneuvered the conversation to the *Allegra*. It became quickly apparent that he couldn't have picked a better subject. Becker needed no encouragement. Starting with a history of the vessel, followed by an account of its two-million-pound overhaul in France, he went on, impressing Kingston with details of its construction, accommodations, engine, advanced communications systems, navigation equipment, safety features, hydraulics, and on and on. After ten minutes—though he admired the man's fervor—Kingston was wishing he hadn't broached the subject. Finally, Becker's pipe went out, signaling the end of the conversation. Kingston went back to his cabin to shower and get cleaned up, ready for their arrival. Two and a half hours, Becker had said. Kingston prayed it would pass quickly and with no nasty surprises.

STANDING ON THE QUAY at Poole harbor before dawn, Kingston breathed a sigh of relief and glanced skyward, thankful that Zander hadn't called Becker and to be safe on terra firma. He watched as Stewart was carried off the boat by two crewmembers and was transferred immediately to the ambulance. Standing at the rear of the ambulance's open door, Kingston saluted Captain Becker, watching from the deck of the *Allegra*. The captain raised his pipe and smiled in return. Kingston climbed into the ambulance and sat next to Stewart, who was sleeping. In ten minutes they were at the hospital.

Stewart was wheeled off immediately for evaluation while Kingston met with the hospital administrator, an efficient woman named Laura Hargreaves. In the fifteen-minute meeting, he explained his relationship to Stewart and described the events that had taken place on the Allegra, telling her that Stewart was a kidnapping victim and that the Hampshire Constabulary and Inspector Carmichael had been working on the case for many weeks. The need for a round-the-clock watch over Stewart was paramount, he stressed. Not only by hospital personnel but also—because it was a criminal matter—by the police. The administrator assured him that the hospital would file a report immediately and inform the Poole police of Kingston's concerns. In turn, Kingston said that he would be contacting Inspector Carmichael as soon as possible. He would also try to reach Stewart's wife and give her the good news. Hargreaves assured Kingston that the hospital would also be contacting Rebecca Halliday immediately, as a matter of routine. Despite Kingston's insistence that he wait at the hospital until Becky arrived, Hargreaves persuaded him otherwise. Stewart would be going through evaluation and a series of tests over the next several hours, she said, and it would be pointless for Kingston to wait.

The meeting over, Kingston provided his contact numbers and completed the admission papers. A few minutes later he was at a payphone in the lobby. His first call, to Becky, went unanswered. He would try again the minute he got home. Likely she was doing her work for the auxiliary or was at her daughter's house. Unfortunately, he

didn't have Sarah's unlisted number with him. Next he
called Inspector Carmichael, to be told by the station operator that he was out for the day. Kingston left his name,
number, and a message asking that Carmichael call him
immediately and informing him that Stewart Halliday was
alive and had been admitted to Poole General Hospital. As
an afterthought, he voiced his concern that when Blake
found out—and he probably had by now—he might try to
pull something at the hospital. At the hospital taxi rank,
he got a cab to Poole station, where he bought a one-way
ticket to Waterloo and a copy of *The Times*. The journey
was a little over two hours, which would give him time
to read the newspaper and maybe get a start on the crossword. As it was, he slept most of the way.

TWENTY-THREE

KINGSTON CLOSED his front door and picked up the mail from the mat. Holding his takeaway dinner bag, he went straight to the living room to check his phone messages. There were none. He picked up his address book, found Sarah's listing, and punched in the numbers. Four rings and the answerphone came on. He left a message for Becky saying that Stewart was safe in Poole General and to call Kingston as soon as she could.

Leaving the mail on the coffee table, he went to the kitchen, where he set the paper bag on the chopping block and withdrew the contents: fresh ricotta-and-mushroom ravioli and a tub of pasta sauce. Filling a stainless-steel saucepan with water, he placed it on the range and turned on the burner to LOW. At last, now he could pour a drink and relax—if that were possible.

He took a soothing sip of Macallan, gave a silent toast to Stewart, and leaned back on the sofa. It was the first chance he'd had to take stock of things since disembarking from the *Allegra*—to speculate on what might happen now that Stewart was in safe hands. What would Blake and Zander do now? He tried putting himself in their place. The evidence against Blake was indisputable. If and when he was brought to justice, he would go away for a long time. Not that Kingston knew how the system worked, but he felt that the case against Zander might be hard to prove. It would depend on whether a direct relationship between him and Blake could be substantiated, if Zander was privy to everything that Blake had been doing. At the very least, Zander would be charged as an accessory, Kingston figured. The use of his house and boat alone would be incriminating enough. Tracking him down should not present a problem, but Blake might not be so easy to apprehend. He had much more to lose and had already proved dangerous. There was no predicting what he might do, if cornered. Where in hell was Carmichael, anyway? Surely he must have got Kingston's message by now. Maybe the hospital was having better luck.

Kingston took another sip of scotch, this time toasting his own good fortune. He'd dodged a proverbial bullet—meeting an inglorious end in a strange faraway land. He cringed as Blake's last words came back to him. It had been some time since he felt this good. He planned to call the hospital first thing in the morning and get an update on Stewart's condition. With luck, Becky would have received the good news by then and would be at her husband's bedside.

He polished off the whisky and checked the mail: three bills and an envelope with LAWRENCE scrawled on it in pencil. The note inside was from Desmond.

Stopped by on the off chance. But you're obviously out chasing the bad guys again. I'm in town only for the day but I'll call later in the week. All being well, I'm opening the Finchley nursery in about two weeks. Too bad you missed a free lunch.
Cheers,
Desmond

Kingston smiled. It would take two or three lunches, minimum, to bring Desmond up to speed on all that had happened since they'd last met.

He picked up his glass and stood, about to head for the kitchen, when the phone rang. "Finally," he muttered. Becky or Carmichael?

Kingston picked up the phone. It was neither. A man spoke.

"Kingston. I have someone here who wants to talk with you. A friend of yours."

Kingston tightened his grip on the phone. He couldn't be certain. Was it Blake?

"Who is this?" Kingston asked.

"You know damned well who it is. Shut up and just listen."

Kingston felt his flesh creep, his body tense. Blake wouldn't be calling to ask whether it was daylight saving time.

"Are you with me?"

"What's this about, Blake? More of Zander's dirty work, is that it?"

"Nice try. You might like to know he's extremely unhappy about what happened on the boat."

Kingston waited. In the pause that followed, he heard a woman's voice in the background.

"Here she is," said Blake. "She's only going to say it once, so listen carefully."

Another pause, then a woman spoke. "Lawrence?" she said faintly.

"Yes, who is this?" He had difficulty recognizing the voice.

"You have to…you must come down here…to The Willows, Lawrence. He's serious…please do as he says. I'm scared." Her voice, no more than a whisper, was quavering so much he was hard-pressed to hear her, to grasp what she was saying.

"I can barely hear you. To The Willows? Is this…Becky?"

"Yes."

"Are you alone with him?"

"Yes."

Kingston expected her to start crying any moment. He struggled to control his rage. "The man that's with you. I know who he is. Let me talk to him."

"That's enough," he heard Blake say, obviously to Becky.

"Are you still there?" Kingston said, straining to remain calm, hoping she was still on the line. "Give him the phone. Tell him I want to speak to him."

Another pause. "Jesus!" Kingston whispered to himself. Had Blake told her about Stewart?

Blake came on again. "I think you'd better do what the lady asks."

"You bastard! Why involve her? Don't you think she's suffered enough? Have you told her about her husband?"

"This is not Q-and-A, Doctor. You heard her, Kingston. What don't you understand?"

"Tell her—"

"I'm telling her nothing, you fool. I'll spell it out for you one last time. It's almost eight o'clock. Be here by midnight and don't come armed. If you're not here by then... well, you can draw your own picture—*Doctor*. And one thing more—if you're thinking of calling the police, *don't*. That'll be a death warrant. And I don't mean yours—that will come later."

Kingston mind was a dizzying whirlpool of questions. Was it Becky? Was Blake lying? How did he know they were calling from the house? He needed to know more.

"I want some kind of proof, Blake. Let me talk to her again."

"Proof? Proof of what?"

"How do I know you're at the Halliday's house and

that Becky is with you? This could be another of Zander's tricks. Like when you stole my car."

"Just be here. That's all."

"Ask Becky what the drummer boy is."

"What the fuck are you talking about?"

"Just ask her, dammit."

"I told you, this isn't a quiz show, Kingston."

"Ask her what it means, or I'm hanging up."

A long silence followed. "Come on," said Kingston under his breath.

"She says it's a porcelain figurine."

Momentarily, Kingston was at a loss for words. He felt cheated, a loathing welling up inside him. He put a hand on the table to steady himself. "Damn you, Blake," he shouted.

Blake said nothing.

"All right," he said, reining in his revulsion and frustration. "I'll do as you say. But you lay a hand on Becky and I swear I'll kill you."

"Before midnight."

"You're forgetting I don't have a car. You stole it, remember?"

"I don't give a toss. Get a cab. Unless you don't think she's worth it."

The line went dead.

Kingston put down the phone, leaned back, and covered his face with both hands. "Oh God!" was all he could say.

Ten minutes later, a cab pulled up outside 346 Cadogan Square. Kingston was waiting at the front door. With Becky's life in the balance, he couldn't risk wasting a minute longer than necessary. It was raining, but traffic shouldn't be a problem, particularly at this time of night, he thought. He got into the cab and slammed the door.

The cab driver slid the separating glass window open

a few inches and turned to Kingston. "Fordingbridge? Right, guv."

Kingston nodded. "Yes."

"Nasty night. Shouldn't be a problem, though. Long drive, so you might as well sit back and relax." He closed the window and drove off.

If you only knew, thought Kingston. If you only knew.

As the cab rounded the corner at Pont Street, the phone rang in Kingston's flat. After a half-dozen rings, right before the answerphone could kick in, Inspector Carmichael gave up.

TWENTY-FOUR

AT THE FRONT GATE of The Willows, Kingston paid the cab driver, pulled his jacket collar up, and watched the cab's taillights disappear. He'd checked his watch a dozen times on the journey but checked it again: ten-fifty. The rain had stopped, replaced by a boisterous south wind that rattled the trees and spun the drying leaves on the lawn into the air, swirling like Catherine wheels, caught in the amber light from the gatepost lamp. He passed under the arbor, the white Iceberg roses visible despite the dark, and started up the brick path that curved to the front door. The only light came from the porch and living room windows. He rang the doorbell and waited. Would Becky or Blake open it? he wondered.

The door opened. Blake stood there. Dressed in a black Windbreaker, he looked paler than Kingston remembered. He said nothing and, as usual, his expression gave no clue to his mood. "Come in," he said, standing well back from Kingston.

"Where's Becky?" asked Kingston, stepping into the hallway.

"The living room." He gestured for Kingston to go first.

On the drive, Kingston had tried to second-guess what might happen when he got to the house. He could come up with only one motive for Blake's actions, and that didn't bear thinking about. Blake was out for revenge—Zander, too, no doubt. In a struggle, could he overpower Blake? With the element of surprise, he might prevail, but Blake was much younger and probably quicker. It could be a mistake to underestimate him. It was all moot because Blake would certainly be armed. It wasn't the first time in his life that Kingston had been scared, but the thought of what he was about to face made the hackles rise on the back of his neck.

Kingston entered the living room and glanced around. The only illumination came from a table lamp by the window, leaving parts of the room in shadow. Where was she? he wondered. Then he saw her, huddled in a large wingback in a corner by the conservatory. She got up, but surprisingly made no attempt to go to him. He started toward her then stopped. The hair? The clothes? He caught the frisson of recognition in her eye and then the penny dropped.

"You two have met before," said Blake, who had moved to one side.

Kingston's stomach heaved. He stood transfixed, staring at Marian Taylor. Now he realized why the strained voice had seemed unfamiliar.

"I'm sorry," she said, biting her lip. "I had no choice."

Blake smiled sardonically. "I'm surprised you fell for it. Maybe I've been giving you too much credit, Doctor." He shrugged. "But then again, we both know what a good actress she is, don't we?"

"Where's Becky, damn you!"

"She's not home. It made it all the easier. Just the three of us, nice and cozy."

Kingston looked at Marian Taylor. "You're with them, then?"

Her eyes darted to Blake, then back to Kingston. "No, I'm not. You've every right—"

"Shut up!" Blake snapped, pulling a black pistol from his jacket pocket, leveling it at Kingston. Kingston felt the acid rising in his throat, a tingling at the back of his neck. Though he had handled pistols and rifles in his army days and witnessed their destructive powers many times, he still abhorred the use of guns for anything but hunting.

"I'll ask the questions, if you don't mind," Blake added.

"Put that damned thing away." For the first time, Kingston noticed that Blake was wearing a tight-fitting cloth glove on the hand that gripped the pistol.

To Kingston's relief, Blake lowered the pistol to his side. "Before we get down to business, let's talk about you first, Kingston." He stepped back and leaned on the edge of a nearby library table, the same contemptuous look on his face. "I doubt if you're even aware of the damage you've done or the amount of money that's in jeopardy, all because of your stupidity, your death wish to be a bloody hero."

Knowing Blake as he did, Kingston knew that interrupting now would serve no purpose. These were the most words he'd heard Blake string together in all their previous meetings combined. He wondered what would come next or if that was the end of Blake's little speech.

Blake looked at Marian Taylor. "And you—you knew all along what he was up to and what did you do? You lied, you told him everything." He shook his head. "But we'll come back to you later, dear," he said, turning his eyes back to Kingston again.

"You're wrong," said Kingston. He felt compelled to come to her defense, despite knowing that Blake's accusation was justified.

"Really?"

Kingston flashed on a piece of advice from his younger days when, as an army captain, he had attended a course with Special Forces, a rigorous training regime in covert operations, survival training, and commando techniques. The advice concerned response to interrogation by the enemy. The cardinal rule was always to give only your name, rank, and serial number. There were exceptions, however, and one of those applied to situations similar to the one in which he found himself now. The drill was to keep the interrogator talking as long as possible, even if you had to fabricate stuff. "Tell me about Miles Everard," he said. "Why did you have to dispose of him?"

"You're delusional, Kingston."

"Was *he* supposed to get the contract? What did he have on you or Zander that you had to get rid of him?"

"The contract? I'm glad you reminded me. Yes. Only fifty million pounds." He shrugged as if it were chicken feed. Then he shouted, "Fifty—bloody—million! That's what the contract was worth. Now it's all going to be pissed away because of you."

"What difference does it make? When the police catch up with you and Zander—which will be very soon—it'll all be over. You can read all about it from your jail cell."

"I've had enough of your lip, Kingston." He turned his attention to Marian.

Kingston was surprised that she hadn't broken down by now, given the way things were headed. She knew that Blake hadn't brought her along just for a drive to the country. He had a gun for good reason. From where he stood, it was hard to read her expression in the dim light.

"As for you, bitch," Blake snarled, "what do you think I should—"

Kingston cut him off. "Do you mean Marian Taylor or Alison Greer?"

Blake ignored the remark. "What would be suitable payback for what you've done? What do you think?" he said, looking at Marian Taylor, swinging the pistol lazily to and fro like a clock's silent pendulum. "There's no need to answer. I already have a solution. I think you'll appreciate it. You, too, Kingston."

The room fell silent, save for the occasional susurration from the conservatory, where the wind-whipped branches of a tree grazed the windows.

"Lost your tongue, have you?" said Blake.

"You've lost your mind," Kingston retorted. "Give up while you can. It's only a matter of time."

The sardonic smile again. Blake's next question surprised Kingston. "You remember the fire at Walsh's house, Doctor?"

"I do, yes." Kingston saw little point in telling Blake that he was there that day. "It was reported in the paper and on TV."

"Right. Walsh killed by a gunshot wound to the head."

Kingston nodded, wondering where Blake was going.

"The gun was never found, was it?"

"How would I know? Was that reported?"

"Not that I'm aware, but I *know* the gun was never recovered."

"How?"

"Because I'm holding it in my hand."

Kingston noticed that Marian had retreated into the shadows. He could just make out the whites of her eyes pivoting about the room in dread, as if the jury was about to announce its verdict.

Blake continued. "Confusing, eh? How could I be holding the gun that was used to murder Adrian Walsh?"

"You killed Walsh? Is that what you're saying?"

"Kingston, give me more credit. Would I be dumb enough to admit that?"

"Why don't you put us out of our misery and tell us—how come you have the gun?"

Blake leveled the gun at Marian. "Why don't *you* tell the doctor?"

Kingston switched his gaze to Marian. Even in the low light, he could tell that Blake's words had hit the mark. She stood as if paralyzed, staring not at Blake but at the gun. It seemed that even the wind outside had sensed the gravity of the moment. Everything was still.

"He's lying," she said finally.

"Why would I bother?"

"You bastard!"

Coming from her, the word surprised Kingston, who was flustered by the dramatic turn of events. Maybe Blake wasn't going to dispatch of them both in cold blood after all.

Blake smiled. "You dropped it, didn't you?"

"No, I've never seen it," she shot back angrily.

"You're the one who's lying. You dropped it as you were leaving Walsh's house the day of the fire."

Marian looked at Kingston. He had never seen such a look of abject fear, her eyes imploring, penetrating his as if he were her only hope of salvation.

"Damn you, Blake. Why not just get on with what you came here for?"

"We're getting to that. You see, Doctor, if this gun were to fall into the hands of the police, they'd find Marian Taylor's fingerprints all over it. You understand the significance, I'm sure?"

"You're suggesting that *she* killed Walsh?"

"Murdered is more like it. She killed him. Then, to cover it up, she set fire to his house. Unfortunately, in her haste to leave she dropped the gun on the terrace outside the door to his study." He looked at Marian. "When you got to the car and realized this, you couldn't go back for it, could you? By then, the fire had taken hold and your only hope was that it would be destroyed in the fire. If nothing else, the fingerprints would be obliterated. Wrong!"

"How the hell do you know all this?" asked Kingston.

"Because I was there. As I drove in, she was leaving—in one hell of a hurry, I might add."

Kingston looked at Marian. "Good God! Is what he's saying true?"

"It was an accident," she whimpered. "I didn't murder Adrian. I loved him."

"This isn't your gun?" asked Blake. "Is that what you're saying?"

"It's not. It belonged to Walsh."

While Blake and Marian were arguing, Kingston was trying to figure out what Blake was planning—what the end game might be. It would be Machiavellian to think that Blake would shoot her and then him with the same gun that she'd used to kill Walsh, then leave it for the police to find. Her fingerprints, along with a ballistics test, would prove beyond all doubt that Marian Taylor had killed Walsh and now him, too. That would confuse the hell out of the police.

"Now you know all about Marian Taylor, Doctor. Quite a piece of work, wouldn't you say?"

"So, that's how you got her to do your con jobs. Threaten to expose her if she didn't do what you demanded. Pretend to be Alison Greer—was that her idea or yours?" As Kingston was talking, buying time, he was desperately trying to think of how to forestall what was starting to look like the inevitable. He was surprised that Blake hadn't shut down the conversation long before now.

Blake waved the pistol at Marian. "Get over there by him," he said. "That's enough talking…"

Suddenly, the room was bathed in white light. In seconds,

it was gone. A crunching of tires on the gravel driveway followed, then silence. A car door slammed shut, then another.

"Stay where you are," said Blake, moving briskly to the window. Covering them with the pistol, he drew the curtain aside a few inches and looked outside. "Shit," he muttered. He turned back to Kingston and Marian. "Big mistake, Kingston. You're going to pay for it."

The doorbell rang.

"Listen to me," Blake snapped, grabbing Marian's arm, pulling her toward the door. "There're two cops out there. Answer the door and leave the chain on. Tell them that Becky Halliday is away for a few days and that you're a friend housesitting for her. If they want to come in, tell them no. I doubt they'll have a warrant. They'll have seen the car in the driveway and assume it's yours. It's a BMW."

The doorbell rang again.

"If you screw up, Kingston's dead. You understand? He's *dead!*" Marian walked out of the room into the hallway. She was a good actress, thought Kingston, but if she could pull this off, it would be a bloody miracle.

TWENTY-FIVE

KINGSTON GRIMACED as Blake's pistol jabbed his side. "Get going, you bastard," Blake snarled. "Into the kitchen and out the back door—quick."

They stepped into the garden, Blake closing the door behind him. The wind hadn't let up and Kingston knew that even if he shouted for help—which could be suicidal—it wouldn't be heard on the other side of the house. A gunshot might, however. He wondered if Marian could pull it off. If she could convince the policemen to leave, what would she do then? Was he about to find out what price she put on his life?

With no lights on in the back of the house, Blake was staying close to make sure Kingston wouldn't try to give him the slip.

The wind and chill had cleared Kingston's head and sharpened his faculties. He was trying to recall the layout of the garden as the two of them stumbled in the pitch darkness across a wide perennial border, trampling plants and sprinkler heads before reaching the lawn. If he could, it would give him a slight advantage, should he get lucky enough to separate himself from Blake. He tried to visualize the garden as it had been on that somber day he and Becky had strolled through it soon after Stewart went missing. The tool shed, he knew, was off to their left; the long wisteria pergola and the shallow flight of stone steps leading to the lower lawn were ahead of them. Beyond that, the pond, then a pasture used by a local farmer for grazing—usually sheep but occasionally horses. What else? The greenhouse, the potting shed, and the small orchard—yes, they were on the right side.

With Blake hard on his heels, muttering the occasional obscenity, they stumbled across the lawn. The farther from the house, the darker it seemed to get. Kingston slowed to a walk, anticipating the stone steps. The pergola loomed overhead and he knew his guesstimate was right. He wondered when Blake would stop—they were running out of garden. The pond and pasture were all that remained. The high brick wall circling the garden was off to the right, and beyond that, the road. Since they'd been in the garden, no cars had passed, not surprising considering the time of night and the fact that The Willows had been chosen by Stewart and Becky in part because of its seclusion. Did that mean that the police were still there? That, of course, would depend on which direction they would head when leaving. As if on cue, a car passed by on the other side of the wall, the high beams lighting the trees and marginally illuminating the lower part of the garden, the willow-fringed pond, and the pasture. "Don't let it be the police car," Kingston said to himself under his breath.

"Stop," said Blake. As the wind dropped momentarily, Kingston could hear that Blake was breathing heavily. Odd, thought Kingston. Their scramble across the garden had hardly been strenuous. Maybe Blake had a medical problem. Emphysema? They stood, barely eight feet separating them, Blake with the pistol at his side, Kingston facing him, tremulous. Was this it? The irony didn't escape Kingston. Was he going to end up facedown alongside the pond where Stewart had made his discovery? Instinctively he started edging back, despite knowing the futility of it. Blake couldn't miss at this range. Regardless, he kept shuffling backward. What was Blake waiting for? Then he saw the pistol raised and closed his eyes.

"Too bad, Kingston." Blake's words were carried off in the wind. The nearby willows rustled as if in protest.

Kingston stepped back, lost his balance, and fell sideways, disappearing before Blake's eyes. It took him a fraction of a second to realize what had happened. He had fallen into the ha-ha, the long, deep ditch used to keep livestock from straying into the garden—commonplace in the English countryside for centuries. He'd completely forgotten that The Willows had one. He remembered seeing it the day he and Becky had walked through the garden.

This was divine intervention, and without even realizing it, he was offering up a silent prayer. He had to take advantage of it, move quickly. The expected shot never came. He rolled onto his belly and started to wriggle in the muddy water along the bottom of the three-foot ditch. It would be only a matter of seconds before Blake realized what had happened. Between now and then, seconds at the most, Kingston had to squirm far enough along the ditch to be out of Blake's sight—in the dark, not too far, fortunately.

Crack! Kingston recoiled at the sound of the gunshot, plunging his head facedown in the mud, instinctively covering his head with his hands. He heard the bullet thump into the side of the ditch several feet behind him, the report echoing off the walls of the house. In his blind rage, Blake must have fired wildly.

Kingston wriggled farther along the ditch, thankful that the wind buffeting the trees made enough noise to drown out the sloshing sounds. He stopped, got to his knees, raised his head slowly, and peered over the edge of the ditch.

His heart skipped several beats.

The blood was pulsing in his temples.

He was staring at the back of Blake's muddy shoes.

He dug his hands into the hard earth at the top edge of the ditch. Don't turn around, don't turn, he kept repeating in his head. But if Blake did, Kingston was ready to give everything he had, exert every last muscle, to grab Blake by the ankles and bring him down.

Kingston remained stock-still, holding his breath as long as he could, letting it out slowly and silently. When he saw one of Blake's feet shift, he tensed, ready to leap forward. Then he saw the dancing light.

Someone holding a flashlight was running across the lawn toward Blake. Close behind was another person. Kingston realized that it was the two policemen but stayed put. He was aware that they carried only batons and sometimes CS spray to incapacitate aggressive customers. The first policeman stopped thirty or so feet from Blake. "Drop the gun, sir," he ordered, his voice calm and steady. It was if Blake hadn't heard him. "Once more," he said, louder this time, "drop the bloody gun."

The other policeman, taller and heavier, had circled to the left, leaving twenty feet between him and his partner. The flashlight was pointed directly at Blake as if he were standing center stage in a darkened theater, transfixed in the spotlight. The policeman gave another order. "It's over. Drop the gun, keep your hands above your head, and walk toward me."

The gun dropped on the grass within three feet of Kingston, and Blake started walking. Only then did Kingston scramble out of the ha-ha, wiping his hands on his jacket. The burly policeman who had walked over to help him had a bemused look on his face. Then Kingston realized what a bizarre spectacle he must present, resembling the Creature from the Black Lagoon, covered head to foot in liver-colored sludge.

The policemen handcuffed Blake and took him into the house while Kingston headed for the bathroom to rinse the mud out of his hair and off his face, and to make himself look as presentable as possible. Later he would shower and look through Stewart's wardrobe and borrow a couple of items. After several minutes, he entered the living room, not knowing what to expect or who to find there. The room was empty. He pulled aside the curtain and looked outside. He saw the rear of the blue-and-yellow police car and the back of Blake's head through the rear window. No sign of either policeman. He was about to leave the room, to see where everybody had gone, when the shorter policeman entered. Kingston's first impression was that he was awfully young for the job. But people were looking younger to him every day.

"Looks like you had a close call, sir. I'm Constable Baverstock, by the way." He pulled out a notepad and pen. "Sit down and I'll ask you a few questions—if you're up to it, that is."

"I'm fine," replied Kingston, sitting in the wingback that Marian Taylor had occupied, trying not to muddy it up too much. Where was she? he wondered. They apparently hadn't arrested her. But why would they have let her leave the scene?

For the first two minutes, Kingston described his relationship with the Hallidays, telling Baverstock about Stewart's kidnapping and what led him to The Willows. Then, step by step, he recounted what had occurred at the house since he'd arrived. When he was finished, Baverstock wrote down Kingston's contact information, and informed him that a second patrol car would arrive shortly to drive him to a nearby hotel if he wished. Kingston declined, saying that he would stay at the house, and that if

Becky hadn't returned by midday the following morning, he would take a train back to London.

The constable stood, about to leave. "You'll be contacted soon to submit a full statement, which may require your coming down to Hampshire."

Kingston smiled. "Wouldn't be the first time," he said.

Baverstock returned the smile. "Well, good luck sir, I'm glad—"

Kingston cut him short. "Where is Marian, the woman who answered the door?"

"We just did a thorough search and it appears that she's gone."

"Sorry, I didn't mean to interrupt. What exactly happened, then?"

"Like you, Dorset Police were unable to reach Rebecca Halliday and we were responding to their request to make a routine check of the property."

"No, I mean when she answered the door."

"She gave us her name and told us that she was housesitting for Mrs. Halliday and that she was alone in the house."

"Did you believe her?"

"Well, yes."

"She was lying, you know. That's what Blake told her to say."

"All I can say is that she's a damned good actress."

"You're right about that."

"She was well dressed and polite, the type of woman that would be housesitting—not like some squatter, that is. We asked if she was okay. Calm as a cucumber, she assured us she was, so we left. Outside, in the car, my partner, Graham, suggested we run a computer check on the BMW. It was a 2005 number plate, seven series—pricey set of wheels. He couldn't picture her driving that kind of car, somehow, unless it were her husband's." He grinned. "A bit macho, old Graham. We waited a bit, then drove off. We were halfway down the street when the info came through. It wasn't registered in her name, but to a leasing company in London. It was then that we heard the gunshot. We whipped around and came back."

Kingston stroked his brow. "Not a moment too soon—thank God."

"Right. We rang the doorbell and hammered on the door, with no joy. So, we went round the side of the house, out to the garden." The constable shrugged. "You know the rest."

Kingston frowned, nodding to himself. "Seeing you come back, she must have hidden in the house until you went into the garden, then took off."

"The only explanation, really. Probably walked to Fordingbridge and got a cab."

"What will happen to her?"

"We've already reported her as missing and wanted as a material witness, so there'll be a warrant issued for her arrest. I would imagine that Blake will corroborate what you told us about her killing Adrian Walsh. By the sound of it, she'll need a good lawyer. So will he."

The following morning, feeling conspicuous wearing a polo shirt, slacks—a couple of inches short—and a yellow golf jacket belonging to Stewart, Kingston took a cab to Salisbury station, where he bought a newspaper, coffee, and a ham-and-cheese sandwich. Ten minutes later he boarded the 10:45 two-coach train to Waterloo and home.

TWENTY-SIX

BECKY'S MESSAGE WAS THE FIRST on the answering machine. She sounded breathless, her words coming a mile a minute: *"Wanted you to know I just got your message, Lawrence. Bless you. I'm leaving Sarah's in the next five minutes for Poole. I still can't believe it. Stewart's safe, thank God. I called the hospital and they said he's doing fine."*

Kingston detected a quiet sob of joy as she paused and then went on: *"I'll call you later, when I get to the hospital, after I've seen Stewart. I have to go now. Sarah's waiting for me outside. I love you. Bye."*

He sat back on the sofa trying to imagine what it must have been like for her getting his message. She was so overjoyed that she hadn't even questioned how it was that Stewart ended up in Poole General Hospital. What did it matter anyway right now? He was safe and in good hands and, from what she'd said, going to survive his ordeal. When they next met, she was going to be flabbergasted to learn what had happened in her very own house and garden, of all places. He smiled and listened to the next two messages.

The first was unimportant, the second from Carmichael. The inspector could wait, Kingston decided. He was famished—the only food he'd had in the past twelve hours was the stale sandwich he'd bought at Salisbury station and eaten on the train. As far as Carmichael was concerned, he must have been informed by now about Stewart's release and was no doubt preoccupied helping other law-enforcement agencies chase down Viktor Zander and Marian Taylor on top of maintaining the peace in Ringwood. Maybe he was calling to say that they'd been apprehended. No, too early for that, he decided.

Marian Taylor? Kingston had spent most of the train ride thinking about her. If what she had said was true—that she had shot Walsh accidentally—why wouldn't she have surrendered to the police at The Willows? The police now had the gun with her fingerprints on it—that is, providing Blake hadn't been bluffing. There had to be more to it. She had clearly been terrified of Blake, to the point of doing whatever he asked. Could it be that he knew more about her than he was telling? Kingston tried putting himself in her position. Having done a runner from The Willows, she wouldn't be aware that Blake had been arrested or that he himself was very much alive. For all she knew, Blake might have carried out his threat. Kingston got cold shivers at the thought. He would never be able to expunge Blake's words and the soulless look on his face when he had spat them out: "If you screw up, Kingston's dead!"

What was Marian Taylor running from—something else from her shadowy past? He knew so little about her, and in a perverse way that bothered him. Why should he be so concerned about her well-being? And how about Zander? Somehow Kingston couldn't picture him and Marian in cahoots. Were that the case, however, it wouldn't surprise him—nothing would anymore. Would that be the last he would ever see of her? Somehow he doubted it.

Conscious of still wearing Stewart's ill-fitting clothes, he showered and changed into comfortable clothes. A half hour later, he was seated in the Antelope's downstairs bar savoring a pint of Fuller's London Pride.

The next morning, rested and looking forward to getting his life back to normal, Kingston finally caught up with

Carmichael. The inspector was in one of his stand-offish moods. No sooner had Kingston uttered good morning than Carmichael started castigating him for going to The Willows alone, never mind that Becky's life was being threatened. "Damned foolish thing to do," he said. When pressed, he conceded that Blake was being turned over to the London Metropolitan Police in connection with the murder of Miles Everard and the kidnapping of Stewart Halliday.

"Everard *was* murdered, then?" said Kingston.

"That's what the Met are saying. From what little I know, telling the difference between 'did he fall' or 'was he pushed' is a tough call. Not to say that it can't be determined sometimes."

Kingston decided not to ask how. It was irrelevant, and given Carmichael's stroppy attitude, he probably wouldn't explain anyway.

When Kingston inquired about Viktor Zander and Marian Taylor, he was less forthcoming. The only information he proffered was that neither had been located.

In the days following, Kingston's abandoned TR4 was discovered by a Royal Parks patrol car. It had been towed to a Chelsea Police garage and stored until the owner could be located. When Kingston picked it up, much to his surprise and relief the car had not been vandalized, as he had feared it might be, and was none the worse for wear. Two days later, he found an unexpected bonus—an expensive pair of sunglasses wedged in the crease of the passenger seat.

Stewart Halliday was discharged from Poole General Hospital eight days after he had been admitted. Ironically, Kingston's diagnosis had been remarkably accurate: Stewart had suffered a mild stroke, from which he was expected to recover fully. Additionally, blood and urological tests had revealed traces of an anxiolytic drug commonly used for sedation. On the phone, Becky had told Kingston that Stewart's physician confirmed that a regular dosage of such a sedative would be consistent with the objectives of Stewart's captors. Moderate sedation, he'd said, would induce depressed consciousness in which the patient could respond to external verbal or tactile stimuli. In this state, normal airway reflexes, spontaneous ventilation, and cardiovascular function would be maintained.

After Stewart's discharge, he and Kingston spoke on the phone often. At first, for obvious reasons, Kingston was careful not to press Stewart too hard, and resisted quizzing him about his experiences at the hands of Blake and company. But inchmeal, like pixels falling into place on a slow-loading computer image, a chronology of Stewart's weeks in captivity unfolded.

Stewart started by telling Kingston about his experiments—first on his own, then with Adrian Walsh—cross-hybridizing water lilies at Walsh's lake at Swallowfield. It had all begun as an amusing pastime, he said, after reading an article on desalination that postulated future wars would be fought over water, not oil. He told Walsh about his "zany" idea of a water plant capable of desalination. Walsh, who was well-off, was intrigued and agreed to go along for the ride and help underwrite most of the costs.

Introducing salt into the lake at Swallowfield led to many failures, wasted time, and money. The toll of dead lilies kept mounting. The two men were about to admit defeat and give up their crackpot scheme when Stewart suggested they give it a last try by cross-hybridizing the giant water lily *Victoria amazonica*. The only drawback was that this genus of water lily was native to equatorial Brazil, growing in calm waters along the Amazon River. This required their building a makeshift greenhouse environment. Hundreds of crosses and eighteen months later, they hit pay dirt.

Aware of the inevitable fallout should the press learn of their discovery, Stewart and Adrian decided to keep it secret until they were certain that it worked on a sustained basis. They also knew that if the process were to be industrially viable, larger-scale trials under more rigorous and controlled conditions would have to be conducted. That meant finding a much larger expanse of water—ideally in a secluded location—the right people, and the substantial funding needed to mount such a project. Walsh told Stewart that he knew a man named Miles Everard, the owner of a large construction and engineering company, who might be persuaded to participate and take the experiments to the next big step. Walsh had never met the man but had once performed as subcontactor in one of Everard's big projects. Soon thereafter, Walsh contacted Everard's company in London by phone and spoke to Everard personally.

According to Stewart, Everard visited Swallowfield twice. After those and subsequent meetings, Everard agreed to partner with them on a full-scale biological desalination project. Under the terms of the agreement, both Walsh and Halliday would receive substantial "sign-on" payments and generous royalties from future sales once the project was up and running and proven to be viable. It wasn't revealed until much later that the person Stewart and Walsh were dealing with was not Miles Everard but his personal assistant, Gavin Blake, posing as Everard. Neither were they aware that, by then, Blake was on Viktor Zander's payroll, nor that the wealthy Zander, who had migrated to Britain in the eighties, had ties to the Russian "Mafia" and was always just one step ahead of the law.

Stewart related how he started working routinely at the new reservoir installation, keeping his and Walsh's end of the bargain. More than once he'd considered telling Becky what he was doing but had been cautioned by "Everard"—with Walsh concurring—to keep the operation under wraps, safeguarded from the inevitable media frenzy, until they had proof positive that the process worked. Knowing her husband's passion for gardening, his affiliation with the garden club, and his friendship with Walsh, Becky had no reason to suspect that Stewart wasn't coming clean about his absences.

For some time, Stewart worked at the reservoir by day, returning home each evening. As the weeks passed, he became uneasy about the prison-like conditions and the conduct of some staff members. What worried him most was that some of the maintenance and security workers carried weapons—not just small arms but semi-automatic assault weapons. When he questioned the need for such extreme protection, he was told to mind his own business. On one occasion, he said, he heard automatic weapons fire some distance from the reservoir. That was when Kingston told him about the ill-fated helicopter ride and the theft of the tape.

When Stewart confronted Blake and told him that he'd decided to bow out of the project, Blake's reaction had confirmed all his suspicions. First, Blake tried to persuade Stewart otherwise, then resorted to coercion, threatening legal action. Stewart said he left the reservoir that day convinced that Blake would take drastic action. He thought about telling Becky but, not wanting to alarm or frighten her about his well-being, decided to wait. He even considered calling Kingston, he said, but again, for whatever reason, opted to hold off. He was sure that if anything happened to him, one of the first people Becky would call would be Kingston. That was when he resolved, on the spur of the moment, the night before attending the conference and just before going to bed, to leave the cryptic clues. In retrospect, he admitted to Kingston with a chuckle, it felt a bit "cloak and daggerish" at the time and was a trifle clumsy, but he was certain that Kingston would solve them.

Kingston asked him how and exactly when he was kidnapped. Stewart reported that it happened on the way to the conference. He'd picked up the drummer-boy figurine from the Salisbury antiques shop—Becky had already told him about the significance of the figurine—and was on an open stretch of the A36 east of Warminster, driving the Jag at a comfortable fifty-five-miles per hour, when he became concerned about a black Land Rover that had been sitting on his rear bumper for several miles, passing up opportunities to overtake him. Then the driver began flashing his headlights. Stewart said that he'd slowed and pulled over as far as he could to let the Land Rover pass. Instead of passing, it came alongside, the driver shouting and pointing to the Jag's right rear wheel. Stewart made out the word "loose" and stopped on the grass verge. The Land Rover pulled in behind.

When two men got out of the Land Rover, he realized that all was not right. They didn't look a bit like Good Samaritans. They opened the door and politely asked him to get out of the car, but their expressions were anything but congenial. He did as they asked, leaving the key in the ignition, the engine running. No sooner was he out of the car than one of the men slipped behind the wheel, slammed the door, and drove off. The other man took his arm in a painful grip and muscled him into the Land Rover. They did a U-turn and took off back toward Salisbury. "Sounds all too familiar," said Kingston.

In their phone conversations after Stewart's return, Kingston had been respectful of his and Becky's need for privacy, recognizing that this was a time of healing for both of them. So, Becky's mailed invitation for Kingston to join them for lunch at The Willows was welcome news indeed. Most of all, it signaled Stewart's return to good health and implied that they were ready to resume their salubrious life in the country. It also meant that, at long last, he would get to see Stewart.

TWENTY-SEVEN

PLANNING A SUCCESSFUL al fresco lunch during an English summer requires two essentials, weatherwise: the luck of a lottery winner and an indoor backup plan. Stewart and Becky Halliday had been granted the first, thereby obviating the need for the second.

The day had started with the sun rising unchallenged and kept improving by the hour. At noon on this agreeable Sunday, someone wandering by chance into the garden at The Willows might imagine that they had stepped onto the set of a Merchant Ivory film. With snowy clouds dawdling across a china-blue sky, the garden looked glorious. A round table with wicker chairs was centered on the upper lawn, mown to putting-green perfection the day before. The grassy smell still lingered. Late-summer color from asters, Japanese anemones, rudbeckia, helenium, and sedum crowded the surrounding beds and borders. A cloak of sweet autumn clematis on a nearby wall perfumed the air.

Underneath a cream-colored umbrella, a table setting for three was laid on antique linen. Crystal wineglasses and water goblets glinted in the sunlight. Before knives and forks were raised, Kingston proposed a simple toast, and afterward produced a small wrapped box from his pocket, handing it to Becky. "Inspector Carmichael asked that I give this to you," he said.

Becky and Stewart smiled, each knowing what the box contained. Becky removed the wrapping, opened the box, and pulled out the Meissen drummer boy. Becky examined it for a moment before passing it to Stewart. He took it, shaking his head. "Who could imagine such a tiny thing playing a part in all of this."

"I'm surprised the police let you have it," said Becky. "Surely it would be considered evidence?"

"It wasn't easy," Kingston replied. "But Carmichael talked to a couple of higher-ups, and they agreed that with the overwhelming evidence they now had against Blake and Zander, it could be released. Whatever you do, though, don't lose it, just in case."

Stewart placed the drummer boy on the table. "Any more news of Zander?"

"There is. I was coming to that, actually. I talked with Inspector Carmichael last week—he was uncharacteristically chatty. He said they caught up with Zander in Paris, of all places. Apparently, he was on his way back to England from Tunisia."

Stewart frowned. "Tunisia?"

"That's what I said when Carmichael told me. It's a guess but I bet that's where Zander was probably negotiating the sale of the desalination plant."

"Where you and I were headed on the *Allegra*," Stewart pointed out.

"It all makes sense," said Becky.

"Anyway," said Kingston, taking a sip of Sancerre, "he's been arraigned and has pleaded not guilty as an accessory in your kidnapping. He was refused bail, so now he's in Belmarsh awaiting a trial date."

"Is that where Blake is?" asked Stewart.

"I don't know. Carmichael didn't say."

Becky rested her knife and fork on the table. "What about Everard's murder?" she inquired, dabbing her lips with her napkin. "You did say it was murder, didn't you?"

"Yes, and Carmichael confirmed it. I'm not sure if I mentioned it before, but shortly after Everard was killed, the Metropolitan Police visited me—routine, they said. They knew I'd been to Everard's office and that I'd met with Blake by going through the visitors' book and interviewing the receptionist. I was unaware of it at the time, but according to Carmichael, the Met had been keeping tabs on Blake for some time. Just prior to Everard's death, his company was about to fire Blake and file embezzlement charges against him. Only now are they discovering the extent of Blake's debts and how much he had taken Paramus for. Apparently, it was well known among the employees that Blake and Everard were on a collision course."

Stewart twirled his wineglass. He looked confused. "What about the Blake-Zander partnership? When did that happen?"

"I asked Carmichael the same question," said Kingston. "The way the police see it, Blake knew his days with Everard's company were numbered and that he was in big trouble—facing the reality of several years in jail. Then, by chance, he intercepts the all-important call from Adrian and, being the devious bastard he is, sees a possible way out. Taking Adrian's word for it—that your desalination discovery could become a huge moneymaker—he makes the first trip to Swallowfield, posing as Everard. Not too difficult to do when you consider he knows the company inside out and the two of you have never met Everard."

"Let me see if I've got this right," said Stewart. "Blake knew that if Everard's company were to partner with Adrian and me, he'd end up with nothing. But if he joins forces with Zander, whom he knows has the wherewithal and the organization to fund and develop the project, he can negotiate a sizable chunk of the business—if the project proves to be a winner, of course."

"That's about right," said Kingston. "Many millions, I'm sure." He took his napkin from his lap, folded it neatly, and placed it carefully on the tablecloth by his wineglass. It was like a metaphor for his next words. "The only thing standing in his way—the only person, I should say—was Everard. Poor bastard."

"So, how did they know it was Blake who shoved Everard off the balcony?" asked Becky.

"He was clever—but not clever enough. Carmichael didn't give me all the details, of course, but it seems that Blake had set up an alibi proving he was nowhere near the office building that evening. He knew that Everard had a habit of working long hours, and with the building virtually empty or possibly closed, the chances of his being seen and identified were slight. He had keys and passes and didn't have to check in."

"He could have been disguised, too," said Becky, now all ears.

"I wouldn't put anything past him," said Kingston, slowly shaking his head. "There was one other thing Carmichael mentioned—a rotten irony. Everard's headquarters were in the only building in Bakers Landing that had balconies and sliding doors to the office suites. All the other skyscrapers have no windows per se—they're all sealed in glass and climate-controlled by HVAC. Brave new world."

Becky sighed. "Blake would have found another way, I'm sure," she said.

"So, how did they prove Blake did it?" asked Stewart.

"Blake was the prime suspect, of course, and the police brought him in immediately for questioning. His alibi held up but meantime the police got a warrant and searched his flat, seizing his entire wardrobe, among other things, hoping that forensic tests on the fabrics might incriminate him. Examining one of Blake's jackets, a sharp-eyed technician noticed that there were two small buttons on one sleeve and three on the other. Where the missing button would have been, the fabric was slightly torn." Kingston paused to finish his wine. He was clearly enjoying the police procedural.

"And they found the button in Everard's closed fist, is that it?" said Becky.

Kingston smiled and shook his head. "In a movie, maybe. But no, that's not how it happened. It was the proverbial 'needle in the haystack.' From what I've learned, this is the way most crimes are eventually solved, by using patience and old-fashioned legwork. For two days, police personnel searched inch by inch a large area surrounding the spot where Everard's body landed. Eventually, they found the button, complete with a minute shred of matching material." Kingston smiled again. "Carmichael said they found it in—of all places—a bed of busy lizzies."

"That's not funny, Lawrence," said Becky. "I feel very sorry for the poor man. It appears he did nothing to deserve such a horrible end."

Kingston nodded. "You're right, Becky."

Becky looked pensive. "Lawrence, I know I've told you this before, but I'll say it again. You risked your life coming down here to save me that night. Or who you thought to be me, I should say. I'm still amazed that this Marian woman could have fooled you."

"On the phone, you mean?"

"Yes."

"Well, to start with, I could hardly hear her, and Blake was clever—he made sure she used very few words. Coming up with the 'drummer boy' answer was what clinched it."

"I must say it was quick of you to think of that," said Stewart.

"Too quick, maybe. It wasn't until it was all over that I realized that Blake could well have seen the figurine after they abducted you, Stewart. It was in your bag, you said, and the first thing they would have done when they got you back to Foxwood House would be to go through the contents."

Stewart nodded in agreement. "Right. Someone—the housekeeper, or even Blake—thought nothing of it and simply put it on the mantelpiece, then forgot all about it."

Kingston nodded. "That's most certainly what happened. Marian wouldn't have known about it."

Lunch continued with the conversation turning to the garden, eventually leading to what happened that windy night and Kingston's deliverance by the ha-ha.

"Brilliant stroke of luck, that was," said Stewart between mouthfuls of poached salmon.

"Or providence," said Kingston with a quixotic smile, raising his glass.

Carrying their empty plates, Becky left for the house to fix coffee and put the finishing touches to her dessert, or "afters" as Kingston preferred to call them. In her absence, Stewart told Kingston how the police had found his Jaguar locked in a garage in Kensington belonging to Zander—further tying him to the crime. Becky had taken the train up to London to pick it up. Kingston also told Stewart about Desmond and Across the Pond, promising to take Stewart to the nursery for a visit in the coming weeks. That led the conversation to water plants and to Stewart's *Victoria amazonica* hybrid that almost made history.

"Give me your honest opinion, Stewart," said Kingston. "Under different circumstances, could the desalination process have been a commercial success? Was it really capable of sustained operation on a large scale?"

Stewart crossed his arms and sighed. "You know, from the beginning, when Adrian and I found that the plants could actually absorb salt, despite our excitement I was skeptical as to how long they would thrive in salt water and adapt to a large-scale, man-made environment. There were all kinds of logistical questions and potential problems. *Victoria* culture is actually quite easy. As you probably know, Lawrence, it's cultivated in many countries. With the right water temperature and lots of fertilizer, they grow fast. I gleaned lots of information on the Internet. The Web site of a Florida botanic garden gave us all kinds of valuable advice, including a fertilizing formula. Life span was another question." Stewart paused, eyeing Kingston's empty wineglass. "There's plenty more wine, old chap. I can crack open another bottle, if you like."

"No, I'm fine," said Kingston. "I've had plenty. I'll wait for the coffee."

Stewart picked up where he'd left off. "Many horticulturists maintain that *amazonica* is a perennial, but our experience suggests that it should be considered an annual. That meant replenishing the tanks every year. I kept telling Blake and the others working at the reservoir that we didn't have anywhere near enough empirical evidence or reliable data to risk investing the megabucks required to build a biological desalination plant. They wouldn't listen. They'd witnessed the early results—which I must say, to our amazement, were brilliant—and thought of it as akin to alchemy: turning lead into gold."

"Given more time and better technology, is it a viable future resource?"

"The answer is, I don't know." He paused, a faraway look in his eyes. "Toward the end, before we abandoned the reservoir, we were starting to run into what I perceived could become serious problems with the plants. Again, Blake wouldn't listen, of course."

Kingston frowned. "What kind of problems?"

"Nothing that's in the books, Lawrence. Something was interfering with the plants' ability to photosynthesize. I think it had to do with the chloroplasts. The normal chain of electron-transfer steps was off kilter somehow and they weren't producing enough sucrose. The plants were slowly dying off."

"The salt, right?"

"Undoubtedly."

"If you'd had more time, could it have been corrected?"

"Hard to say."

"So, if you were to try again—"

Immediately, Stewart was shaking his head. "Out of the question, Lawrence."

"I realize, but if you did, you're saying that you'd have to start from scratch with a different *Victoria* cross?"

"That's right."

They paused, seeing Becky emerge through the French doors carrying a large tray loaded with coffee, the dessert, plates, and silverware.

"Let's put it this way," said Stewart, standing. "It wouldn't surprise me one bit if I pick up a paper a couple of years from now and read that somebody's pulled it off."

"Scientists are certainly going to be trying to finish what you started," said Kingston, starting to clear a space on the table.

Becky lowered the tray onto the table and sat down. "Phew, that was heavy," she said. She poured the coffee and spooned portions of sherry trifle onto their plates. "Lawrence," she said, stirring her coffee, "in the kitchen,

I was thinking about that woman who was here with you that night—Marian Taylor."

Kingston smiled. "Or 'Alison Greer.'"

Becky smiled back, nodding. "Either will do. Did the police find her yet?"

"No. Not as of when I last spoke with Carmichael, that is."

Stewart looked puzzled. "I still find it impossible to believe that she would have killed Adrian. She seemed such a nice person on those occasions when we met at Swallowfield. Particularly that first day—I remember it well. It was unusually warm and we were all out on the lawn having drinks. Adrian introduced her as his secretary. As the day went on, I couldn't help notice how she fussed over him, almost doting at times. To tell the truth, I think it embarrassed poor Adrian a bit. On the other occasions when the three of us were together, she treated him in much the same way." He shook his head. "Who would have ever thought that she would end up killing him?"

"I'm afraid there's no doubt about it," said Kingston. "She admitted it." There was a trace of melancholy in his voice. "To start with, she wouldn't have done Blake's bidding if she could have proved her innocence. It all boils down to whether, as she claimed, it was accidental."

"But why run from the police?" Becky asked.

Kingston sighed and shook his head. "I've asked myself that a dozen times."

Becky picked up her coffee cup and stopped before taking a sip. "If I didn't know better, Lawrence Kingston, I would say that you have a soft spot for her."

"The confirmed bachelor?" Stewart exclaimed.

Kingston gave them a sheepish grin—uncharacteristic for him. "All right, I admit that at one point, the idea of—

shall we say— companionship had crossed my mind. But I soon realized that was fatuous on my part."

"Maybe it's not too late," said Becky.

Kingston shook his head. "No. As I've said before, I've come to realize that I'm now married to being single. Besides, no one will ever be able to take Megan's place."

"Not take her place," said Becky. "But you could make a new place in your life for someone else."

AT TEN THE NEXT MORNING, Stewart and Becky—his arms around her waist—stood under the Iceberg roses at the front gate of The Willows, looking for all the world like a newlywed couple. From the seat of his TR4, Kingston gave them one last farewell wave and, with a smile of fulfillment, drove off. He glanced in the rearview mirror before turning the corner at the Cricketers. They were still standing by the gate and he was still smiling.

THE PLAIN ENVELOPE bore no return address. It was postmarked London W14. Putting the other mail aside, Kingston opened the envelope and withdrew the letter. The handwriting, in blue ink on ivory stationery, was neat and unquestionably feminine. He started to read.

Dear Lawrence,

My behavior over these last months has no doubt left you disappointed and, I daresay, offended. I'm writing this letter to tell you how deeply sorry I am for what I've done and the shameful manner in which I treated you.

I read in the paper about what eventually happened that night at your friends' house, and was much relieved to learn that you were unharmed and that Blake is now behind bars. What a despicable man. I had no choice but to leave after the police arrived. What follows will explain why.

I chose to write this letter because you deserve an explanation for my irrational and hurtful conduct since you and I got mixed up in this beastly mess. Over these last months, I have gained considerable respect for you as a kind and honest person. Your tenacity and courage in the search for Stewart Halliday were remarkable. Few men would have persisted when misled so often and their life placed in such jeopardy.

I want to set the record straight so that you will not go through the remainder of your life thinking ill of me. Much of what Blake said that night was true. What he and you don't know is that the gun wasn't Adrian's. It was mine. I went to Swallowfield to confront him when, after constant pleadings, he refused to recognize my child as his (it is) and wanted to end our relationship. I simply couldn't accept it. I was desperately in love with him. In the bitter argument and struggle that followed, he wrested the gun from me, and it discharged, killing him. My first thought was to call the police and tell them there had been an accident, but I quickly realized what a hopeless mess I was in. They would never believe me. It was my gun, with my fingerprints on it. And to make matters worse, I foolishly tried to cover it up. Even with the best barristers in the country, a jury would convict me in no time for premeditated murder. You know the rest—how Blake was able to blackmail me. Ironically, as long as he had the gun, I was relatively safe. I must presume the police have it now and it will be only a matter of time before they uncover what they perceive to be the truth. That's why I have made the decision to leave the country—for good.

There's not much left for me to say, Lawrence. I dearly wish that none of this dreadful business had ever happened and that we could have met under different circumstances. I think I would have liked that. Most of all, Lawrence, I beg your forgiveness.

God bless,
Marian Taylor

EPILOGUE

A COUPLE OF DAYS after receiving Marian Taylor's letter, Kingston was readying to leave for dinner with Andrew— Japanese, this time—when the phone rang. He thought about letting the answerphone kick in, but with time to spare, he picked it up anyway.

"Kingston here," he said cheerfully.

"Oh, I'm so terribly glad I've been able to reach you," a soft-spoken man answered. His accent was "frightfully" British, leading Kingston to wonder if he was about to be invited to Highgrove or the Queen's garden party.

"How may I help you?" asked Kingston.

"First, if I may, let me introduce myself. I'm Aubrey Lloyd-Smith, the vicar of St. Andrew's in Woolstead."

Woolstead? Why did the name sound familiar? Then Kingston remembered—the pretty church with the Norman turret, near the reservoir. It had to be the same. There couldn't be too many Woolsteads. "Ah, yes. In Hampshire, not far from New Milton."

"That's right. Not too far from Viktor Zander's house."

Hearing Zander's name caught him unawares. Where was all this leading? Kingston wondered. "What's this about, then?" he asked.

"It's about what happened recently. You know, the business with the kidnapping. We all read about you in the newspaper. How you saved that colleague of yours and, of course, the unspeakable behavior of that man Blake. I must say, that was an extraordinary—"

"Yes, yes. But why are you calling me, Vicar?"

"Well, you see, the story mentioned that you were a famous horticulturist and that a few years ago you'd helped restore a famous garden. In Somerset, I believe it was."

"Yes, that's right."

"Let me see…how should I put this?" He paused for a few seconds.

Kingston could picture him sitting in his book-lined rectory, sipping tea from a willow-pattern cup, tugging at his dog collar.

Then he sighed, probably for effect, thought Kingston. "We have an awfully pretty garden here at St. Andrew's," he said, "but I'm afraid to say that it's become rather shabby over the last year or so. It's dreadfully overrun and, sad to say, quite a few things have passed on."

Kingston smiled to himself. In all his years as a botanist and a gardener, he had never heard of plants "passing on."

"And you want me to look at it? Is that it?" he asked.

"That would be awfully nice, if you could, Doctor. We do have a gardener, of course—old Billings—but he's getting on in years, and frankly I'm more than a trifle worried about his health. What we need most of all is for someone like you to give it a complete face-lift, as it were. We have plenty of willing hands, by the way—volunteers from the parish."

Kingston smiled to himself but said nothing.

Aubrey-Smith rattled on. "We're quite happy to pay you, of course. Though I have to be honest—it wouldn't be much. We just spent most of our meager funds on a new roof. And you know how costly those can be."

While the vicar had been talking, Kingston's mind had flashed back to that night in the Hallidays' garden when he was about to meet his maker at the hands of Gavin Blake. Was it luck that he happened to be standing on the edge of

the ha-ha? Or was there another hand in his deliverance—
a higher power?

"Vicar," he said, hearing the doorbell ring, "I'd be more
than happy to come down and take a look. I've wanted to
see your church and the village anyway. And it won't cost
you a penny. How's that?"

The doorbell rang again.

"I must go," said Kingston. "Give me your number and
I'll call you back in a day or so."

Kingston wrote down the number and promised to
phone.

"Thank you so much," the vicar gushed. "Your good
deeds will be most appreciated by our parishioners, and
I'm sure the Lord will reward you."

"I think He already has," Kingston replied and rang off.

* * * * *

REQUEST YOUR FREE BOOKS!

2 FREE NOVELS
PLUS 2 FREE GIFTS!

W()RLDWIDE LIBRARY®
Your Partner in Crime

YES! Please send me 2 FREE novels from the Worldwide Library® series and my 2 FREE gifts (gifts are worth about $10). After receiving them, if I don't wish to receive any more books, I can return the shipping statement marked "cancel." If I don't cancel, I will receive 4 brand-new novels every month and be billed just $5.24 per book in the U.S. or $6.24 per book in Canada. That's a savings of at least 34% off the cover price. It's quite a bargain! Shipping and handling is just 50¢ per book in the U.S. and 75¢ per book in Canada.* I understand that accepting the 2 free books and gifts places me under no obligation to buy anything. I can always return a shipment and cancel at any time. Even if I never buy another book, the two free books and gifts are mine to keep forever.

414/424 WDN FVUV

Name	(PLEASE PRINT)	

Address		Apt. #

City	State/Prov.	Zip/Postal Code

Signature (if under 18, a parent or guardian must sign)

Mail to the **Harlequin® Reader Service:**
IN U.S.A.: P.O. Box 1867, Buffalo, NY 14240-1867
IN CANADA: P.O. Box 609, Fort Erie, Ontario L2A 5X3

Want to try two free books from another line?
Call 1-800-873-8635 or visit www.ReaderService.com.

* Terms and prices subject to change without notice. Prices do not include applicable taxes. Sales tax applicable in N.Y. Canadian residents will be charged applicable taxes. Offer not valid in Quebec. This offer is limited to one order per household. Not valid for current subscribers to the Worldwide Library series. All orders subject to credit approval. Credit or debit balances in a customer's account(s) may be offset by any other outstanding balance owed by or to the customer. Please allow 4 to 6 weeks for delivery. Offer available while quantities last.

Your Privacy—The Harlequin® Reader Service is committed to protecting your privacy. Our Privacy Policy is available online at www.ReaderService.com or upon request from the Harlequin Reader Service.

We make a portion of our mailing list available to reputable third parties that offer products we believe may interest you. If you prefer that we not exchange your name with third parties, or if you wish to clarify or modify your communication preferences, please visit us at www.ReaderService.com/consumerschoice or write to us at Harlequin Reader Service Preference Service, P.O. Box 9062, Buffalo, NY 14269. Include your complete name and address.

WWLl3

ReaderService.com

Manage your account online!

- Review your order history
- Manage your payments
- Update your address

*We've designed
the Harlequin® Reader Service
website just for you.*

Enjoy all the features!

- Reader excerpts from any series
- Respond to mailings and
  special monthly offers
- Discover new series available to you
- Browse the Bonus Bucks catalog
- Share your feedback

Visit us at:

ReaderService.com

RS13

REQUEST YOUR FREE BOOKS!

2 FREE NOVELS
FROM THE SUSPENSE COLLECTION
PLUS 2 FREE GIFTS!

YES! Please send me 2 FREE novels from the Suspense Collection and my 2 FREE gifts (gifts are worth about $10). After receiving them, if I don't wish to receive any more books, I can return the shipping statement marked "cancel." If I don't cancel, I will receive 4 brand-new novels every month and be billed just $5.99 per book in the U.S. or $6.49 per book in Canada. That's a savings of at least 25% off the cover price. It's quite a bargain! Shipping and handling is just 50¢ per book in the U.S. and 75¢ per book in Canada.* I understand that accepting the 2 free books and gifts places me under no obligation to buy anything. I can always return a shipment and cancel at any time. Even if I never buy another book, the two free books and gifts are mine to keep forever.

191/391 MDN FVVK

Name _____ (PLEASE PRINT) _____

Address _____ Apt. # _____

City _____ State/Prov. _____ Zip/Postal Code _____

Signature (if under 18, a parent or guardian must sign) _____

Mail to the Harlequin® Reader Service:
IN U.S.A.: P.O. Box 1867, Buffalo, NY 14240-1867
IN CANADA: P.O. Box 609, Fort Erie, Ontario L2A 5X3

Want to try two free books from another line?
Call 1-800-873-8635 or visit www.ReaderService.com.

* Terms and prices subject to change without notice. Prices do not include applicable taxes. Sales tax applicable in N.Y. Canadian residents will be charged applicable taxes. Offer not valid in Quebec. This offer is limited to one order per household. Not valid for current subscribers to the Suspense Collection or the Romance/Suspense Collection. All orders subject to credit approval. Credit or debit balances in a customer's account(s) may be offset by any other outstanding balance owed by or to the customer. Please allow 4 to 6 weeks for delivery. Offer available while quantities last.

Your Privacy—The Harlequin® Reader Service is committed to protecting your privacy. Our Privacy Policy is available online at www.ReaderService.com or upon request from the Harlequin Reader Service.

We make a portion of our mailing list available to reputable third parties that offer products we believe may interest you. If you prefer that we not exchange your name with third parties, or if you wish to clarify or modify your communication preferences, please visit us at www.ReaderService.com/consumerschoice or write to us at Harlequin Reader Service Preference Service, P.O. Box 9062, Buffalo, NY 14269. Include your complete name and address.